At the third cruel stroke of the lash, she turned on her tormentor . . .

Moaning in pain, Melanie turned on York, as the lumber king raised his whip for the next stroke. The lash caught her on the cheek, raising a weal on the golden-bronze skin, but her fingers found York's throat and the momentum of her unexpected charge threw him off balance. He fell heavily, with Melanie's weight atop him, striking his head against the massive mahogany cabinet.

She rolled away, but he lay crumpled, the right side of his head covered with blood. She felt for his pulse and found none.

She seized her clothes and looked about for a means of escape. She must put miles between herself and the village before dawn.

And then she heard the tramping just outside—the heavy footsteps of the guard patrol . . .

The Making of America Series

THE WILDERNESS SEEKERS
THE MOUNTAIN BREED
THE CONESTOGA PEOPLE
THE FORTY-NINERS
HEARTS DIVIDED
THE BUILDERS
THE LAND RUSHERS
THE WILD AND THE WAYWARD
THE TEXANS
THE ALASKANS
THE GOLDEN STATERS
THE RIVER PEOPLE
THE LANDGRABBERS
THE RANCHERS
THE HOMESTEADERS
THE FRONTIER HEALERS
THE BUFFALO PEOPLE
THE BORDER BREED
THE BOOMERS

THE
BOOMERS

Lee Davis Willoughby

A DELL/BRYANS BOOK

Published by
Dell Publishing Co., Inc.
1 Dag Hammarskjold Plaza
New York, New York 10017

Dell ® TM 681510, Dell Publishing Co., Inc.

ISBN: 0-440-00688-0

Printed in the United States of America

First printing—September 1981

THE
BOOMERS

1

On a brisk October morning in 1852, Alan Travers sat in the handsome lobby of the Imperial Hotel in New York City pondering his immediate future. His mood was glum; he was contemplating the situation in which he'd suddenly found himself and concentrating on where he would go from here.

Alan was jobless, though not quite penniless. He had about $3,000 cash in a New York bank; he had his youth and ebullient good health at 26. He also possessed a fine education that meant absolutely nothing to him at the moment, since it couldn't earn him a living except as a private tutor. A job for the half-educated, he felt, not for a man who'd already taught for three years at the venerable and distinguished Plato Academy for Boys.

Alan's carer at Plato had come to an abrupt and, some would say, a rather unsavory end. Willie Morton, son of a minister, had been trying to steal some school funds when Alan chanced to surprise him ransacking the headmaster's office. Willie was an honor student, a bright liar with great charm. Willie was already in trouble with Alan who had caught him cheating at his exams. When Alan reported Willie to the headmaster, Dean Jasper, Alan's superior turned on him and accused him of abusing the boy—even worse; of attempting to seduce him.

Alan had never hit it off well with Dean Jasper; he refused to knuckle under to the old man's antiquated teaching methods, so it was understandable that Jasper would accept Willie Morton's version of the incident: a gross lie that smeared Alan's good name with the shame of an unspeakable act that had never entered his mind.

The Morton case, however, was Alan's undoing. In one swift and unforgettable day, Alan was sacked and sent packing from Plato Academy. He had asked, begged, for a letter of recommendation, or a written acknowledgment of tenure, but Dean Jasper had stoutly refused his request.

"You dare ask for a clean bill of health?" Jasper had raged. "You're fortunate you weren't indicted. I suggest you leave Boston by the first available train and lose yourself in New York, or some other suitable Sodom or Gomorrah."

"What will I do for a living? Dig ditches?" Alan asked. "Teaching's the only job I know."

"You should have thought of that when you

tried to lay hands on young Morton," Jasper responded coldly.

"Sir, the whole story's a fabrication. I never so much as hinted such a thing to the boy. Can't you see he's turned everything around? I've tried to treat my pupils as my equals. I've never curried favors nor have I caned them."

"Yes, you always were unorthodox," Jasper observed. "Well, now you can indulge your whims on your own time. I wish you success."

"I won't be able to teach on the Eastern seaboard without a paper from you, sir," Alan pleaded.

"Then go west," Jasper snapped. "Go to Australia. They welcome criminals. You'll be right at home." Jasper handed Alan his final check. "This will bring your pay to date. And you won't need credentials in Australia; they'll welcome you with open arms, I've no doubt. Your genial manner, your gentle speech. Oh yes, you'll do nicely. *Bon voyage*, Travers. We have nothing more to say to each other."

Alan shrugged, realizing the futility of any further discussion with this intractable disciplinarian. "Someday you'll realize how you've misjudged me."

"I doubt it."

"I pity you, Jasper," Alan said, beyond anger. "I pity you for your dirty, narrow mind, which indicates something very wrong with your own nature."

"Get out!" Dean Jasper shouted, red-faced in fury, as he pointed towards the door.

Without further words, Alan picked up his two

pieces of leather luggage and left the grounds of Plato Academy forever.

Alan spent a few days in New York, attempting to find a school job without a letter to cover his first three years of professional teaching employment at Plato. It took him just that long to realize that Jasper's unfeeling advice was right: he would have to go west. He thought briefly of California but suspected that he would find the same reception there as in New York without proper credentials. A mere diploma from an obscure Vermont college meant nothing without some practical experience gained since graduation three years ago.

On Alan's fifth day in New York he came upon an advertisement in a morning paper. Passage was offered aboard a schooner sailing two days hence for Sydney, Australia. The ad emphasized that only gentlemen of education and quality need apply: accountants, lawyers, teachers. For such skills, the ad stated in glowing terms, Australia was the land of golden opportunity. Proof of education was all that was needed to secure bargain-rate accommodations aboard the comfortable ship, *Invincible*. Jobs would be waiting at the end of the voyage, etc.

Alan lost no time hurrying to the Hudson River docks to inspect the Australian-bound schooner. The vessel turned out to be a creaking, scruffy coffin of a tub, alive with vermin and commanded by a bleary-eyed, seedy, fast-talking captain. The crew appeared to be a dirty, shifty-eyed gang of pirates; and thus far there were no professional passengers signed for the voyage. The reality of the *Invincible* had sent Alan back to his room at

the Imperial Hotel in a despairing mood. Feeling
isolated and alone, he hadn't even the heart to
take the train to his family in Vermont, to talk
with them and get their advice. And he couldn't
even write to them, since he had no substantial
news to convey.

Something, he knew, had to be done soon. Jasper had told him to go West, and much as he
now loathed Jasper, this seemed the wisest move.
But how would he go? By sea or by land? Land
travel seemed preferable to the long marine odyssey: a ship from New Orleans to the Isthmus of
Panama, then the perilous, disease-ridden march
across the jungled isthmus to the West Coast and
another ship bound for San Diego or San Francisco. Yet, he really had no choice. He couldn't
stay in New York, and he certainly wasn't going
to Australia.

As he sat in the Imperial Hotel lobby, he was
thankful for the legacy from his uncle Seth that
would carry him West, but he had very little else
to be grateful for beyond his good health. Now it
remained for him to bestir himself, take a train for
New Orleans and find a Panama-bound vessel to
carry him to the Isthmus. That was as far as he
wanted to think this morning. He would somehow
pull himself out of the grim mood that had en-
veloped him like an evil cloud and enjoy his final
day in New York: a fine luncheon, a stroll through
the great stores, a dinner in the evening and a
seat at the theatre, then afterwards early to bed
and on his way tomorow.

A new life was about to begin. But it wasn't
easy for Alan to convince himself that it would be
a happy, productive life, the one he had planned

for himself. How could he know at that moment that what was about to happen to him would lead him to a life beyond his most extravagant expectations?

As Alan scanned the theatre listings in his newspaper. he heard voices close to him—a man's and two women's. He glanced up to see a well-dressed trio—a distinguished, bearded gentleman in his forties, attired in black; a fair and comely gentlewoman, a bit younger than the man, wearing dark purple; and a very lovely young woman, not much more than a girl really, fair-haired and blue-eyed, wearing a dress and cape of soft rose, with a bonnet to match. A family, Alan thought: father, mother and daughter. The girl had the woman's dark blue eyes and the man's broad forehead and strong clear gaze, and she was pleading with the bearded gentleman as the three of them took an unoccupied sofa and chair opposite Alan.

"It's unnecessary, my dear," the man said to the young woman. "Where would you wear such a gown? It could be six months or more before you'd have a chance to show it off. Perhaps not ever, where we're going."

"But father," the girl pouted, "you promised it to me for my eighteenth birthday. You know it's the only present I want."

Alan saw that the girl seemed genuinely close to tears, which made her quite adorable, he decided, and quite the prettiest, freshest blonde he had ever seen.

The man said, "I'd rather you bought something more practical, my dear. A necklace of garnets, perhaps, or a gold bracelet."

"Now, Guy," the woman in purple remonstrated, "Let her do as she wishes. White *is* practical, whatever you think. It will never go out of fashion."

The bearded man smiled. "Practical for weddings, yes, but Janet's not ready for one yet. At least not for some time, I hope."

"Oh, father, really," said the girl named Janet.

"Guy, please let her have it," the woman said gently but with a practised firmness that took the stern expression from the father's eyes.

"Oh all right, all right," the man said quickly. "You women do as you wish. I wash my hands of the whole affair."

At that, Janet jumped up from the sofa, perched herself on the arm of the chair where her father sat, and gave him a peck on his forehead, which ended the discussion. The mother rose from her seat.

"Come, Janet," she said to the girl, and to the man, "We'll be back in two hours."

"And I hope without sending me into bankruptcy. I'll see you to the street," he added, rising.

As the trio moved off, Alan saw the man's wallet fall from his frock coat pocket onto the parquet lobby floor. where someone would pick it up.

Alan dropped his newspaper, retrieved the thick leather bill case and hurried to catch up with the group.

"I beg your pardon, sir," he said to the father, "but I believe you just dropped this case." He held out the man's wallet, smiling.

The family turned to study him.

"Well, well," the bearded man observed, "so I have. Thank you, young man." He took the proffered wallet and opened it. "I'd like to reward you for your honesty, if you'll accept a token of my gratitude"

Alan shook his head and flushed as the young woman smiled warmly at him.

"Thank you, sir, but I really couldn't accept anything. I simply did what had to be done."

"Others wouldn't think so," the man observed wryly. Then, nodding toward his companions he said, "I'd like to make your acquaintance. I'm Captain Guy Kelsey, this is my wife, my daughter Janet . . ."

Alan acknowledged the introduction. "I'm Alan Travers, lately of Boston. I'm a guest in the hotel."

"As are we," said Kelsey. "Would you care to have coffee with me? As you may have heard, my wife and daughter are off to deplete my fortune at one of the big department stores."

Alan grinned. "I couldn't help overhearing," he said, and Janet laughed.

"We'll go on then," Mrs. Kelsey said. "Nice meeting you, Mr. Travers."

"The same, Mrs. Kelsey, Miss Kelsey," Alan replied.

The women moved away with a rustle of skirts and the two men headed toward the Imperial's small, red damask-walled lounge for their coffee.

With the coffee, Kelsey expansively ordered two brandies.

"Might as well enjoy the interlude," he said. "You know, Travers, you're quite unusual. I'll wager almost nobody else would have returned my case. I'm carrying several hundred dollars in it, unwise in New York, but necessary, since we're only here briefly on business."

"Well, sir," Alan said, "I have a conscience. In this case it didn't get me into trouble. Should I call you Captain Kelsey or Mr. Kelsey?"

"Plain Guy suits me fine, lad."

"Good. And please call me Alan."

"Done. I'm tired of formalities anyway. Captain's fine when I'm aboard ship, and the crew wouldn't dare call me Guy. But here, in this pleasant room, we'll be two cronies, eh?" Kelsey said, toasting Alan.

"Do you like the sea?" Kelsey asked.

"I've not sailed, sir, except to Nantucket Island one summer when I was a boy."

"Ah well, that's not much more than an outing in a rowboat on a pond, from my point of view. Just wait until you've been around the Horn. Then you'll know what I mean by sailing."

"I'm not sure I want to."

"That would depend upon the ship. Mine, the *Prince Rupert*, is as sound as a new-minted dollar. It can stand up to the most hellish weather imaginable. . . . By the way, Alan, what's your profession?" Kelsey asked abruptly.

Alan decided to be candid, up to a point. "Until last week I was a school teacher." He was tempted to tell him about the Willie Morton incident and of his dismissal by Dean Jasper but instinct restrained him.

Kelsey studied him a moment. "Let me guess why. You're on your way West. No young man wants to waste time teaching raw, stupid boys and girls when the world's full of high adventure for the taking."

Alan smiled, partly with relief. Kelsey had eliminated the need for confession. "Well," he admitted, "I was thinking of going to Australia until I inspected a schooner called the *Invincible* this morning. It was headed there."

Kelsey frowned. "Good God, Alan, you didn't book passage on that wretched rat trap, I trust?"

"No, sir. I'd just come from looking at it when you folks sat down next to me. I wouldn't have sailed aboard it free."

"There you show good sense," Kelsey said, exhaling sharply in relief. "Old Pitt, the skipper, is a rogue. It's a wonder they even let him dock in New York. If you wait another month, the *Capetown* will be back from England, and you'll have safe passage. But steer clear of the *Invincible.*"

"I shall," said Alan.

Kelsey consulted his pocket watch.

"Look here, Alan, I hate to run, but I'm expecting the arrival of my client. We're to meet in a few minutes, and he's always punctual. Sorry to leave you . . ." Kelsey signalled the waiter and paid the bill over Alan's protests.

"I've an idea," Kelsey said, rising. "Unless you're determined to go to Australia."

"Not really. It was just a notion. I'm about ready to go anywhere that looks right, and do almost anything except teach, for the time being anyway. I'm no pauper, sir. I have modest funds; they'll last a while anyway."

Kelsey stopped in the lobby, and shook hands with Alan.

"Say no more, lad. Meet me at six in the hotel dining room. I'll be with my wife and daughter and my client. I'd like to have you join us."

"It would be an honor, sir."

"All right then. Six o'clock . . ."

Kelsey walked through the crowded lobby, a tall, imposing figure. Alan stood looking after him, wondering what he'd let himself in for. What if that dropped wallet was some kind of confidence game, and the women, though ladylike, merely lures? Stranger things had happened to gullible out-of-towners in New York. Yet, on the other hand, what could he lose by accepting an invitation to dinner with the Kelseys—if that's who they really were? And, honestly, he was intrigued by two other factors—the identity of Kelsey's client and the precise nature of Kelsey's seagoing business, which the captain had carefully bypassed.

As Alan headed upstairs to his room he saw Captain Kelsey standing just inside the front entrance of the lobby, hands clasped behind him, obviously waiting for his guest.

Alan was tempted to linger and eavesdrop but instead he continued on to his room. He would bathe, dress carefully and be in the dining room promptly at six. After all, if nothing else happened he could always feast his eyes on the refreshing loveliness of Janet Kelsey—if that's who she really was. But whatever or whoever she was, Alan knew one thing; he wanted to know her better, and he would.

2

ALAN TRAVERS WALKED into the sumptuous dining room of the Imperial at precisely six o'clock. The headwaiter led him to the Kelsey table, dominated by the distinguished figure of a tall, rather elegant man in his mid-thirties, impeccably attired, handsome, clear-eyed and deep-voiced. Alan was quite impressed as Kelsey introduced him to Bruce Randall, of Boston.

The surname Randall struck an immediate and familiar note with Alan. There were prominent Randalls in Boston; the family had come over as immigrants in the late years of the eighteenth century and had made a fortune in shipbuilding. From Bruce Randall's obvious breeding and glow-

18

ing self-confidence, Alan assumed that the captain's guest must be a member of that branch of the Randall family. Or again, Alan reminded himself as he sat down at the table to Randall's left, the man might merely be an actor posing as the scion of a wealthy Boston family, appearances often being accepted at face value in New York.

Nonetheless, Bruce Randall asked all the right questions, said all the right things, and dinner proceeded smoothly and enjoyably for Alan. There was much small talk of ships and sailing, of supplies and ports of supply. Randall directed no special questions toward Alan, to Alan's relief, and no mention was made of the fact that Alan was a currently unemployed schoolteacher.

The meal continued through forty minutes of delicious food and a variety of topics. As dessert was being served, Bruce Randall finally directed his attention to Alan.

"Captain Kelsey tells me that you're thinking of going West, Travers."

"It was on my mind, yes," Alan replied.

"Where exactly, may I ask?"

"Well, first I'd thought of Australia but I changed my mind today."

"He inspected the *Invincible*," Kelsey added.

"Now I'm not sure where I'll go or what I'll do," Alan said. "I might try the West Indies."

"Wretched climate," Randall said. "You'd do best to travel to the west coast of America. As Captain Kelsey might have told you, I've chartered the *Prince Rupert* for an important voyage. At least, important for me. We're sailing shortly for California and the great Northwest territory."

Alan brightened at the news, which was certainly more information than the cagey Kelsey had given him. "I didn't know," he told Randall.

"Yes, tomorrow we load equipment. Barring unforeseen complications, we sail the day after tomorrow. A voyage of discovery, I'm calling it. Going into unfamiliar territory and taking all the risks attendant to exploration. My rather romantic hope is that I'll find a new life for myself."

"For all of us, Bruce," Kelsey added graciously, while Marian Kelsey concentrated silently on her lemon meringue pastry, and Janet smiled conspiratorially at Alan from across the table.

"I've recently become independent of my family business in Boston," Randall went on. "This has enabled me to do something on my very own for the first time in my life. We're a tradition-bound bunch, we Randalls, and not prone to take off on whimsical expeditions in commerce. I've decided to break that tradition and become an explorer and strike out on my own."

"I think that's exciting, sir. What will the new business be?" Alan asked, feeling that he was either being used as a possible sounding board, or that he would soon be asked to donate to the Randall cause.

Randall smiled knowingly at Alan. "I see that you're a bit skeptical. I admire that quality; it shows prudence and native good sense. My business, Travers—and Captain Kelsey's, too, for the duration of our association—will be to carry equipment around Cape Horn, God willing, and to open up new land north of San Francisco in which a lumber business can be developed. We'll be sailing with enough material to set up a small community and logging operations in the vicinity. Land has already been negotiated for by agents in California, and with due modesty, I've sufficient funds to purchase all the virgin timberland a company can handle for the next several decades."

Naturally, Alan was impressed. "There are Indians to the north in Oregon Territory, Mr. Randall. Many are hostile. And there are no towns of any size."

"Yes, yes, we know that. And it's my very reason for wanting to start from scratch. That's all part of the challenge."

Randall snapped his fingers at their waiter who immediately arrived with a silver champagne stand and glasses. When all were served, Randall raised his glass for a toast.

"To a successful voyage and a successful new life for one and all," he declared.

Alan raised his glass hesitantly; Randall said: "To your good fortune as well, wherever you go, Travers."

The men drank heartily; the ladies merely took token sips and set their glasses down.

After the champagne, Bruce Randall insisted on paying the check. The ladies rose and excused themselves while the three men retired to the hotel lounge for cigars and brandy. Alan bought the first round, which was quickly downed. Kelsey ordered the next, and the talk turned again to technical matters concerning the impending voyage. After twenty minutes Alan excused himself, thanking both men for a most agreeable evening, shaking hands.

"This isn't the end of it, lad," Kelsey told Alan. "Come down to the river docks tomorrow and watch us load the *Rupert*. We'll show you around and open your eyes."

Randall said, "The captain is serious about the invitation, Alan. And so am I." His smile was genial.

"I'm honored, sir," Alan replied. "I'll be there—"

Kelsey and Randall watched Alan leave the crowded lounge.

"Fine youngster," Kelsey observed as he puffed his cigar.

"First rate," Randall agreed. "If there's one thing I've learned from my association with the family business, it's an unerring instinct for character appraisal."

"You surprise me. I thought we had all the personnel you wanted."

"Alan Travers may be the wisest choice of all, Guy. We'll see . . ."

Alan went up to his room in a light-hearted mood, unaware that his fate was being decided in his absence.

Early next morning Alan went down to the docks. He found the *Prince Rupert* moored to Dock Five on the Hudson River and was favorably impressed with the neat 160-ton brig. It was well-kept, sparkling with fresh paint; a two-masted, square-rigged vessel that looked as though it could sail around the world and back without a mishap. What impressed Alan even more was the orderly, jovial crew that supervised the loading of various supplies under orders from a burly first mate. The cargo included drums of cable, kegs of nails, giant two-handed saws, crates of axes, and many other items Alan couldn't identify, all appropriate to the expedition's needs, he decided.

Bruce Randall and Kelsey stood to one side with papers checking the disposition of the cargo while the first mate directed the loading of the holds and the arrangement of deck space.

The Kelsey ladies, Alan noted, were nowhere in sight, presumably either out shopping or else already settled aboard. It was noon before the heavy supplies were positioned to Randall's and Kelsey's satisfaction. After the crew knocked off for lunch, Randall invited Alan to eat aboard in the small officers' mess. The hearty stew was much to Alan's taste, and he ate it eagerly, sopping up his plate with fresh bread.

After luncheon, Captain Kelsey excused himself to go into the city to join his wife and Janet who, it turned out, were still staying at the Imperial. After thanking Bruce Randall for the meal and the visit, Alan said he would go along with the captain.

Bruce Randall protested. "No you don't. Come into my cabin. I'd like to talk with you about a personal matter."

Kelsey agreed. "Better listen to him, Alan. Besides holding the purse strings, Bruce is a man of shrewd taste." Kelsey patted Alan on the shoulder and left the men to themselves.

Following Bruce to his cabin, Alan wondered if he were about to get the pitch that he'd been expecting and readied himself for a solicitation of needed funds. Inside the small cabin, Bruce gestured for Alan to sit on the lower bunk, closed the door and leaned against it, and began speaking without further preamble.

"First off, Alan, let me say that I like you."

"Good to know," Alan replied with a grin.

"You're bright, alert, well-mannered, quick to air your views, yet still modest, and intelligent. Quite a set of virtues in a young man these days. And, just as important," Randall continued, "you're exactly what you claim to be."

"How so, sir?" Alan asked with faint trepidation.

"You have funds, you've a degree to teach."

"That's correct, sir."

"And second, we—Guy Kelsey and myself—are exactly what we claim to be. I'm a Randall, for what it's worth, and Guy Kelsey's probably as fine a skipper as you're likely to encounter on the seven seas, an extremely tough and able man of strength and integrity. I'm financing the entire project, but of course there's more to my involvement than mere joyful enthusiasm and the desire to explore undeveloped country."

"I imagined there was, sir."

"Stop calling me 'sir', Alan. It's Bruce from now on."

"As you wish, Bruce."

"We all have our hidden sides, dark places that will probably remain unexplored. I have mine, and I imagine that you have yours."

Alan started to speak but Bruce continued without giving him the chance to say anything.

"It didn't take us very long after you left us in the bar last night to decide to offer you passage on the *Prince Rupert.* Even without checking on your credentials, we were certain you were right for our party. So, we've decided to suggest that you go with us to the west coast of America. Nominally, this means San Francisco. From that point on you're under no further obligation. How does that strike you?"

"I'm dumbfounded," Alan said. "How much will it cost me?"

"That's what I'm trying to say, Bruce. You'll be one of us. We're going to leave our eastern manners right here on the dock, and grow a new set on the trip for the world we'll encounter. Guy and I feel that you'd be a definite asset to us. You'll have duties. You'll work on the voyage to pay for your passage. But you'll be learning the fundamentals of life at sea, how to patch a sail, scrub a deck, keep logs, even a diary of your own, if you like. In all, a thousand things you never thought you'd learn, and certainly not on a vessel as neat as the *Rupert*. Later on, of course, you may want to explore the West alongside of me. But that's considerably into the future and will have to work itself out. I have a strong premonition you'll be first-rate at whatever you turn your hand to. Well, what do you think?"

"Incredible," was all Alan could manage.

"Then you'll accept the offer?"

"With great pleasure," Alan replied eagerly.

"Good. Oh, and also, Alan, if you find that the voyage isn't to your liking, you're free to leave the ship wherever and whenever we put into a port for fresh supplies. You'll have to find your own way home, of course, from that point. Aboard you'll be responsible to Captain Kelsey first, whose word is law on the high seas. And you'll be responsible to me as my guest . . . so, if you come aboard tonight before midnight, you'll be sailing with us before dawn tomorrow. How does that strike you?"

Alan could say nothing for a few moments. He stared at his hands clenched together between his knees. So much had happened so suddenly that he was unable to gather together the proper words of response. Finally he looked up at Bruce Randall who was regarding him intently.

"I want to go with you and Captain Kelsey, Bruce," he muttered softly. "I think it's the best thing that could possibly happen to me right now."

Bruce Randall clapped his hands together. "Excellent choice, excellent!" Bruce checked his watch. "Now, there's just enough time for you to get to your bank and arrange for a letter of credit in San Francisco. Check out of the Imperial and sign aboard this evening. As I said, we'll be sailing sometime before dawn with tomorrow's tide."

Alan sat motionless on the bunk as Bruce turned to open the cabin door, still stunned from the rapid resolution of his future. Bruce glanced questioningly at him.

"Anything wrong?"

Alan nodded. "There's something I should tell you. You mentioned dark sides."

"I'm not asking for confessions, Alan."

"I know. But you said a few minutes ago that I was just what I claimed to be—fairly solvent, with a teaching degree. But what you don't know is why I'm not teaching right now. I was just sacked from a very good job. I can't get a letter of recommendation, which means I can't work anywhere on the east coast."

Bruce leaned against the open door, studying Alan.

"Why not?" he asked evenly.

In painful embarrassment, Alan told Bruce the

story of Willie Morton and Dean Jasper and his unpleasantly prejudicial departure from Plato Academy. When he was through with the details he lapsed into silence, awaiting Bruce's cold dismissal. The story was preposterous, he realized, and not easy to believe. But instead of reprimanding him, Bruce broke into laughter.

"Oh Christ," he chuckled, shaking his head, "that's the classic case of the pot calling the kettle black. You won't believe this, but I know that sly bastard Jasper, the old pervert. He was a master at Plato when I attended school there as a boy."

"*You* went to Plato?" Alan gasped.

"Unfortunately. Jasper wasn't in charge then, but he was a rotten apple if there ever was one. How he managed to maintain tenure and achieve his present eminence is just one of the many reasons why I've come to detest Boston and its hypocrisy. I believe you, Alan. And what's more, I admire you for having the courage to tell me your story. Damn that son of a bitch Jasper! I'd like to break his neck."

"So would I," said Alan with vast relief.

"Now, let's just pretend this little conversation never took place, shall we? It will remain our grim private joke."

"If you say so," Alan responded gratefully.

"I do, most emphatically. Kelsey will never learn anything of this, I promise you. Now, go and make your arrangements and come aboard as soon as you can."

"Where will I bunk?"

"Why here, of course, on the upper ledge. I hope you don't snore."

"No complaints so far."

"Good! Otherwise you'll be out with the crew. Now get going."

Alan arranged his affairs at the bank and withdrew a fair amount of cash to place in the captain's safe. He paid his bill at the Imperial and boarded the *Prince Rupert* in the early evening. The Kelseys, Bruce Randall and crew were already there.

The brig sailed long before dawn. Alan was on deck as the graceful craft moved slowly down the river, out into the Bay and toward the open sea. He watched the twinkling lights of the city's low skyline diminish against the morning sky, then finally disappear altogether. He could hardly believe that he was embarking on what would surely prove to be the big event of his life, but he made himself accept it as the truth. He would learn and grow and change, and who knew, he might even become a giant in the new country that awaited him.

Of course, he told himself, countless, endless days of sailing lay ahead, perhaps even as much as six months. There would be moments of intense boredom when the very sea would spell monotony; there would be other times when he would long to be out of earshot of the human voice. But all in all, there would be much to learn, and he felt relaxed about his impending adventure, at ease, strangely enough, for the first time since his dismissal from the academy. In fact, he didn't even resent Dean Jasper much. He had no fear of the unknown that lay ahead, nor did he worry about the voyage. His life was just beginning, and only that was important.

"Aren't the birds beautiful?" a soft voice at his elbow remarked as he leaned against a pile of deck cargo. The voice belonged to Janet Kelsey, and she was pointing to the gulls that circled lazily above the ship.

"Yes, they are," he said, glad to see her.

"You'll like the sea," Janet said. "I do. I can tell when people respond. I've an instinct. I've been sailing since I was six."

"You've been everywhere then?"

Janet's answer was interrupted by the abrupt appearance of Marian Kelsey, who seemed to materialize out of thin air, the eternal chaperone.

"Come, dear," Mrs. Kelsey purred at her daughter. "It's time for morning tea."

Without further ado and with no apology, she whisked Janet away and Alan was once more alone with the sea, the screeching gulls, and the soft slap of the waves against the *Prince Rupert*'s sleek prow.

A stiff breeze sprang up and took the sails. Alan went forward to the prow and leaned into the wind, letting it ruffle his wavy brown hair, enjoying the sting of salt spray on his cheeks. If the whole voyage could be as lyrical as this moment, he thought, he might even turn to the sea and forsake teaching forever. But he was too much of a realist to expect such joy to continue.

As for Janet, he had seen Bruce Randall's long, speculative glances in her direction. It took no great insight on Alan's part to determine that even if Janet might prefer someone nearer her own age, or his, both Guy and Marian Kelsey were undoubtedly aware that Bruce Randall was a wealthy bachelor and would make a superb mate for their highly eligible daughter.

That brought Alan to another disturbing thought. He was already foolishly, imprudently smitten with Janet, and this could easily turn to love soon enough. Aboard ship this could be fatal, or at least uncomfortable. But better not to anticipate anything.

"Travers!" a loud voice was calling to him from mid-ships. He turned to see Captain Kelsey beckoning him with none of the friendly deference he had shown at the Imperial. Alan hurried to join him.

"Your first assignment, Travers," Kelsey announced. "Ship's papers, the job of purser. Come along. Might as well start you right out . . ."

Falling in behind the captain, Alan felt that his life at sea had at last truly begun.

3

ALAN TOOK READILY to the routine that sailing demanded. He found, to his surprise, that without exception the hand-picked crew held a highly professional view of their duties, executing them summarily upon Kelsey's orders. They seemed to accept the close quarters and the endless monotony of the seascape as a fact to be lived with as comfortably and efficiently as possible. Alan soon found out that shipshape meant exactly that; a place for everything and everything in its place.

There were fair days and windy days as the *Prince Rupert* moved southwest toward its first port of call, the Spanish city of Havana in the West Indies. With the ship at anchor, he was glad to go ashore with Kelsey and Bruce and see the sights.

He was advised by Bruce not to follow the crew
to their special hangouts, and he continued to
abide by this suggestion all through the voyage.
He was, in any case, too interested in Janet to go
hankering after the flesh of foreign ladies of
pleasure.

The weather remained fair but rough as the
Rupert left the West Indies behind and sailed
down the coast of South America. At Belem, not
yet the rubber capital of the world and still under
Portuguese rule, the *Rupert* put in for supplies and
remained several days in the torpid heat of the
port, while a fierce storm marched down the coast
a hundred miles or so to the east of them. The
blood-thirsty pirates who once plagued the area
were long gone; even so, Alan was fascinated by
Guy Kelsey's stories of another era when Belem
was a military post for the defense of northern
Brazil against French, English and Dutch renegade
plunderers.

It was a long voyage from Belem to Recife, but
again, with the chance to learn celestial navigation
and the complete workings of a vessel as well-made
as the *Rupert*, Alan found no time for boredom.
There were nights when the weather was soft and
mild, the sailing smooth and swift and the stars
seemed very close. After meals in the gentle darkness, everyone would sit on deck and listen to the
first mate and the cook, amateur musicians, play
Spanish guitars and sing songs in a variety of lan-
guages, gathered on their many trips across the
globe. The lustier songs, of course, had to wait until the ladies and the captain and Bruce had retired. These would be sung far into the night,

muted, naturally, so as not to bring down Kelsey's
wrath—which was considerable when something
did not suit him precisely.

Recife, in the state of Pernambuco, Brazil, was
the next important land-fall. Crisscrossed with brilliant waterways, it was called the Brazilian Venice.
It had a fine natural harbor enclosed by a coral
reef and exported great quantities of cotton, sugar
and coffee. Founded in 1548 as a port for nearby
Olinda, it boasted two universities and a seven-
teenth-century cathedral. Its people were charming, multi-lingual and extremely hospitable.

The Kelseys, Bruce Randall and Alan were
wined and dined in Recife by the local gentry,
taken to see the nearby cane fields and sent on
their way loaded with gifts by their Brazilian hosts,
who were generous to the point of embarrassment.

Captain Kelsey employed the time-honored system of always carrying supplies which would
guarantee the *Rupert*'s welcome in port. And from
one port to the next he would carry goods that
could easily be bartered where no currency was
acceptable.

Salvador in the state of Bahia, Brazil, was the
Rupert's next port of call. Tobacco for the crew,
sugar, hardwoods, even a pouch of industrial
diamonds, were taken on here. The tiered city was
the seat of unrest for Brazil's independence even
as early as the *Rupert*'s visit. Built on a peninsula
and settled by a motley group of merchants and
insurgent intellectuals, Salvador caught Alan's
imagination. He wouldn't have minded staying on;
the cultural vitality of the city charmed him, as
did the beautiful, black-eyed young women who

smiled at him everywhere. If it hadn't been for
Janet, he could easily have given his heart to the
city.

Rio de Janeiro was as breathtakingly beautiful
as the crew had assured him it would be. If he
had almost fallen in love with Salvador, Rio cap-
tivated him completely. The warmth and humidity
were offset by the generous hospitality of the
Cariocas, who could not entertain the captain and
his guests often or splendidly enough. There were
parties daily while the ship lay in the harbor, long
luncheons, sparkling dinners, music, entertainment.
All in all, a world that Alan could never have
imagined existed, and one he was reluctant to
leave. Janet, of course, was besieged by suitors, to
the point where either Kelsey, Bruce or Alan had
to act as escort to the ladies whenever they went
ashore. Alan was delighted, for this not only gave
him the opportunity to explore the city, he also
had much more time with Janet. Never alone, with
her, however, for Marian Kelsey was always present, keeping a subtle but perpetual vigil. It was a
sad day for Alan and the entire personnel of the
Rupert when the brig sailed out of the harbor on its
voyage south, leaving behind a whirling social life
of lavish glitter, beautiful subtropical parks,
stately palaces, and a land of apparently endless
fertility.

Montevideo, Uruguay was just recovering from
the effects of a vicious civil war in 1852. Its independence newly won, it opened its gates to the
Rupert and other ships making the voyage around
South America and north with a special warmth.
To survive, Montevideo encouraged commerce and
it was already a small, bustling capital that would

later become one of the most handsome cities on the southern continent. The climate was benign, the beaches exquisitely beautiful, the cuisine and native fruits exotic and delicious. The *Rupert* sailed off across the wide Rio de la Plata toward Mar del Plata and Peninsula Valdes, bypassing Buenos Aires. From Valdes south to the Gulf of San Jorge, the weather gradually became blustery and the seas much rougher. The *Rupert* was beginning to feel the effects of the winds and currents sweeping up from the Antarctic. Seasickness began to plague Marian Kelsey, a couple of crew members, and Bruce Randall, even though they were experienced sailors. Alan delighted in the stormy weather, not knowing what was still to come.

By the time the *Rupert* set its course for the narrow Strait of Magellan, the narrow waterway separating South America from Tierra del Fuego and the islands south of the continent's tip, the weather had turned nasty and the brig was forced to move directly into a raging storm. While Alan had enjoyed the rough weather up until now and found it exhilarating, and although Kelsey had briefed him on what to expect as they approached the Strait, Alan was unprepared for the sea's fury once it struck.

Sails were ripped loose, and the brig, though tight, shipped crushing waves, sometimes almost disappearing between two mountainous crests, deep in a wave trough. Rising again, the *Rupert* would shudder on the crest of the next wave before it plunged down with sickening speed into the watery abyss.

During this passage into the Strait, Bruce Randall lay sick in his bunk, vomiting and groaning.

Even Captain Kelsey looked rather white around the gills, the crew's standard expression for seasick passengers, which Alan could well understand now.

At one point, not too far from the Strait, where the storm was at its fiercest, Bruce could stand the stench and confinement of the cabin no longer. Weakly, he pulled himself up on deck, unnoticed by either the crew or Alan, panting for a breath of fresh cold air.

The force of the teetering brig tore away Bruce's hold on the handrails and threw him into the rigging just as Alan was rounding the bulkhead in Bruce's path.

With a shout lost in the storm's howling winds, Alan sprang forward and threw himself across Bruce's body just before a giant wave crashed across the brig's starboard bow, inundating them both.

Gasping for air, Alan managed to hang onto the rope ladder, shielding Bruce from the direct force of the icy wave. As the ship righted itself, Alan was able to grab Bruce around his waist. Aided by the force of the tilting ship, he dragged Bruce to the nearest hatch and pulled him through, closing it behind him. If Alan hadn't managed his timing precisely, both men would have been swept overboard and lost in the icy marine holocaust.

Sturdy brig that it was, the *Rupert* rode out the peak of the storm. Some seven hours later it sailed through the mouth of the Strait of Magellan and into thankfully calm waters. Fog made the passage difficult, but the Strait provided refuge from the storm that more than compensated for the trick navigation needed to reach the Pacific Ocean. The

Rupert put into Punta Arenas for fresh water, staying longer than planned because Bruce Randall had developed pneumonia.

During Bruce's illness, Alan never left his side. He had nurtured a fine rapport with Randall and feared for the older man's life, doing all he could to hasten his recovery. Finally the fever subsided, Randall began to eat again, and more than ten days later than scheduled, the brig set sail for the Peninsula Tres Montes and the open Pacific.

Two weeks later Valparaiso, Chile, rose from its narrow waterfront terrace on steep hills, a welcome sight gleaming and beckoning in the dazzling sunlight. The wide bay had just recently been visited by a devastating storm but was now calm and hospitable to the *Rupert* after its rough passage around the tip of South America. The Spanish city was just beginning to grow industrially; its wines were choice and already in demand for export, its wools the finest.

The *Rupert* lingered on in the refuge of Valparaiso's harbor until one of the crew deserted ship, presumably in love with a Chilean woman, and Kelsey and Randall decided that they must sail on, or else sustain further crew losses.

From Valparaiso to the port of Lima, Peru, the *Rupert* was never far from land. Sailing weather was magnificent, with occasional storms, but none to compare with those in the region of Cape Horn. They crossed the Equator again without celebration. While such ceremonies were traditional aboard most ships, Kelsey disliked them as disorderly, and forbade them, both on the east coast of South America sailing down, and again, on the voyage north to Mexico.

Ports of call on the way north included Panama, the Gulf of Tehuantepec in Mexico, Melaque in Jalisco, and then on to San Diego, skirting the arid shores of Baja California, on the other side of which lay the Sea of Cortez.

For Alan, the voyage seemed almost over at San Diego. Here he could speak to his countrymen again, he was in a truly American atmosphere, although the tempo and folkways were far different from those in the eastern United States.

After a few days in San Diego Bay, Captain Kelsey set a course for San Francisco. Christmas had been celebrated near the Equator. Alan observed St. Valentine's Day with a silent message for Janet while nearing San Francisco Bay. He hadn't the courage to confess personally to the Kelsey girl that during the weeks and months he had been observing her, his admiration had increased, and his love become full-blown. Nor had he the courage to say anything of his feelings to Bruce Randall, who had become his firm confidant in all other matters.

San Francisco was not what Alan had thought it would be. Fed upon tales of the Gold Rush of 1849, Alan was not prepared for the sudden changes that had been wrought on San Francisco. He didn't particularly like it, and told Bruce so.

"Well, at least you've got to sort it out for yourself, Alan," Bruce told him. "Check out the teaching positions here. See if you might want to linger on."

"I don't," Alan responded stoutly. "It's not my style at all. There's too much of the circus to it, too many gaudy people."

"You could go inland to Sacramento, or south."

"I'm really not interested."

"But I thought you intended to settle here."

"I did. But now I want to go north with you."

Bruce Randall had given this idea much thought since Alan had saved his life at the risk of his own during that nightmarish storm near the Strait of Magellan. Also, he might not have survived the bout of pneumonia had it not been for Alan's constant vigilance. Yes, Bruce knew that he owed Alan far more than he could ever repay him, and he reflected on this unsentimentally. He wanted Alan to come north, but at the same time he didn't feel it was his right to push the issue. Until now. He knew clearly why Alan didn't want to stay behind in California: Janet.

"Very simple," Bruce said. "If you decide to come along with us and find your fortune in the northwest, nobody will be happier than I'll be."

"You really mean that?"

"Alan, you ought to know me well enough by now. I don't say one thing and mean another."

"Dear God," Alan sighed, "that's the best news I've heard since we landed in San Francisco Bay."

Bruce knew he owed Alan much more than just the trip north. But this entailed some serious thought and would be decided upon later, if things went at all the way Bruce hoped they would. And at that time, Alan would become a close friend for life.

But now there was something he could do. He could persuade Captain Kelsey to take off his blinders, the ones he'd been wearing during the entire wearisome trip, make him see that Alan and Janet were in love, even though they hadn't been given a single moment to think about it. It was about time that something was done to give the young people a chance. But practically speaking, this time would have to be postponed until the *Rupert* was safely headed north. If the subject were brought up in San Francisco, Kelsey was just bullheaded and protective enough about his daughter to leave Marian Kelsey and Janet behind in San Francisco when the brig sailed.

It took Bruce the better part of a fortnight to set up the machinery for his business operations in the northwest with various San Francisco business houses. The *Rupert* would be used to make frequent round trips between San Francisco and Puget Sound, for so long as Kelsey wished to continue the operation, or until Bruce decided to buy his own vessel.

When all business details were arranged to Bruce's satisfaction, and Kelsey had obtained provisions for the *Rupert*, the brig sailed out through the Golden Gate on a glorious early spring morning to make its last leg of the odyssey to the Pacific Northwest territory. The *Rupert* was to be followed in a few days by a second brig, leased for only the single trip north and carrying the men Bruce and Kelsey had recruited to establish what Bruce hoped would one day become a vast logging empire.

The blue and golden day was serene, the wind right, the crew jolly. Bruce and Alan stood on the deck studying the coastline until the Mendocino shoreline and the forests began to appear, tipped with the fires of sunset.

"What a sight!" Alan exclaimed.

"There they are," said Bruce, passing the hand

telescope to Alan. "The sequoias, California's green gold, its coastal redwoods. Our riches begin right here and go as far north as the mind can reach."

"I've never seen anything so impressive or so immense," Alan said almost reverently. "They're incredibly beautiful."

"Just waiting for man to take them," Bruce replied, with a touch of irony in his voice. "Kelsey says the giant sequoias only mark the beginning. The forests range all the way north as far as anyone wants to go. At Puget Sound the Douglas fir stands are so thick that the light of day rarely falls on the earth."

"I can hardly wait to see it all," Alan said eagerly, speaking for both of them. They handed the scope back and forth in the fading light, hungry for the sight of such wealth and magnificence.

The first sight of big trees might not have been such a joyful one had Bruce and Alan known of a certain Henry York, already entrenched at Puget Sound. The man held dreams similar to Bruce's of building the greatest lumber empire the world had ever known. York had made a solemn vow to himself that he would let nothing stop him in his quest for supremacy. That meant that he would discourage all comers and competitors by whatever means he found necessary—sabotage, even murder.

Night fell swiftly as the brig sailed past Mendocino and held to its course toward Oregon Territory. In his small lounge, Captain Kelsey sat up late talking of the Northwest with Bruce and Alan. Guy Kelsey was doing most of the talking, since he was the only one of the three who had seen the land before on two voyages to the west coast.

Alan was the first to retire, giving Bruce the opportunity he wanted to discuss Alan and Janet with the captain.

"I'm delighted," he began, "that Alan's coming along with us. He'll be a companion for me, but I worry about his getting lonely."

"No need for you to be lonely," the captain pointed out. "Janet admires you a lot."

"She's a fine young woman," Bruce said, not pleased with the direction the conversation was taking. "She'll make someone a marvelous wife."

"Someone?" Kelsey's heavy eyebrows shot up. "She'd be perfect for you."

Bruce shook his head. "I wasn't thinking of myself. I have no inclination to marry anyone at present, not even your charming daughter."

"But you've escorted her to wherever we've put into port on the voyage," the captain protested. "Surely you have some interest in her."

"Purely avuncular," Bruce advised. "Guy, don't you see what I'm trying to say? Alan's in love with Janet, and I don't think I'm off the mark by observing that Janet is equally taken with him."

"My God, Bruce, you can't be serious! Travers hasn't the means to make a life for Janet. Why, he'll be no better than a lumberjack up north, and without even proper training at first. The fact that he left school teaching speaks for his lack of stability."

"I wouldn't say so. As for his prospects, I think they're quite good. I'm going to make him my general manager and see how things turn out. After all, this isn't to be a summer's outing, Guy. I'm dead serious about settling here permanently, as you know, and Alan is just as intent on it."

"I'm firmly against the match, Bruce. I might as well say it right out. But to be fair to your ideas, and to young Travers, who isn't a bad sort, I'll discuss the matter with Marian, see what she thinks."

"I'd be much obliged, Guy. I understand your sentiments, wanting the best for the girl. I think she'll be getting that. Do you realize that not once in all our ports of call did Alan go ashore to carouse? Not once. He's a steady, solid young man and deserves consideration."

Kelsey got to his feet. "Very well, Bruce. I'll talk it over with Marian and let you know. Goodnight."

Bruce sat alone in the lounge a few minutes longer, pondering the wisdom of his words with Kelsey. Maybe he'd done the very thing that would keep the young couple apart forever; he sincerely hoped not. Anyhow, it was done; he had fulfilled part of his obligation to Alan, at least.

It was several days before Captain Kelsey found the propitious moment to bring up the subject of Janet's future to her mother, Marian.

Mrs. Kelsey had been a great Boston beauty in her younger years, from a good though not wealthy family. She had been her parents' one hope of aligning themselves with a bloodline of quality and money, for Marian was being courted by a most eligible young man. Then she had met Captain Kelsey at a party, fallen instantly in love with him, as he had with her, and had broken with her family in her determination to marry the dashing young sea captain without a penny to his name.

Marian, in fact, had finally run off with Guy

Kelsey to the West Indies, married aboard ship,
settling in the Virgin Islands where Kelsey's shipping firm was based. Janet had been born at St.
Thomas and spent her early childhood there. If
there was one hope Marian Kelsey held to firmly
it was a good marriage for Janet. Alan Travers,
while a charming young man with intelligence
and good breeding, was not what she had in mind
for her pretty daughter. Bruce Randall was the
object of her eye, and it was in hopes that Bruce
would find her daughter irresistible that she had
been willing to come along on the arduous voyage
around South America with Janet.

"The answer is no, Guy," Marian told her husband when he finally broached the subject of
Alan Travers in their cabin one night. "An absolute, unequivocal no. You know how I feel about
love matches."

"We haven't done too badly," Kelsey told his
wife. "We own the *Rupert*, we've got a few invest-
ments, the cottage on Cape Cod."

"Yes," Marian conceded, "you've done the best
you could. I have no complaints. But I want even
more for Janet. If it's not going to be Bruce Randall, and it certainly looks as though it isn't, then
we're returning directly from the Northwest with
you and you'll deposit us in San Francisco."

"San Francisco!" Kelsey exclaimed. "My God,
you're not thinking of turning Janet into a demi-
mondaine, I hope!"

"Don't be crass," said Marian. "I'm thinking of
staying with the Bradys. They gave us a standing
invitation while we were in town. I didn't tell you
for obvious reasons, which have now altered the
entire picture."

"Marian, let's relax. If Janet likes Alan well enough to respond to the idea of marrying him, why not?"

"And let her live like a savage in the north woods while the men are making a fortune for themselves?"

"Which she'll enjoy in due time," Kelsey pointed out.

Marian shook her head. "You're mad, Guy, absolutely mad." But she was a practical woman and there was a certain element of logic to Guy's belief that Alan might eventually make a fortune.

"The only trouble is," she pointed out, "it's going to be Bruce Randall's business, not Alan's."

"I have an idea that might change. Bruce feels obligated to Alan for saving his life. Let's wait things out."

"You mean, let the young folks alone, do my crocheting elsewhere than within earshot."

"Right! Let them have the lounge once in a while in the next two weeks. No harm in that."

"No, I suppose not."

Kelsey turned to his wife and took her in his arms.

"Tell me, have you ever been truly sorry you married me? Have I made you unhappy, denied you anything you really wanted?"

"No, Guy, you haven't," Marian conceded. "I've had no regrets."

"All right then, why can't we let nature take its course and see what happens?"

Marian sighed, laying her head against her husband's shoulder. "I shall miss her terribly if she decides to stay up here with him," she murmured. "My baby—"

"Now, now," the captain comforted her. "Lie down, like a good girl, rest, relax. Remember how it was with us," he said, kissing her firmly while she responded, . . . "and still is.'

During the following days Mrs. Kelsey relaxed her constant vigil over Janet. She said nothing to the girl, nor did Alan have an inkling that he and Janet had been the subject of some intense discussion between the Kelseys and Bruce Randall.

The weather was cool and brisk, with some tail-end winter storms, although nothing as fierce as the weather outside the Strait of Magellan. But sharp weather couldn't keep Janet and Alan inside when they could lean against the bow of the *Rupert* and hold hands covertly, expecting at almost any moment to be interrupted, and surprised when they were not.

In lieu of physical contact, the lovers found a thousand obscure subjects to discuss, always skirting the issue that meant the most to them: how would they be able to make legitimate and permanent their as yet undeclared love for each other? Eventually it was Janet who brought up the problem one sunny afternoon off the coast of Washington Territory.

"Do you think there's any hope for us at all?" she asked Alan as they faced into a biting wind only two days out from the Strait of Juan de Fuca.

Alan slipped his arm around Janet's waist, not caring if the captain or Marian Kelsey did catch him.

"The only hope, dearest, is if your father will consent to marry us. And I don't see much chance of that."

"Nor do I," Janet sighed sadly.

"Well, at least one of us has finally spoken up. I wanted to, but I wasn't sure how you felt."

"Now that we're both sure," Janet said, "we must declare our intentions to my mother and father. You do want to marry me, don't you?"

"More than anything! But we should wait to tell them until we see what the territory's like," Alan told Janet. "I don't want to subject you to primitive conditions that you may come to hate, and me along with them."

"That's nonsense. You forget, dearest Alan, that I was raised in the West Indies. I've travelled most of my life and I'm used to adapting."

"True. But I still think we ought to wait."

"You're not having doubts, are you?" Janet asked playfully. "It's been known to happen."

"Where you're concerned there's no such thing as cold feet," Alan assured her.

Janet studied Alan's strong profile against the distant shore, certain that she was much surer of her love than he was of his, and that she would have to be the strong one always, if and when they married.

"Then you do care for me?" she asked.

Alan turned and took her in his arms and kissed her deeply and soundly, for the first time. He released her and said, "There's no one else. There never has been and never will be. And I come to you as you come to me, completely. Also—" and he chuckled softly—"completely inexperienced."

"Oh Alan!" He had made her blush. She pushed away from him, turned and fled coyly down the deck toward her cabin.

At least, Alan reflected happily, she loved him,

making this the single most important moment in his life, or at least as important as his first step onto northwestern soil would be. The alliance with Janet couldn't have come at a better time, as far as he was concerned, and he was sure that Janet felt exactly as he did.

4

THE DAY that the *Prince Rupert* sailed through
the Strait of Juan de Fuca marked its 171st day out
from New York. It was also the first time that the
brig had passed another vessel within hailing distance. All during the voyage from New York to
the Northwest the *Rupert* had sailed discreetly
distant from other vessels—it was Captain Kelsey's
policy to avoid close contact until proper signals
were exchanged, or unless the other ship happened
to be in genuine distress.

As the *Rupert* passed the lower promontory of
Vancouver Island, it was approached by the brig
Hope, captained by one Horace Shell. Shell was an
old sea-going comrade of Guy Kelsey's from his
early sailing days between New England and the

West Indies. The men had served together during their apprenticeship under other masters and had always been friendly, so their coincidental meeting just inside Juan de Fuca was a happy moment for both. The ships drew bow-to-bow and a small boat brought Horace Shell to the *Rupert*. The two captains, one tall and black-bearded, the other rotund and flame-cheeked, embraced one another, clapping backs, exchanging laughs, and were quickly comparing data, past and present. Talk soon got round to where the *Rupert* might find the most felicitous anchorage in Puget Sound, invaluable since Guy Kelsey had not been in the area for several years.

"Where'd you say you were going?" Shell asked Kelsey.

"Proctor Bay. Do you know it?"

"Sure thing. Got charts that'll help you. Don't go any further southeast around the point, though."

"Why not?"

"Indians?" Bruce asked.

"No sir, not Indians. Needn't worry about Indians for the time being. They're docile enough. It's the whites you want to watch out for. I've just delivered supplies to a man named Henry York. A meaner cuss I never met. Downright inhospitable. Lucky you'll have the whole point's forest between the two of you. He's a man to beware of."

"Is he close to Proctor Bay?" Bruce enquired, not pleased with Shell's news and hoping he had overstated the case.

"A few miles or thereabouts. A tough route through the forest, not so bad by water, but a lot longer. Take my word for it, stay clear of York and go about your business in peace."

"It's not likely our paths will cross," Bruce said.

"You're going to be in the lumber business," Shell pointed out. "York's in it, too. He'll brook no competition."

"I should think, with all the natural resources available, there'd be plenty of room and timber for a thousand Yorks."

"There is at that," said Shell, "but York wants it all."

"We won't be tangling with him," Bruce said.

"Well, maybe so," the captain of the *Hope* allowed. "All the same, don't go any further south than your harbor unless you're armed. How're you fixed for supplies?"

"Fine, for the time being," said Bruce. "Horses, small boats, the men and equipment are following."

"Good, good. You'll be into fine weather soon. It's God's country up here, all right, with the finest timber in the world, and enough of it to build houses around the globe. And empty, empty, nothing but forest."

Bruce smiled. "I thought the sea was pretty empty myself, at certain points during the voyage."

Both captains stared at him in astonishment.

"The sea empty?" said Shell. "Ha! That's a real joke, sir. The sea's boiling with life. A million voices, a million furies. It's constantly on the move, hiding or revealing its secrets. All the forest does is stand still and grow."

"That's enough for me at the moment," said Bruce.

"Yes, well, you may have a point," Shell said, as Kelsey broke out the brandy and the four men drank a toast to the *Rupert*'s safe arrival and to their respective futures.

Captain Shell then paid his respects to the Kelsey ladies and departed for the *Hope*. Final goodbyes were shouted across the water and the two brigs sailed away on opposite courses, the *Hope* out through Juan de Fuca to San Francisco, the *Rupert* to the upper passage that led south to the mouth of Puget Sound, where the ship anchored for the night.

"Who's this man Henry York?" Randall asked Kelsey at dinner that evening.

"I can't ever recall hearing the name before," the captain replied, "but apparently it's someone rather nasty or old Horace wouldn't have given us the warning he did. I've seldom heard him say a bad word about anyone, never unless they were already generally known as villains."

"I don't see any reason why York should give us trouble," Bruce said. "We have legal access to the bay and the point to begin operations, both from the former claimants and the U.S. Government."

"Well, Horace didn't indicate that York goes much by the book," Kelsey pointed out.

"One thing we don't need is trouble with white settlers," said Bruce firmly. "We'll mind our own business and never see York."

"The best idea is to ignore the man," Kelsey declared. Bruce was in complete agreement, though uneasy about his new neighbor.

It was mid-morning the following day before the *Rupert* reached its final destination and sailed into the wide mouth of Proctor Bay, named for the first white man ever to set foot on the small peninsula, three decades earlier.

As the *Rupert* eased along the deep bay channel, it became apparent to Bruce and Alan that the small harbor was absolutely ideal for the *Rupert's* accommodation and an excellent shelter against winter storms, as well as the perfect spot for a settlement. The bay was long and narrow at its southernmost end, with a wide sloping beach, gentle lapping surf, and an excellent deep-water anchorage that brought the brig close to land. It didn't take much for Bruce to visualize a small community rising rapidly at the edge of the heavily wooded land, and to see the business he would start growing just as rapidly.

Behind the handsome silver crescent of beach rose the forest, the reason for their long voyage. It stood massively silent, dark and serene, drenched from a brief shower that had passed over an hour earlier. Its pungent earthy scent spiced the clear air, quite the most intoxicating smell that Alan could ever remember inhaling.

In a flash of insight he thought how sad it was that these beautiful, vulnerable earth giants of nature, now growing right down to the beach in their vigorous and pristine glory, would soon be leveled to serve puny man's need for shelter and barter. The human need to conquer was never more cruelly revealed to him than in this moment, but all he could do was to sigh and dismiss the forest's destruction as inevitable, something over which he had no control.

"This spot staggers the imagination," Bruce exclaimed as the *Rupert* dropped anchor. His thoughts were much like Alan's, although he was thinking of production rather than preservation. "Look at those magnificent trees. I think we ought to call the settlement Green Bay. Never mind Proctor."

"Good idea," Alan agreed, along with Kelsey.

"Plenty of timber for everybody," said the captain. "As anyone can see, it's practically endless."

It was. The dense forest that touched the white beach stretched across the far promontory of the bay's western flank with solidly verdant thickness, a forest so rich that it would be almost impossible to ride a horse through it without a marked trail, the gloom so dim that one could scarcely see inside it, even with bright sunlight overhead.

This and the other forests of the territorial region were so vast that no one could even estimate in 1853; the volume could only be guessed at. The variety of trees was astonishing. Outstanding among them were Douglas fir, cedars, pine, spruce, hemlock. They covered a large portion of Washington Territory, surpassing all forests around the globe in size, number and prime quality. And besides their overwhelming abundance, they were ruggedly beautiful.

In another fifteen years more than a dozen sawmills would be located in the Puget Sound area alone. Nearly two hundred million board feet of lumber would be cut from the timber stands, the vast cuttings scarcely taxing the resources of these primeval forests.

Beyond Green Bay's western reaches lay open water, blue-green and delicately white-capped. And beyond that, some thirty miles distant, stood the heights of the Olympic Peninsula with its range of more-than-mile-high peaks dominated by Mount Olympus. All were still snow-crested, glittering like heaps of diamonds in the pure air, a ravishing sight.

If Bruce Randall had held any doubts about the

wisdom of his venture during the long voyage West, these were now dispelled for all time. Even a blundering fool, he thought, could make a fortune here quickly, providing he could get ships to sail this far north. The mountain would have to come to Mohammed, so to speak, and in fleets. But once the business got going, this was easily possible. The incredible riches that lay close to hand, as close as the sharp blade of a willing axe, were enough to make multi-millionaires of a hundred men and satisfy their wildest ambitions.

Yes, he would do well here, Bruce reflected. He knew this instinctively. And so would young Alan. But the acquisition of a fortune would not be a tranquil undertaking, not if Captain Shell had characterized the man York accurately.

The first boatload ashore included Captain Kelsey, the ladies, Bruce, Alan and the boatswain. Although they didn't know it at the time, Marian and Janet were the first white women to step ashore at Green Bay. Soon there would be others, south of them, but none of these could be called ladies.

Standing on the white beach in the bright sunshine, Captain Kelsey said, "I would like to make a small prayer . . ."

Janet and her mother knelt in the sand; the men removed their hats, their eyes reverently downcast.

"May God bless this land in which our little party is about to settle," Kelsey intoned solemnly. "May the earth yield goodness, health, wealth and happiness to all who come here. May the settlers grow strong in Thy name, O Lord. Amen."

In the brief silence that followed, the only

sounds heard were the songs of birds in the deep forest, the lapping of waves against the small boat, soft breezes rustling the trees.

"Where's the river?" Alan asked Kelsey, who had the territorial charts in one hand. "It's supposed to be close by."

Kelsey spread out the map on the silver-grey trunk of a long-fallen spruce. "Just to the south, beyond that clump of rock and trees, I would imagine."

"Let's explore," said Alan, followed by Bruce.

The two men took off down the beach toward the sharp finger of land that projected into the bay. Climbing up between the lichen-covered boulders to the summit, they were unprepared for what they found beyond.

Forty feet below them a broad river emptied into the bay. It was sixty feet or so wide at its mouth, narrowing down to a channel of twenty to twenty-five feet as it curved gently up through the gradual rise of the forest, lost in the dense dimness of trees.

"It's magnificent," Alan exclaimed, "exactly what we want."

"Made to order," Bruce agreed.

"Let's explore the river bank a ways."

"Later," said Bruce. "Right now we'd better start thinking about felling some trees, setting up a central log house for the mess and services and getting the tents up with floors to them. Our supplies will be along in a couple of days."

"Meanwhile we're living aboard ship," Alan reminded Bruce. "Come on, let's see the river now, before the supplies arrive."

"All right," replied Bruce, responding to Alan's enthusiasm.

Bruce turned back to Kelsey and the others, shouting down to them, "We've found the stream. We're going to follow it up a bit."

"Is that wise?" Kelsey said. "We might encounter bears, and we're not even armed."

"We'll be all right," Bruce assured him, not at all certain that they would be. Until that moment he hadn't even thought about the threat of wild beasts.

The two men climbed down to the stream and followed its shoreline for nearly half a mile, picking their way carefully over rotting logs, piles of stone and hummocks of sand deposited by the spring floods. The river was clear and swift, eight or ten feet deep, and narrowing when they had gone some distance to a width of no more than fifteen feet.

Bruce and Alan stopped at a point where a large tree trunk had fallen across the stream to make a bridge. Exhausted, unaccustomed to the exertion of walking after so much time aboard ship, they plopped down on the trunk and dangled their feet over the cold clear stream.

They sat for a while in silence, savoring the rich wonder of the forest around them, feeling the sun hot on their backs, rich earthy odors enveloping them.

"We know one thing," Bruce broke the stillness, "we've come to the right place. Everything can be used—the river to float down the trees we fell, the bay to make our booms for towing, and the bay-side land itself as our new home. Once the sawmill's operating, we'll be in business."

"It's ideal," Alan agreed. "But the river has no name on the captain's charts," he pointed out.

"You're right. I hadn't thought of that. Let's name it right now. After all, it belongs to us."

"To you," Alan corrected.

"Nevertheless, I'd like *you* to name it."

"All right. Why not call it Green River, to match the bay?"

"Excellent. Green River it shall be," said Bruce.

They lingered for twenty minutes more, reluctant to return to the landing party. A sense of peace and well-being made them feel closer to each other than ever before; the vastness of forest around them seemed to seal their friendship.

"You remember," Bruce said, "the story you told me about Dean Jasper and that Morton boy?"

"I'm not liable to forget it," Alan replied.

"Well, I've a story to tell you. This seems as good a time as any."

Alan glanced up quickly at Bruce and saw his features grimly set, a look of pain across them.

"Can it wait?" he asked.

The older man sighed deeply and nodded. "Yes, I suppose it can. No need to rush things. Anyway, it's done and gone. Another time . . ." He stood up and stretched. "What a splendid beginning," he breathed softly, "for a new life. I suppose we should go back and join the others."

By the time they returned to the beach the women had gone back aboard the *Rupert* and the crew had come ashore. Some were racing up and down the beach like schoolboys at recess, wrestling one another, delighting in the open space and braced by the pristine beauty around them.

Two of the crew had set up tents where they would spend the night and were talking next to a roaring campfire. The boatswain and the first mate, armed with rifles, had gone into the forest to hunt for small game, possibly deer.

Kelsey, Bruce and Alan settled on the warm sand to enjoy a leisurely hour before the sun would start setting on the western horizon.

"We'll remain only until the *Plover* arrives with your supplies," Kelsey told them. "Then we'll sail back to San Francisco and I'll supervise your next order. This is a primitive place, so the sooner you get your operation going, the easier it'll be for your people."

"We'll be all right," Bruce said.

Alan wasn't so sure. From the tone of Kelsey's voice it didn't sound like the captain would consent to Janet staying at Green Bay under any circumstances. Alan went aboard ship late that afternoon with a heavy heart. After dinner he sought out Janet and they retired to the bow to talk.

"You'll have to ask father to marry us tomorrow," Janet told Alan. "He'll raise a storm, but it's the only way. Otherwise I'll sail back to San Francisco, stay with those stuffy Bradys and attend the Presbyterian church every Sunday. I'll meet some idiot young men about town, not one of them will measure up to you, and . . ."

"All right, all right, I'll beard the old fox in his den, if that's what it takes."

"Oh, Alan, that's wonderful! I love you for being so agreeable."

Alan took Janet in his arms. "My darling, I'm a lot more than agreeable. I'm the most passionate man in Green Bay right now, father or no father."

"Why, Alan, what brass you have," Janet said, throwing her arms around his neck and kissing him deeply.

Alan found the proper moment to speak with her father late that same night. The captain was sitting up in his cabin after Bruce had retired to go over the lists they were preparing for Kelsey's next round-trip voyage to San Francisco.

"Sir," Alan said, entering the lounge, "may I have a word with you?"

Kelsey turned and frowned, knowing what Alan had in mind and vowing that he wouldn't make it easy for the lad. He had decided to let Alan cool his heels in Green Bay while he and the *Rupert* were in San Francisco. Then, all things considered, he would make a final decision about Janet's future.

"That would depend upon what the word is, Alan," Kelsey replied. "Sit down."

Alan slumped nervously into a chair.

"It's about Janet and me. I guess you know."

"I surmised."

"Well sir, we want to get married."

Kelsey's eyebrows shot up in mock surprise. "Married, you say? This is the first I've heard about it."

"I'm asking your permission, sir."

Kelsey pushed back the stack of papers and lit his pipe.

"So that's the way it is. Yes, I've thought as much for some time. Both Mrs. Kelsey and I have observed certain glances passing between you two that could only be interpreted as . . ." The captain cleared his throat. "Well, the truth is, I know a thing or two about being attracted to a member of the opposite sex, but there are other considerations besides being in love, which I assume that you two are."

"We are, sir. You've only to ask Janet."

"I know Janet. I don't have to ask her," said Kelsey. "You have my consent, if you'll agree to a decent period of reflection."

"What do you mean?"

"That Janet goes back with us to San Francisco. I'll wed the pair of you on the next trip to Green Bay. If, of course, you haven't found an Indian maiden by then, or Janet a rich husband in the city."

Alan's expression was one of total disappointment. "Guy," he said, dropping all pretense of etiquette, "man to man, I don't think I can stand a separation. If you're going to insist on that, I'll return to San Francisco with you, take some kind of a teaching job there or in Sacramento, and marry Janet right off."

"Threats," Kelsey mused. "I wouldn't have thought you'd resort to threats. I don't want my daughter subjected to the perils of this place now, not until a decent community's been established."

"But she wants to stay here," Alan said.

"Be that as it may, we'll discuss the matter in the morning."

Alan saw that it was useless to pursue the subject any further with Kelsey, so he said goodnight and retired to his cabin, where Bruce was already asleep.

*   *   *

Janet wasn't asleep, nor was her mother, who sat on her daughter's bunk in the tiny cabin which was once Janet's nursery and stared at the girl in genuine shock.

"I don't believe you," she said, on the verge of tears. "After all we've done, all we've taught you, protected you, tried to give you a sense of decent values."

"It's true, all the same," Janet said. "Alan and I are already lovers, in the physical sense."

"I should tell your father," said Marian, "but I'm afraid he would kill young Travers. Janet, how could you do such a thing?"

Janet was beginning to regret her story. "Mama," she confessed, "it's not true."

"You're sure?" Her mother stared at her, mouth pursed. "Then why did you lie?"

"I saw no other way to break you down. Anyway, weren't you and papa lovers before you married?"

"Certainly not!" Marian snapped. "Not until we exchanged vows."

"All right. But I *will* become lovers with Alan if you don't consent. And you know that's not an idle threat!"

Mrs. Kelsey sighed. "I guess your father and I don't have much choice, do we? You'll be married aboard the *Rupert*." Mrs. Kelsey began to cry softly.

"Oh mother, please don't . . ." Janet knew she had gone too far to achieve her ends, but there was no stopping now. She reached out for her mother and embraced her, and the two women's tears mingled.

* * *

The following morning, the sound of axes began to break the early stillness of Green Bay for the first time since the *Rupert* anchored. Frames were made by the crew for tent bases, filled in with dry pine needles and sod, and logs for the central cabin were cut. The real work would begin when the lumberjacks arrived with the *Plover* in a couple of days, but Bruce Randall didn't intend to wait for the supply brig. It could be delayed days by a storm, and meanwhile, hands would be idle.

A week later, the *Plover* entered Green Bay to the vast relief of Randall and Alan, and of Captain Kelsey, impatient to return to San Francisco. It dropped anchor alongside the *Rupert* and the lumberjacks came ashore, the reluctant horses following after them. Supplies were two days unloading. When this was accomplished, both the *Rupert* and the *Plover* were readied for the return voyage to San Francisco.

The night before sailing a large party was held ashore. Among the lumberjacks there was a short, wiry man named Bill Dexter, about forty, with a grizzled beard and a hard grey-eyed gaze that brooked no interference with his wishes. Dexter was chosen by Bruce Randall in San Francisco because of his honest reputation. No one would ever have taken Dexter for a physically formidable adversary because of his size, which was definitely small. Dexter always went armed with a knife and a pistol, and knew how to use both. He was known among West Coast loggers as a tough timber boss, a bull of the woods, as expert as any around. His disposition had just about finished him in the California area, however, and Dexter was happy to sign on as Bruce's foreman when Randall found him.

"For the time being anyway," Dexter had agreed. "Don't know if I'll like the Puget Sound. Got to see the area before I can fall in love with it."

Dexter's presence as timber boss was effective from the moment he stepped onto the beach. His crew, unlike Kelsey's sailors, went right to work ashore under his command, and in two days the framework of a community was laid out and parameters established. Both Bruce and Alan could scarcely believe their eyes, in light of their own hard work. They were lucky to have Dexter and they gave him full rein.

By the time the *Plover* and the *Rupert* were ready for departure, even Marian Kelsey wasn't feeling too unhappy about Janet staying on in a private cabin with her husband-to-be.

On the afternoon before the two ships were to sail away, Captain Kelsey married Alan and Janet on the *Rupert*'s deck, in a simple ceremony that moved even the toughest of Kelsey's crew. Janet wore her white New York dress.

That night Kelsey broke out grog for his crew and the men of the *Plover*, and the two crews stayed ashore to celebrate the wedding in their own way. It was crude, however, and fights broke out between the two crews. A grog-filled sailor off the *Rupert* wrestled a *Plover* crewman into a bonfire, setting his clothes ablaze. These were quickly extinguished, thanks to Bill Dexter's quick thinking. He rolled the man down the beach slope and into the bay, then dealt with his opponent.

When another fight broke out between the

lumberjacks and a couple of sailors, Bill Dexter jumped up on a pile of split timber and shot his pistol into the air, bringing Kelsey and the *Plover*'s captain to the railings of the *Rupert*. They were celebrating the happy couple's marriage with a small dinner there, graced by gamehens shot in the forest.

With a bellow of rage, Dexter shouted, "Now listen to me, one and all! Any more trouble and I'll not be shooting my weapon into the air! Calm down, all of you, and let's have some peace and quiet!"

The lumberjacks quieted immediately, and while there was some grumbling among the ships' crew about taking orders from Dexter, they nevertheless obeyed him. The brawling group gave way to silence.

When the bride and groom had gone below to Alan's cabin for their wedding night, Bruce said to Kelsey, "I think we made a wise choice in Dexter, eh, Guy?"

"Absolutely. I feel a lot better about Janet staying on with you and Alan. Dexter will keep things in hand."

"Everything's going to be just fine," Bruce declared. "Don't you worry about anything."

"I'll worry all the way down to the Golden State and all the way back," Kelsey said, "and Marian will worry even more. When I think about what you've bitten off here, Bruce, I wonder why you didn't buy yourself a sugar plantation in the West Indies and live a gentleman's life."

"I'll probably wonder myself before long," Bruce said. "But I've made my bed, so to speak, and now I'm going to lie in it, although I don't suppose there'll be much sleep for me for a long time to come."

"I'll miss you," Kelsey said. "And while I'm sure Alan will make Janet a good husband, in my judgment you'd have made a better one."

Bruce shrugged. "At least I can be her guardian while you're away. She'll come to no harm. Trust me."

Kelsey put his arm around Bruce Randall's shoulders.

"You're a good man, Bruce, a real gentleman."

"Thanks for the compliment," Bruce said, "but it's you who has acted like a gentleman."

"I know what I see and hear," said Kelsey. "I'm a good judge of men."

"I'll take your word for it," Bruce said, smiling, pouring them each another brandy.

"Here's to commerce and success," he toasted Guy, raising his glass. "Here's to green gold!"

In the darkness of the cabin, Alan undressed and crawled into the lower bunk alongside Janet and took her in his arms. His teeth were chattering with excitement as he said, "You don't know how often I've dreamed of us like this."

Janet laughed. "No more than I. And no more eagerly."

"What beats me," Alan said, "is how easily your mother persuaded your father to marry us right away."

"She saw it as inevitable," she said evasively. "I've great powers of persuasion."

"There's got to be more to it than that."

"If I tell you, promise not to be angry with me?"

"How could I be angry with you, angel?"

"Well, I told mama that we'd been . . . that we were already lovers, so we might as well get married, the damage was done."

"Why, for God's sake?" Alan exclaimed. "It's not true."

"Oh, don't worry about it, darling. I admitted it was a lie afterward."

"Well, thank goodness at least for that. No wonder she was giving me such funny stares during the ceremony," Alan said. "There'll always be a question in her mind." All thought of passion with Janet evaporated. He had even lost his rigidity.

"Oh, be sensible, sweetheart," Janet cooed. "What's done is done. Let's get on with the love-making."

"I feel like a scoundrel," Alan moaned.

"Don't!" Janet ran her hands lightly over his body; he began to respond. "Darling, there just simply wasn't any other way to bring matters to a climax." Janet giggled over her pun. "One of us had to make a practical move. *You* certainly hadn't."

"I guess you're right," Alan admitted. "Otherwise you'd be heading back to San Francisco tomorrow and we might never have been married."

"Now you're making good sense," Janet said. "It will all work out, you'll see . . ." She drew him closer to her. "Kiss me, darling," she murmured, "and make me *know* we're truly married . . ."

Realizing how much they both had to learn, Alan took Janet in his arms once again, holding her tenderly. When their kisses had reached a peak, he rolled on top of her and began to make love, as easily and naturally as if he'd been doing it for a thousand years.

It was dawn before they fell into an exhausted sleep, locked together, happily entwined, breathing in quiet rhythm, about to meet the first new day of their marriage, the very first marriage of a white couple on the peninsula.

5

DEXTER'S HAND-PICKED CREW included highballers, expert lumberjacks who peeled the trees after the felled trunks had been sawed into manageable lengths. A bunkhouse for twenty men and a mess-hall to accomodate two cooks were the first buildings to be completed after a cabin for Bruce, and another for Janet and Alan, were built.

Housing soon went up for the men who would be operating the central mill in a short time. A log platform with planks was built and launched close to Green River, so that when the *Rupert* returned from San Francisco it would be able to tie up at this floating dock, instead of unloading by the arduous method of small boat.

With the help of Bill Dexter, Bruce had purchased much of the strategic supplies and equipment needed to start a logging camp. It would be several months before the forest immediately behind them could be subjected to what Dexter called a cruise—that is, an estimation of the approximate value of the standing timber in Randall's holdings of some 200,000 acres.

Janet and Alan were in that state of wedded delight where even minor misfortunes, including the hardships of settling into a rugged way of life, had their comic rather than dismal aspects. They laughed a good deal more than they cried, and Bruce noted that Alan proved to be even more filled with optimistic enthusiasm than usual. During the *Rupert's* absence Janet did no pining for her parents. Instead, she pitched in at the messhouse and baked bread for the men, biscuits on Sundays, and generally won the respect and admiration of the entire crew. They adopted her as their mascot. Any fears that Guy and Marian Kelsey may have had about Janet not adapting to camp life, or being in any danger, were baseless, Bruce was glad to see.

As Dexter's men made their forest surveys, some of them became aware that they were being watched by unseen eyes. Then one day, out alone with his rifle and notebook, Bruce was confronted by an Indian in a clearing. The Indian immediately strung his bow, and Bruce gripped his rifle, wondering whether he would die here in the forest before he could fire a shot.

Indians in the region were peaceful, inclined to cooperate with the settlers, since the latter hadn't moved into the territory yet in threatening numbers. There were only a few thousand whites along the entire coast from Canada to San Francisco.

Bruce did the only sensible thing he could. He laid his rifle on the ground at his feet, held out his hands, and smiled across the clearing at the silent, buckskin-clad Indian. He waved his hand at the man, beckoning him. Slowly the Indian approached, grinned and said distinctly, "Tobacco?"

Bruce pulled a pouch from his jacket and tossed it to the Indian, who opened it, sniffed it, then accepted it. On the chance that the Indian might know a few more English words, Bruce tapped his chest and said, "Friend . . ."

The Indian, perhaps in his late thirties, close to Bruce's own age, nodded gravely but did not smile.

"Enemy," the Indian mumbled and pointed over his shoulder.

Bruce was relieved. The man's vocabulary meant that he'd been exposed to some white civilization. Then another thought occurred to him that was not quite as comforting. The Indian could have come from Henry York's camp.

"Enemy where?" he asked the Indian.

"Down land," said the man, nodding south.

"York?" Bruce ventured.

The Indian's eyes narrowed, glittering with unconcealed hatred. He nodded.

Bruce tapped his chest again.

"Friend," he repeated, and the Indian nodded noncommittally, apparently satisfied, indicating that Bruce could now pick up his rifle. He did, slinging it over his shoulder.

"What you want here?" the Indian asked.

It seemed too laborious a task to explain that he was the legal owner of the land on which they stood. He had come out into the forest to scout for

sugar pine, which Bill Dexter's first assistant had
said was growing not far from the clearing.

Bruce took out his pencil and notebook and
drew a rough sketch of the sugar pine cone and
tree. The Indian grasped his meaning instantly.

"Come," he said, "I show." And Bruce followed
him into the forest, regretting his foolishness in
venturing out alone. He had laid down a rule
against this himself. But Alan had been occupied
and no one else was free. Well, he would simply
have to take his chances.

Bruce accompanied the Indian in silence as
they crossed several small brooks that trickled
toward Green River. At least, he reflected, he knew
where he was; and since his guide had elected to
precede him, Bruce didn't think he would be
murdered suddenly in his tracks.

After about a twenty-minute walk, they arrived
at a thick stand of giant sugar pines. The big
cones hung far above Bruce's reach; there was no
way to climb up to the lower branches. Bruce took
his rifle, aimed into a tree and shot down a cluster
of cones.

Before he could pick the cones off the forest
floor he was surrounded by four other Indians, all
younger and much fiercer-looking than his companion. For a moment he thought that his time
had come.

A heavy silence ensued, perhaps the longest
half-minute Bruce could ever remember, as he
stood with his rifle useless in his hands, not even
a pistol or knife in his belt.

At last the English-speaking Indian produced
Bruce's tobacco pouch, tossed it to the Indian
nearest him, said something in his own language,

and all five of the men began to laugh together. The crisis was over; he had been accepted . . .

On the way back to Green Bay camp, the English-speaking Indian introduced himself as Black Deer. His tribe, he explained, had always lived at the southern neck of the peninsula and used the dense virgin forest only for hunting; it was their time-honored preserve, always rich in game simply for the taking.

Black Deer was a Siwash, as were his companions. He had learned his English from a missionary-school teacher who had visited the region twenty years earlier, he said. Before they reached camp Bruce realized that Black Deer spoke really fair English, not the monosyllables he had at first used. This could mean that he was now beginning to trust Bruce a little, which Bruce hoped was the case. However, it was not until they reached the shore of the bay and Black Deer dismissed his four companions with a gesture of his hand that Bruce was certain of acceptance. Black Deer had come to trust him. If York were the enemy, then he would do everything he could to make Black Deer his friend.

On arrival in camp Black Deer caused a sensation. All work ceased; men came running from all directions to see the aborigine that Bruce had brought out of the forest. Most of the loggers had never seen a northwest Indian before; they crowded closely around Black Deer to inspect him.

Trinkets, tobacco, various small supplies, were all offered to the smiling Black Deer, and when he was the happy possessor of more articles than he could carry in his arms, Janet stitched up a

sling for him from a remnant of the *Rupert*'s can-
vas sail. He said goodbye to Bruce and went back
into the forest to join his companions, but not
before thanking Bruce for his generosity.

"Tomorrow," he told Bruce, "I come tomorrow.
Talk then."

True to his word, Black Deer arrived the following morning with his belongings carried by four
youthful Indians. They set up his tent at the far
edge of the cleared land already prepared for the
growing community, a discreet distance from the
bunkhouse, cookhouse, community store and the
cabins belonging to Bruce, and Alan and Janet.

With reservations, Bruce watched the operation
that established Black Deer as part of Territorial
Mills. He was tempted to tell Black Deer that
he'd not been invited to move in. On the other
hand, he had a feeling that Black Deer would not
have come unless there was to be a fair exchange
of services. Bruce waited in his office for the Indian
to approach him; the visit came in mid-afternoon.

"Good place," was the first comment from Black
Deer. "Good people. Not like down there."

"Will you stay long?" Bruce asked.

Black Deer smiled. "Long enough," he replied.
"Until winter. You need meat here."

That couldn't be denied, Bruce thought. "We
need all we can get."

"Plenty in forest. Me, my tribesmen, we hunt
for you. You give us tobacco, guns maybe, some
cloth for my village. Good exchange."

"Whatever we can provide, we will gladly give
you," Bruce promised.

"Friend?" said Black Deer.

"Friend," replied Bruce.

After this simple exchange Black Deer relaxed; he smoked his pipe and told Bruce all he needed to know about his neighbor to the south. York had arrived about a year ago, on the east shore of the peninsula. From what Bruce could gather, York had set up a brand-new steam sawmill, similar to the model that Bruce would receive in his next shipment of goods from San Francisco.

"Now he cuts many trees, makes much lumber," Black Deer surprised Bruce by saying. "You get more machines, you make more lumber than him."

"Why are you so interested in my doing more business than York?" Bruce asked.

"York enemy," said Black Deer. "Bad man. Him take, take, take. Never give. Make promises, no keep, no good."

Still skeptical about just where Black Deer stood with his loyalties, Bruce said, "And yet you trust me."

Black Deer smiled. "I can tell. I know in the forest you all right. You no try to kill Black Deer."

Black Deer was right. Bruce even had a difficult time killing needed game.

"York will take all the forest here. He like nobody else to make business. He will come for you, sooner or later."

"Why hasn't somebody killed him?"

"Kill?" Black Deer hunched his shoulders. "No good. Indian use bow and arrow, knife. White man will know, and soldiers come for my people."

It appeared that the flaw in Black Deer's reasoning was a way simply to run out Henry York by ruining his business with competition. But this was an impossible goal, Bruce reflected. In the first place, York was already established, he had ships to carry his finished lumber from mill to southern port. He had his township already flourishing, soon to encourage family life, banks, saloons, even whorehouses. He and Alan had done little more than set up the basics; he would never catch up with York, and saw no need to. It was obvious that Black Deer was infected with a phobic conviction that York's enterprise might eat up the entire Northwest, especially the game preserves closest to his home.

"So, what you have to do is stay clear of York," said Bruce, which only made Black Deer frown.

"I stay with you, go back to my village sometimes. My men will look after you when I am gone. No need to worry. You treat us right. We are honorable people."

And just what that meant specifically was not defined.

"You agree?" Black Deer reiterated.

"I agree," Bruce replied. "And if I can't always answer your questions, go to my man, Alan Travers, and he will."

"Good man," Black Deer said. "I can tell."

"Come to me if you have trouble with any of my men," Bruce said. "We don't want fights and feuds."

"I understand," said Black Deer. "I go now . . ."

During the next two weeks there was a marked change in camp life. As the buildings went up Black Deer suggested access routes to the inner forest and the river. He advised where the pier should go. He taught Alan nature craft: how to hunt small game, where to set traps, how to ward off curious bears that might invade the camp looking for food. In short, he was invaluable. He and his men worked silently, came and went unobtrusively. Bruce had issued strict orders for no one to offer the Indians anything but tobacco, and since the liquor supplies were kept under lock and key in the community store, this matter posed no immediate problem.

By the time the *Rupert* returned the following month, a landing platform had been built. Not exactly a deep water pier, but it made the unloading of the sawmill equipment easier.

An additional cabin was erected next to the Travers home, where the captain and Marian Kelsey could stay nights when they came ashore, and which made it easier for mother and daughter to see each other. Marian was delighted with Janet's contentment, and Kelsey brought back news from San Francisco, of prodigious new markets for lumber, even as far away as China. He had also picked up a report on York's operation, which appeared unprofitable despite its volume.

"A poor businessman," Kelsey said, "he owes everybody. A man to avoid, at all costs, which I see you've done so far. By the way, York's shipped in some women, his saloon's going full-blast. The money he pays his men stays on the premises. You can look for word of this to get through to the men you picked from my crew. You know how sailors live on scuttlebutt."

"I think our men are just too busy to think about making a trip across the peninsula to satisfy their urges. They all seem too intent on saving money, or at least Bill Dexter says so. Most of them are happy to work Sundays for time and a half."

Kelsey frowned. "You may have a problem with Bill Dexter, Bruce."

"How so?" Bruce asked. "He's reliable."

"Well, just last week, I understood in San Francisco, York received a shipment of goods and one Egan Connelly, his new logging master. It's well-known in lumber circles that Dexter and Connelly have a long-standing feud going. Whenever the two are in the same neighborhood there's some kind of confrontation. Size and degree depend on how many men are working for each. They appear to fight in gangs."

"You're saying I can look for trouble?"

"Not necessarily. But you ought to be aware of the possibility."

"I'll cross that bridge when I come to it," Bruce said, and the talk turned back to the lumber market.

"As I said, prodigious," Kelsey advised. "We could have a fleet of ships up here tomorrow if we had the sawmills to supply them."

"What we can't haul out of the forest we can float down the river around to our mill," was Alan's suggestion as he sat in on the conference.

"With a little luck, you can have the tightest little operation in the Northwest," said Kelsey.

"Except for York," Bruce reminded him.

"Forget about York," Alan said spiritedly. "We're not going to let him ruin a good thing."

"I suppose not," Bruce said. "We're fine just so long as we don't lose Dexter."

"We won't," Alan assured him. "And Black

Deer is better than a newspaper. There isn't a tree felled at Yorkville that the Indians don't know about, and I get a day-to-day report."

"You haven't mentioned it," Bruce replied.

"Why should I bother you with petty details? There hasn't been much of interest in Black Deer's news except for the woman who just arrived with several others. She's half-Cherokee, half-Irish. Beautiful and single. Not exactly a whore but there's some question about her virtue. Even Black Deer's scouts are impressed. She was raised in Kentucky and God knows how she got out West. Probably by wagon train. Anyway, she seems to be making her own rules with York, and she's giving orders. But whether or not he's taking them is anyone's guess."

"I think," Bruce observed, "we've given enough time to the discussion of York and Yorkville. Now, about the erection of the sawmill. I'd like to see the site ready by tomorrow, Alan, if you don't mind. To hell with the competition! Let's restrict our energy to ourselves!"

6

MELANIE CLOUD was an exceptionally beautiful woman. She had a luminous bronze complexion, startling green eyes, curly black hair, rich, thick and unruly, and an unusually full figure for her height. Melanie had always commanded male attention wherever she went.

Because of this and her natural alertness and innate keen judgment, she could assess a man just by looking at his clothing, his bearing, his manners, but most of all, by how he looked at her. Very few men ever tried to see beyond the regular features, the proud walk and the serene smile that was Melanie's trademark. And when one of them did, it was only to find out if she was as passionate as her exterior seemed to indicate, and to gauge his chances of success with her.

When Melanie heard about the operation called Yorkville on Puget Sound, and that its owner Henry York had sent out a call for women, she decided to meet that challenge. She knew that there were already fifty men at the job site and that the operation was booming. Soon there would be a hundred lusty lumberjacks with no place to spend their hard-earned pay except in York's store and saloon, gambling, drinking and brawling, or in the whorehouse that York would eventually build. So Melanie organized her own stable of clever young doxies, set herself up as madam, and sailed north to Yorkville with her entourage.

Melanie was twenty-four, born of a Cherokee mother and an Irish father, married off at fourteen to a ne'er-do-well southerner who was killed for unpaid gambling markers a year after they were wed, putting Melanie on her own. She was taken in by a Kentucky farm family, made to feel like one of them, and stayed with them for some years. When the family decided to go West, Melanie went along with them. The trek in a covered wagon was harrowing. En route the father, Jeb Muphy, died of pneumonia, and Melanie helped Jill Murphy and the two small children reach California, where another branch of the Murphy family lived.

By the time Melanie arrived in California she was twenty and attractive in the eyes of many men. In San Francisco Melanie decided that she had one commodity which she could exchange for an easier life than scrubbing people's floors

and doing their laundry—menial jobs she was rele-
gated to because of her mixed blood. She could
either become a prostitute, a dance-hall girl, or
she could find some man to keep her. She found a
man, an eastern businessman who was deeply attracted to her, had no reservations about her heritage, and who set her up in a small apartment.

When Melanie's businessman decided to go East
permanently, Melanie remained behind. She felt
she had enough experience by this time to survive,
but as yet had no contacts. Then she met Madam
Flora, an octoroon who ran a posh brothel fre-
quented by San Francisco's elite. Flora taught
Melanie that it wasn't the favors you gave that
made you popular, it was the favors that you with-
held. Early on, Melanie learned to ration her favors, which accounted for her popularity as a
dance-hall girl.

Finally Melanie reached a saturation point with
San Francisco; her instincts, on which she relied
heavily, told her to move on, her destiny was elsewhere. So when she heard of Henry York's needs
in the Northwest, she decided that this was the
situation for her. Where a more timid woman
would have hesitated going north, Melanie welcomed the challenge of life in a small growing
lumber town.

It was unusual for a young woman to be boss
of a stable of four working girls in a place like
Yorkville's, and it wasn't a job she could run away
from if the going got tough, Melanie realized. At
the same time, it wasn't the last resort. She had a
strong premonition as she sailed north with her
girls that she was fulfilling a destiny that had not
yet been revealed to her. She kept this awareness

to herself, telling no one. She wore it like an amulet, and it gave her the strength she needed . . .

The balmy spring day on which Melanie and her four girls disembarked from the schooner at Yorkville could not have been more auspicious for their arrival. It was a Saturday, rooms were available at Yorkville; the saloon was open and the lumberjacks would be paid late that afternoon.

Melanie saw to it that her girls were attractively dressed in gay pastels, and that they acted decorously—no giggling or staring boldly back. They were advised to play no favorites on this or any other day, but to handle clients courteously, perform their duties and report any unseemly demands or behavior immediately to Melanie.

"I'm the police chief around here as far as you're concerned," she told her girls as they gathered nervously in the ship's salon for inspection just prior to docking. "The clients will expect you to be sluttish and ladylike at the same time, so you'll just have to do the best you can. Hold back when possible, play up to them, make them think they're getting more than their money's worth, and refuse all drunks. All right, ladies, here we go!"

As Melanie preceded her girls down the gangplank, she recognized the heavy-set, bull-jowled man standing on the wharf as the nastiest customer she could remember meeting at the Silver Star Saloon in San Francisco, where she had worked briefly as a hostess. The man had ice-water in his veins and his hooded grey eyes were lifeless. She felt her own blood run cold for a moment, remembering what had happened when she once refused the man's invitation to go to bed with him. He had waited for her outside the saloon until closing hours and had tried to rape her in the alley. Her screams had finally sent him running, only moments before two bartenders had come to her assistance.

Apparently York didn't recognize her now, which was fortunate but understandable. She had lost weight, she wore no make-up; she was doing her hair differently, and her clothes were now subdued where before they had been garish. Her friend Emily with the dress shop had taken her in hand at the Splendide and shown her how to dress, and she had learned quickly.

With a knowing smile on her lips and in full view of the males in the area, Melanie walked down the gangplank, took Henry York's proffered hand, and stepped lightly onto the wharf.

"Madame," York purred, his frosty gaze taking her in from beneath the brim of his grey fedora, "welcome to Yorkville. I am Henry York, owner and manager of York Mills."

"Thank you, sir, for the welcome," Melanie told him in genteel tones, making a half-curtsy. "May I present my ladies?"

The girls lined up, properly demure, their eyes on the ground.

"Dolly, Trixie, Alice and Martha . . ."

York inspected each quickly, showing his regular teeth, quite small for a man of his bulk.

"Charmed," he murmured to each girl in turn as she nodded and curtsied to him.

He turned to Melanie. "Quite the nicest packet of lovelies I've seen in a long time. I only hope my crew won't take the bloom off these lilies."

Melanie smiled at him. "I think not, Mr. York.

My girls are exceptionally talented, healthy and ingenious."

"Call me Henry," York said in a rich baritone, offering Melanie his arm which she accepted while repressing a shudder of repugnance.

"There is the hotel." York nodded toward a low, rambling two-story building ahead of them, looking as though it had been built quickly and recently, which was the case. "You'll have your own suite, the girls will be assigned rooms and we'll rent the others out. You and I will discuss the operation at my house over drinks. By the way, the girls will go to work tonight. You already have a backlog of eager customers."

"They will go to work when I say so, Mr. York," Melanie corrected him gently. "And, by the way, I don't drink, sir."

"It's Henry—"

"Henry—" He still hadn't recognized her, thought Melanie; one point in her favor.

"I don't drink," she told him, "I don't smoke, and I do not consort with the customers. The girls will be available tonight for light entertainment and socializing in the saloon, but that's all. I want them to get to feel at ease here. And besides, eagerness sometimes breeds trouble. Wouldn't you agree?"

York shifted uncomfortably. "I was counting on business tonight if the ship arrived in time. I'd hate to let the men down."

"Oh, they'll be happy enough with our little party. Don't you upset yourself on that score."

"I want to begin tonight," York said, and now his voice was steely.

"I think not," Melanie replied undeterred. "And if I can't persuade you to change your mind, we have an arrangement to go back aboard ship and return to San Francisco in the morning. The captain tells me he'll unload the ship in eight hours and sail at dawn."

"Well, well," York said as they approached the hotel, the girls a discreet distance behind them, "you have everything figured out, haven't you?"

"I should say so, yes."

"You puzzle me."

"In what way?"

"I keep having the odd feeling that we've met somewhere before."

"I don't think so, Henry. I would certainly have remembered a man with your grace and charm."

"Nonetheless, I seem to remember you. Weren't you in San Francisco about a year or so ago?"

"Definitely not," Melanie replied. "At that time I was travelling west in a wagon train. There are lots of brunettes around these days who look like me, Henry. Half-breeds, part Indian, part white. I can understand your confusion. We tend to look alike."

York shook his head. "Well, be that as it may. We'll have your little party tonight and we'll start operations on Sunday. Of course, we won't be able to run on Sunday when our first church opens here, but that's in the future."

"Do you have a piano? Martha plays."

"We do indeed," York said.

"I would have been surprised if you hadn't," said Melanie, entering the hotel. "Now, if you'll just show me around, I'll settle in my girls . . ."

* * *

Later, Melanie went to York's quarters, feeling that the eyes of the entire community were burrowing into her back as she walked sedately across the dusty square to meet the man who thought he was her boss. She hated what was going on in the minds of the gawkers watching her, but knew with satisfaction that eventually they'd all pay dearly for their present thoughts. If they did not make her rich, at least she'd be in command of the situation.

At Melanie's side marched Dolly, her favorite, a dainty blonde who had learned the martial art of jiu-jitsu from a sailor who worked the schooners between San Francisco and Shanghai. Small as she was, Dolly could pacify the rowdiest lumberjack alive.

York admitted the ladies, disconcerted by the fact that Melanie was not alone. He smiled politely, but Melanie could read his irritation, and was pleased.

"What a delightful parlor you have, Henry," Melanie observed, enjoying the moment. "You must spend many pleasant hours here."

"I hope to," Henry said meaningfully. "What will you ladies drink?"

"Tea," Melanie said instantly.

York stared at her. "Tea? I've been saving some champagne for the occasion."

"Oh, no thank you. My girls and I never drink anything stronger than tea. Tea is often passed off for whiskey in the San Francisco dance halls," she added pointedly. "You'll just have to get used to our abstinence."

"Very well," York said, "we'll conduct our busi-

ness over tea," and went to give orders to a servant
in the rear of the house.

On his return, York got right down to specifics,
naming hours of operation, fees to be charged,
services to be rendered. By the time he was finished Melanie was boiling inwardly. If York
thought for one minute she would abide by his
rules, then she and the girls would indeed be sailing back to San Francisco at dawn.

"Well," said York when he was finished with his
recital of regulations, "what do you think?"

"I think we'll be returning to San Francisco."
She stood up, Dolly following. "Nice to have
known you."

The color drained from York's features.

"Wait a minute! You can't do this to me. I've
made promises to the men; they've already seen
you. They'll go on strike if you don't stay. My operation could close down."

Melanie said, "There are ways of persuading us
to stay, Henry, and I don't mean force. I think the
men would side with us in that case."

"What ways?" York asked, dubiously.

Melanie opened her large reticule and drew
forth a folded sheet of linen bond paper. "My demands are all written down here, Henry. I think
I've covered everything. When you've gone over
the list carefully, I'll be waiting in the hotel lobby
for your answer. If it's negative, then we'll board
ship at once. If it's positive, we'll have our little
party tonight. We may be soiled doves, Henry,
but we aren't bird-brained. We don't intend to
leave the Northwest territory empty-handed when
the timber rush is over and the demand for us has
dropped off. No sir, not by a long shot."

Melanie swept to the door, Dolly marching behind her. "I'll be waiting for your answer," she said.

York stood and watched her go, clutching the paper in his fist, livid with fury. The arrogant slut! he thought.

Melanie trilled a final *"Au Revoir!"* as she sailed out the door. Let that hold the slimy bastard until he came around, she thought with a smile, for come around he would. Otherwise, his men would raise holy hell, and he knew it.

York sat down heavily in a brocaded chair and opened the paper containing Melanie's list of demands. She wanted twice the regular fees; she wanted a percentage of the bar sales and the house gambling take, and free rent and meals, with the right for any of her girls to take off for four days during menstrual periods.

"You bitch!" he muttered. "I'll get you . . ."

He crumpled up the list and threw it into a corner of the office. Melanie Cloud might think she was untouchable, but not for long. He'd get to her, by God, if it was the last thing he ever did. Suddenly he recalled where he met this damned half-caste, and how she'd been so high and mighty toward him once before. Well, this was the north woods, his land, his township, his kingdom. No female on this earth was going to tell *him* what to do!

"Just wait," he said to himself, "just you wait!" and went to cancel the order for hot tea.

"Off to a good start," Dolly said as they crossed the square to the hotel. "You sure gave the bastard hell, honey."

"I'm keeping my fingers crossed," Melanie replied. "Keep yours crossed, too."

"I'm proud of you, Melanie. You're spunky."

Well, whatever she was, Melanie was shaking now, her palms sweaty, her armpits streaming, and her knees about to buckle under her. She may have bitten off a bigger hunk than she had bargained for, but shed be damned if she'd let a son of a bitch like York make slaves out of her and the girls. She might not get what she wanted from him, but *he* wasn't going to get what he wanted from her either. At this point she would gladly settle for modest profits and a truce in the battle that seemed to be just beginning.

The saloon piano was old and battered. The only remarkable thing about it was that it had survived the trip around the Horn, the last years of Spanish rule, and had ended up in the great Northwest, far from things musical. But the tone of the instrument wasn't nearly as important to the crowd of lumberjacks gathered in York's smoky saloon as was the entertainment it was soon going to help provide.

It was eight o'clock, and the concert had been set for that hour, and Melanie was determined to keep her part of the bargain. So, on the dot of eight, she arrived at the small, crowded room smelling of sweat, liquor and smoke, with her quartette of girls in tow.

First the lumberjacks cheered their arrival with greetings and obscenities, then applauded as the girls made a semi-circle beside the piano on a small, improvised platform at one end of the room, away from the bar.

Melanie rose, motioning for silence. She was magnificent in a red velvet gown, cut low in the bodice. Jewelled combs glittered in her piled black hair. Dolly, on a chair behind her, was dressed in white; Trixie in powder blue, dainty and frilly; Alice in an orange outfit two shades lighter than her red hair; and Martha in dark blue.

When the lumberjacks roared louder than ever in answer to Melanie's request, she stepped forward and shouted, "You will all stand and sing the national anthem—if you still remember it!"

Instant silence fell on the crowd: Melanie couldn't have quieted them more effectively. One and all, they were on their feet, those who wore them snatching off their battered hats and clutching them in their hands. Martha at the piano struck up an off-key chord, and all of them began to sing, *"My country 'tis of thee . . ."*

After that, Melanie had the audience right where she wanted them. Each girl did a specialty. Dolly's was a suggestive song about a girl who lost her heart to a lumberjack and had to chop him down to size. Thunderous applause followed. Trixie recited poetry in her little girl's voice to the audience's noisy approval. Alice did a dramatic monologue roughly improvised from Ophelia's mad scene in *Hamlet*. Martha played piano interludes, ranging from Chopin adaptations to popular songs.

The program lasted forty-five minutes, with Melanie delivering patter and announcements between the entertainment numbers. The lumberjacks had never seen anything like it on the west coast—crib girls doing theatre and doing it well. These weren't ordinary whores, the men realized, and by the time the program was completed their attitude had changed from rough-and-ready to a genuine interest in their performance. It was more than Melanie had hoped for, and more than she had any right to expect. She had taken a chance, but instead of being laughed off the stage, she and the girls were roundly cheered for five minutes when the show was over.

One of the lumberjacks took over the piano after that and played light music for dancing. York stepped forward to take Melanie's hand, and the dancing began. Except for the fact that this was a lumber camp, and too few women in ratio to the men, it could have been any Saturday night in pioneer country.

"Well, how did we do?" Melanie said as she danced with York.

"Fine show," York said. "You're a popular success."

"That will depend upon you, Henry, and whether we can keep the men in line when we open for business."

"Oh, I doubt if you'll have trouble in that respect," York replied. "It's a question of your demands."

"I was wondering about that. Have you changed your mind? We can always get back aboard; its not yet even midnight," Melanie said, feeling reckless, heady with success.

"Oh no, I haven't changed my mind. I'll meet your demands for three months. Then we'll rewrite the contract. Unless there's trouble."

"There won't be, for one simple reason. I want two of your strongest men to be on duty at the hotel every evening we're operating. They'll act as bouncers, and strong-arm any customer who gets out of line."

"That's ridiculous. This isn't a dictatorship!" York said indignantly.

"If it isn't"—Melanie smiled her sweetest at him —"then it's a darned good imitation of one. Let's just say it looks like some little kingdom in the Balkans, and you're standing in for the king."

The music for the first dance ended. Melanie stepped away from York's embrace and bowed to him, then turned and walked calmly off the floor. York watched her go, knowing that she had won another point from him. He boiled inwardly.

When the hotel opened for business with Melanie's girls, the line was long. At first the lumberjacks—money in one hand, their trouser snaps in the other—were put out with the arrangement at the desk: business by appointment only. But on reflection it seemed like a sensible arrangement. No long waits, twenty minutes to a customer was ample time for the body's urgent lusts; they adapted to the schedule at once.

Within a week, all was going well. There were a few lumberjacks, of course, who preferred their own sex. These went discreetly off into the woods on occasion to satisfy their needs, and no one in camp, not even Henry York, deigned to notice such behavior. As for Melanie, she had all the business she could handle; her girls, who soon took over the dice table in the saloon when not on duty at the hotel, were now serving drinks to the lumberjacks, allowing hands to roam over them in exchange for huge tips.

One thing Henry York had to admit; the booze-buying never slackened off, but the brawling did. Which meant that in his self-created world without the normal component of women and domesticity, things were going well indeed. Efficient Melanie Cloud and her four associates were paragons of good behavior, and still made excellent money. York had no complaints about Melanie's business acumen, at least.

Work at the sawmill went well. Ships arrived empty, were loaded, paid off, and sailed away. York's private bank grew and prospered; he had never been happier and would have remained so indefinitely until it was time to renew Melanie's contract had not Bill Dexter across the peninsula gotten curious.

It didn't take long for word of Melanie's arrival to reach Green Bay. Black Deer's men came daily with reports of the good looking women available for a steep price (and worth it) at Yorkville's hotel, and about the stunning half-Indian woman who managed the same versatile quartette at musicales in the saloon on Sunday afternoons. Bill Dexter listened carefully, having another reason to visit Yorkville: Egan Connelly. Word had reached Dexter that Connelly was setting a new record for felling the big trees and Dexter wanted to see with his own eyes if this were true, and if so, what new equipment and techniques he might be using.

Dexter knew he'd be going into enemy territory, but he was confident that he could pay a visit and get away undetected. Another new load of twenty-five lumberjacks had arrived in Yorkville the day before, Black Deer reported, and a strange face would hardly raise an eyebrow in camp. Dex-

ter could slip through the forest, appraise what
was going on, maybe grab himself one of the girls,
then be on his way quickly and back at Green Bay
before Bruce or Alan even missed him. And all in
one piece or so he intended.

With the connivance of one of Black Deer's men,
Dexter borrowed a swift Indian pony familiar with
the trails. He rode off two hours before dawn with
a guide, making the trek beyond Green River into
enemy territory. He arrived in Yorkville when the
Sunday morning sun was barely up, and no lumberjacks were about. He inspected the facilities
and the mill, and was planning to see the girls
when he rounded a corner of the hotel and
bumped smack into Egan Connelly coming out of
the building. His timing couldn't have been worse.

Egan Connelly was no larger than Bill Dexter,
but both men were as touchy as a bag of angry
bobcats, and the meeting was not timely.

"Why you little spying son of a bitch!" Egan
Connelly shouted. "You got no business in this
camp. I'm gonna peel your hide, you pipsqueak!"

The feud between Dexter and Connelly was an
old one and had begun over a game of cards where
both had accused the other of cheating, and neither might have been guilty. But with their fiery
tempers well-matched, the feud was on. A fight ensued. Bill Dexter had an ear lobe torn loose, Egan
Connelly's right nostril was gouged. This was in
San Francisco, some years back.

Months later, the two men found themselves
both competing for the favors of a dance-hall girl,
again in San Francisco, and again with the result
that Egan Connelly got kicked in the groin and
Bill Dexter got kicked in the buttocks. Neither

man got the girl, and both ended up in jail for the night.

Connelly had now been with York for a year. He knew the operation well, and like Dexter was one hellishly good bull of the woods. Connelly loved his job, especially the power that York wisely gave him; he was making York more money on his investment than the owner had ever seen in his life before. Which in turn brought Connelly handsome bonuses. One thing he wouldn't tolerate was interference, nor would he put up with spies from the enemy's camp. And Green Bay was just that, and here Dexter was, scouting out York's operation.

"Easy, Connelly," Dexter said, knowing that his horse was beyond the edge of the clearing and a good two hundred yards away, being held there by his guide.

"Just came down for a little poontang, partner," he went on. A fight with Connelly would bring Yorkville men, and he'd be beaten to a pulp. Better play it easy.

"You stay away from our women, you filthy bastard," Connelly said in a loud voice. "I'm comin' after you, worm!"

And with that, Connelly stepped quickly forward and swung at Dexter, who ducked, stumbled, and sprawled in the dust. The fight was on. Connelly jumped on Dexter and started to pummel him. But Dexter was a good wrestler, throwing Connelly, sitting astride him, beating him in the face.

Bill Dexter knew his luck couldn't hold out for more than another minute or two. He had a pre-arranged signal with his Indian guide; he used it now—a high piercing whistle.

Instantly, the Indian was on his mount and leading Dexter's at a sharp gallop, closing in on the two men brawling in the square.

Before Connelly knew what was happening, Dexter was on his feet, swinging himself onto his mount and galloping away with dust flying.

Connelly shook his fist at the departing Dexter and cursed him, but by that time Dexter was out of earshot. He had found what he'd come for, evidence that Henry York's operation was soon to double its output, and that it was only a matter of time until the two camps would be linked by a wagon road. York was planning one that would touch the shores of Green Bay only a mile or so below the Randall camp itself and the river.

Since Green River was the only deep stream on the peninsula that led to Green Bay, and part of the land south of the river was still partly open territory, it figured that Henry York would set Egan Connelly and his men to fight a dirty little war. They would create any kind of disturbance just to discourage Bruce Randall's enterprise from surviving and prospering.

The sailing time was a lot shorter from the Green Bay Community to the Strait of Juan de Fuca than was Yorkville, some eighty miles closer by the east shore. Now that the community was functioning, it stood to reason that York and Connelly would play tough for the control of open land on which to build their second port.

As he rode back to Green Bay, Bill Dexter decided that he'd been lucky in his encounter with

Connelly. Maybe the next time he might not be so fortunate, for surely with Connelly there would be a next time. York would make sure Connelly saw to it—and soon, Dexter judged.

Dexter returned to Green Bay with the bad news, made all the worse by the fact that, in order to tell Bruce and Alan what was going on, he'd have to admit that he took it upon himself to spy at the enemy camp.

7

BILL DEXTER CLEANED up after his forest trek, ate some lunch at the messhouse, and went reluctantly to Bruce's cabin to tell him what he'd learned.

Bruce was tempted to lecture Bill Dexter, but he had to weigh his irritation against the fact that Dexter was invaluable. There was no need to make him feel any guiltier than he already did over his unauthorized trip, which could have been disastrous. He might even have been killed.

Instead, Bruce called Alan over so the three men could discuss the situation at Yorkville in detail.

"If your survey's correct," Bruce said, "it makes me wonder what use there is in owning land. York will take what he wants from whatever grove he desires. I could be a lessee instead of an owner, and maybe a lot better off. Isn't that so, Bill?"

"You're right in a way, Mr. Randall. It's happened everywhere I've ever worked. With owners either there or absent, some stealing will go on; nothing can stop it. You got to realize that we can't control it, not even if you owned the whole damn peninsula. And if York *doesn't* get what he wants, he'll start to make it so tough for us that we won't be able to operate at a profit."

"He may even want a share of Green Bay," Alan said, voicing the thought that was in all their minds.

Bill Dexter banged his fist on his knee, enraged. "Damn York! If he thinks he can scare us out— Connelly too—then he's got another thought acoming. They may have a more advanced set-up than ours, and they've been here longer, all their equipment's arrived. But there's no need to be greedy, there's plenty of timber here for a hundred sawmills. Hell, Mr. Randall, I just don't know what to tell you to do."

"I feel like going down to see York and making a deal with him," Bruce said. "I didn't come out here to fight a war with Indians or whites. We're all settlers, we've come by our land legally, and business ought to be conducted that way."

"Wonderful in theory," Alan agreed, "but not in fact. I'm with Bill. Those devils are spoiling for a fight."

"We'll wait until they start something," Bruce said. "Did you find out anything at all about York himself?"

"Didn't see him. But I learned something from

Fog, Black Deer's lieutenant who took me south. Up until two months ago York's wife was with him," Dexter announced.

"His wife? Well, that's news," Bruce observed.

"Not good news for York, it seems. The minute he started talking about bringing up a madam and some girls, Mrs. York up and sailed back to Frisco. Guess she didn't much like the idea of a whorehouse in her front yard."

"I can see her point," Alan said. "Neither would my wife."

"Anyway you look at Yorkville, it's trouble," Dexter told his bosses. "Now, am I forgiven for pussyfooting in enemy territory?"

"Of course," Bruce said. "Thank God you're in one piece."

"Always will be," said Dexter, "where that bastard Connelly's concerned."

"I'm going to hope the same luck holds with York," said Bruce, "and hope it works like a charm."

With the departure of the *Rupert* and the arrival of another ship carrying more sawmill equipment, the Green Bay community was too busy to think about feuds with its neighbor. The weather was mostly fine and sunny, with occasional showers sweeping down from the north. In the lumber yard, a magnificent array of timber was awaiting shipment. Bruce could not have wished for better progress. The men seemed to be working well together; there was very little grumbling, due to good wages, despite the fact that Green Bay was a womanless camp. Except for Janet, who was now pregnant and still the sweetheart of the loggers and their mascot.

Bruce Randall had plenty of lonely moments, the self-imposed isolation of Green Bay. But he was satisfied that he had had the courage to go into an unknown business, invest money in an area where no one else had settled, and become a pioneer of sorts. This gave him great pride, and although he was a peaceful man, he wondered just how far he would actually go to protect his community and the forests that ranged beyond them. He knew, with a little luck, that he had many good years ahead of him; and he liked to think that he could cull out the great forest he managed with sensible restraint and still come out in ten to twenty years with a fortune that would make his stuffed-shirt Bostonian relatives recognize him as the most successful Randall of them all.

As for that dark period in his life that had brought him to the Northwest, he dwelt very little on it. It was a closed and finished chapter in his life, a matter over which he now had no control, unless he wanted to surrender to the continuing anguish of remorse, and he had neither the time nor the energy for this. Better to think of ways to contain his new empire. . . .

The first sign of trouble between Yorkville and Green Bay came in the late summer, a few weeks before the heavy rains began, and the dusty clay soil turned to the consistency of molasses, a harbinger of winter.

With horses purchased from the Siwash, Bruce and Alan had taken to making guided tours of Territorial Mills property to survey the immediate cutting areas, and to familiarize themselves with the forest itself. What the Indians knew intimately looked to Bruce and Alan at first like a continuous belt of green with no distinguishing features. Gradually, both men came to understand the signs that the Indians posted as trail references. In this they would always be ahead of York's men, for whom no Indians would work.

It was on one of these short scouting tours that Black Deer, Bruce and Alan came out at the river, right at the point where the two Americans had sat down on the bridge log that first day of discovery and contemplated their new world.

This was to be the point where felled logs would be rolled down the steep banks of Green River into the stream and floated down to the bay. There they would either be assembled into a boom raft or beached at the sawmill and sized. But where the fallen log bridge had rested there now lay a colossal jam of much smaller logs, intricately latticed to form a sturdy net that would catch and hold all debris that floated downstream like a beaver's dam. The net hadn't stopped up the river, but it had dammed it and created an imposing obstacle that would be difficult to clear.

Black Deer stared at the obstruction in stony silence for a moment, then turned to the two men.

"York's work,' 'he muttered. "I know. He learn from Connelly, bad man."

"I'm glad Dexter isn't here," said Bruce. "We'd have a hard time holding him back."

"What do we do now?" Alan asked practically. "When the rains start and the river gets twice its present size, we'll be in real trouble. We won't be able to open up the stream until spring."

"Better get Dexter," Bruce sighed. "Tell him not to waste time being angry, there's work to do."

Black Deer brought Dexter in half an hour, and Dexter's rage, all directed at Connelly rather than at York, was monumental.

"I want your permission, Mr. Randall, to take some men and burn down Henry York's big mill," he asked. "Late at night. I know every dirty trick there is."

"I don't doubt it," Bruce said, "but we can't afford that kind of retaliation. In a fortnight neither Yorkville nor Green Bay will have a camp. We'll all be out of business, the forests will be ashes, and all our work gone for nothing."

"Then what do you suggest, sir?" Dexter asked.

"Bring some men out, all you can spare. We'll clear out this mess before the heaviest rains start."

"It may take a week, sir. Those devils knew what they were doing. They'll try floating down saplings to reinforce the screen. We'll have to hurry to cut it away before the storms start."

Operations halted at the sawmill and north of Green Bay while the net was cut and cleared away. Men camped on the banks at night, just in case York's men were prowling the southside of the stream and intending trouble. But there was no trouble, only hard work in which one man nearly drowned, cutting out some tree limbs below the river's surface, and another lumberjack broke his wrist in a fall from a slippery log.

In five days the river was once more open, ready for floating operations. The fallers moved into the river basin and began to fell trees close to the river bank, so they could be floated down to the saw-mill for processing when the rains came. The biggest trees in the forest could wait until the following sunny spring, or until appropriate equipment was available to pull these giants into Green Bay. Although the land was hilly and rose to a central spine of peaks, Green River was the only floatable stream. It's water source, a small lake a few miles from camp, did not encourage the utilization of flumes from the great fir groves to the bay. The area was not ideally set up for logging, as Bruce found out the hard way, but its riches of green gold were fantastic. A cruise of any new area with Black Deer always turned up more potential riches. Bruce considered himself lucky that the former owners hadn't sold to the opposition. But although they hated York they hadn't told Bruce about his ethics, either.

Each passing week brought a new brig to Green Bay, empty and ready to do business. Bruce and Alan decided to continue processing operations right through the rainy season. When the first storm came, as it did shortly after the blockage was removed from Green River, the crew built extensive roofing over the mill to give the operators as much comfort as possible during the winter.

As the weather grew colder, the community's output decreased in volume, which was to be expected. Even an offer of double pay on Sundays didn't bring out much of a work force, nor would Bruce pressure his men if they didn't feel like working. He seriously considered importing sporting girls, but thinking of Alan and Janet made him decide against such a move. Anyway, girls weren't always morale-boosters. There were times, during the long winter nights, when Bruce grew curious about the women in Yorkville, especially the beautiful Melanie Cloud. Of course some of his more adventurous loggers had gone south to inspect

Yorkville, returning with stories even though they had no permission to make the trip. So long as they didn't desert, and none had so far, he ignored their visits.

Black Deer and his men were now running a flourishing tourist business, furnishing mounts, guiding loggers south and bringing them back. Bill Dexter, to Bruce's relief, made no further move to go after Connelly, nor did Connelly venture north. This had nothing to do with a truce between the two men; Bruce doubted if that could ever exist. When spring came again and the river swelled with melting snow from the peaks around the lake, trouble would start up again. York would either want to use Green River for his own trade or else would try to prevent Bruce's men from using it. Bruce didnt' even have to make a bet with himself about what would happen—it seemed inevitable.

Word of Melanie Cloud reached Bruce from several sources. The loggers who had seen her not only extolled her beauty but thought her one shrewd packet who took no guff from Boss York, and had him eating out of her lovely hands. Black Deer had seen her, he told Bruce, when she took occasional outings with one of her girls, the one named Dolly, reputed to be trained in the art of self-defense.

"Pretty squaw," Black Deer said, in a rare burst of opinion, his black eyes bright. "She has very long eyes. You would like her. Unusual woman."

Bruce had smiled at this and changed the subject, but the image of Melanie Cloud, enlarged by his vivid imagination and the lack of female company, would not let him alone. He dreamed of her, all bronze loveliness, bathing in a deep, sunlit forest pool. She held out her arms to him, smiling, and he entered the water, took her satiny body in his arms, and together they floated through lily pads to a cave where he made love to her, to the musical tinkle of tiny waterfalls. An absurd dream, but nonetheless, a very disturbing one.

One day far south of the river, venturing out further than he ever had before, he and Black Deer stopped to rest on the bay's narrow white beach. Although winter had come and the air was brisk and hinted at snow, the sun warmed their backs as the two men dismounted, smoked their pipes and enjoyed the wild beauty of nature and the first snow settling on Mount Olympus far across the Olympic Peninsula.

Bruce enjoyed the company of Black Deer, a man who seldom spoke unless spoken to first, a fantastic guide, a man who missed absolutely nothing. He had become invaluable to Bruce, in a way that Alan never could be. While Alan had picked up logger operations quicker than Bruce had thought possible, and was a good sincere friend, his knowledge was limited. Black Deer not only knew the Indian lore of his own people, the Siwash, he had correspondingly great knowledge of everything that went on in the Puget Sound area. He was also a one-man weather bureau. He could predict an Arctic storm that would sweep down and hurl itself at the continental coast to the exact degree and time that it would strike. He knew when there was tension at the mills, giving Bruce an edge on situations that might arise either at work or in the bunkhouses, where the men were forced to stay in close quarters during the bad weather. It was even Black Deer's suggestion that Bruce build a recreation room—something few jerry-built logging communities ever thought about—so that the men could stay up late, if they wished, reading old newspapers the schooners brought in, playing cards, darts, or merely exchanging scuttlebutt.

The new social room, they decided, should have a corner with a raised platform in it, so that any of the men who wished to put on a show could perform. One logger owned a guitar, another a banjo, several had harmonicas, one of them had a concertina. And more than a few had fair voices which they loved to raise in song on Saturday nights, when Bruce opened the community bar and sold modest rations of grog to his employees.

On this particular day, when the two men had paused for a rest stop, Bruce asked Black Deer what he thought about building a few more cabins and bringing up the wives of several of the married loggers, so that a genuine community could be developed.

"Good idea," Black Deer observed. "First, a wife for you, chief, then for the others."

"I wasn't thinking about myself," Bruce said, faintly irritated that Black Deer should take his question personally.

"You should," said Black Deer. "You are very lonely, and no reason . . ."

"Yes, well, be that as it may, I don't think the situation is going to change much in the immediate future. I have a lot of time to think about such matters."

"Look at Alan," Black Deer pointed out, "and his wife. Look at Captain Kelsey. Happy men."

Bruce tamped out his pipe on a stone. "I think it's time to move on," he murmured, rising.

Black Deer's face broke into one of his rare grins. "Yes," he replied, "time you move on, chief. And get a wife. . . ."

The two men hadn't gone five hundred yards down the narrow beach when they heard a high, piercing scream. It came from the forest to their left, and apparently it meant more to Black Deer than Bruce, for he took off at a gallop through the woods, aiming directly for the source of the scream, which came again. Bruce followed.

In a clearing about an eighth of a mile inland, Black Deer located the source of the scream. Two women were clinging to the lower branches of a half-fallen tree, just barely beyond the reach of an enraged grizzly bear.

Before Bruce could respond, Black Deer raised his rifle and shot the grizzly neatly in the chest. With a bellow of surprise and pain, the grizzly rolled away from the leaning tree trunk and lay inert on the ground. Black Deer shot the grizzly once more as it reared up from where it had fallen. The second shot stilled it forever.

The women descended calmly from their perch. One of them advanced toward Bruce and Black Deer. Bruce didn't need an introduction to know that this was the extraordinary Melanie Cloud. She wore a buckskin suit that fitted her figure perfectly, and a fur cap. The small blonde woman with her wore a similar outfit, but made of cloth. They had obviously come out on a picnic, and gotten lost in the forest, when they encountered the grizzly, a female, who probably had a mate somewhere in the vicinity.

"Thank heaven you came along," Melanie said to the men. "You saved our lives."

"Thank my assistant," Bruce said. "Its a good thing he heard your cry for help."

Melanie studied Bruce as he sat on his horse. "You're from Green Bay, aren't you?"

Black Deer said something to Melanie in Siwash, which to Bruce's surprise, she apparently understood.

"Of course," she murmured, "you're Bruce Randall. I'm Melanie Cloud and this is my assistant, Dolly."

Bruce acknowledged the introduction. "This is Black Deer, but you probably know that."

"Yes, I do. There is very little about you we don't hear down at Yorkville."

Bruce recalled his dream and smiled at Melanie. She couldn't have heard about that, he was certain.

"I wonder why everyone's so interested in us?"

"Oh, not everyone," said Melanie. "Just Henry York. He is especially curious about you."

"We could solve that by getting together."

"I think you would do better not to," Melanie declared. "You know the old saying about familiarity breeding contempt."

"I thought he already had contempt for us."

She surprised him by saying, "He also is somewhat afraid of you. Maybe with good reason."

"How will you get back to Yorkville?" Bruce asked.

"Why, the same way we came up. On horseback. We left our mare tied up about a mile down."

"On the beach?"

"Yes. We'll find her by ourselves. If she's not already gone."

"The least we can do is escort you safely to her," Bruce said, and dismounted. "Here, take my horse."

"Thanks," Melanie said, and swung gracefully into the saddle.

Black Deer followed Bruce's courteous gesture and set Dolly astride his mount. The four of them moved through the forest toward the bay.

As they turned south and walked along the shore, Melanie asked suddenly, "Do you like it out here, Mr. Randall?"

"Yes, I do," Bruce replied, wondering where she was leading. "Do you?"

"I hate it!" she replied. "It's suffocating . . . What brought you? Dreams? Money? Scandal?" Her eyes met his.

"Curiosity, Miss Cloud. And challenge. Isn't that what brings most people West? What brought you?"

"Necessity, Mr. Randall. Things were intolererable in Kentucky. Almost anything looked better. Even this."

"Is that the reason why you came to the North-west?"

"It's one of the reasons," Melanie said, and fell silent.

They walked along for nearly half a mile without speaking. Then, as they rounded a bend in the shore, Melanie pointed ahead to her horse, which was tethered to a fallen log.

"There she is!" Melanie cried out.

It was folly for the women to have come out un-armed, Bruce thought, but he made no comment. After all, it was their business—or York's—not his. But thank God the mare was where they'd left her, and unharmed.

Melanie pulled in the reins of Bruce's mount and jumped lightly down from the saddle.

"There," she said, with what sounded like re-lief, "I think this is as far as you'll want to go, Mr. Randall. Or should I say, as far as it's prudent to go?"

Bruce nodded. "A pity things have to be this way."

"Do you know Henry York?" Melanie asked.

"I've never seen or met the man."

"You're fortunate," Melanie observed with a hint of bitterness. "You're that much ahead of the game."

"So I'm told," Bruce replied noncommittally.

"Yet even Henry York has dreams."

Bruce didn't want to discuss the subject with her. He said, "Perhaps we'll meet again?"

"That wouldn't be unlikely," Melanie said softly, studying him carefully with her green eyes.

Black Deer helped Dolly off his mount and she thanked him. Melanie thrust her hand out to Bruce who held it in his.

"Thank you again," she told him, "for the melo-dramatic, nick-of-time rescue." Her voice was al-most mocking. "You know the old Chinese proverb, don't you? Save someone's life and you're respon-sible for them always?"

"I don't believe I do," Bruce said.

"Well, anyway," Melanie shrugged her shoulders, "it's just a saying. Unless you believe in omens . . . Goodbye, Mr. Randall, and thanks again."

"Will we meet another time?" he repeated.

"That would depend upon fate," said Melanie. "I sincerely hope that it will be kind to us both."

"So do I," Bruce replied solemnly.

At this, Melanie called Dolly to join her, then marched briskly off down the beach without looking back, her pert companion at her side.

"You sure gave Randall the red carpet treatment," Dolly observed from behind Melanie as they rode the dappled mare back to Yorkville.

"He rated it," said Melanie. "He's a gentleman."

"So was the Indian," Dolly observed.

"And that's why we thanked them both courteously. We still have our manners."

So Bruce Randall was also a dreamer, she thought. She was deeply pleased that he was a man of character and manners, gentleness; decent, and . . . considerate—that was the surprise. She couldn't under any circumstances imagine York offering her his horse. He would consider someone else slaying the fierce grizzly as consideration enough, and would probably give her a rough lecture about venturing so far into the forest and leaving her horse on the shore. He wouldn't think of her as an individual, only as a commodity which, if lost, would cost him money.

"I saw the way you looked at him," Dolly said. "It wasn't the way you look at most men."

"Unless I'm a poor judge of the sex, he's not like most men."

"Do you think he'll come down to Yorkville?"

"Not to see you girls," Melanie said, acutely aware that she was suddenly jealous of the idea that one of her quartette might entertain Bruce Randall.

"Oh, well," said Dolly, "*I* can certainly live without him, if you can."

"I'll try," said Melanie. "Now, not a word about what happened," she cautioned Dolly, and dug her heels into the mare's flanks.

That evening, Bruce took his late meal with Janet and Alan. He couldn't resist relating the details of his unexpected meeting with Melanie Cloud and one of her girls.

"What was she like?" Janet was anxious to learn.

"Not like you," Bruce teased.

"Oh Bruce, tell me—"

"Like no one I've ever met," he told Janet soberly. "Not at all like the reports we've had."

"That doesn't tell me anything," Janet pouted. "Was she pretty, beautiful. Or was she homely, coarse-featured, or common, or . . . ?"

"Not exactly."

"Describe her, Bruce, before I die of curiosity."

To his dismay, Bruce found himself incapable of describing Melanie to the Travers. Why? Was he so taken with her that he couldn't trust his vocabulary or his emotions? Or was it because he wished Melanie were as naive and eligible as Janet had been before her marriage? Did he love her? He thought not. Besides, he didn't trust love, not after what he'd been through.

"I found her a remarkable woman," Bruce declared, "and not at all as she's been described. She has manners, sensitivity, charm, and looks—I suppose you could call her beautiful, but not in any conventional way."

"You sound as if you were impressed," Alan observed, and Bruce glanced at him sharply.

"Whatever I sound like, I wouldn't mind seeing her again," he declared, and changed the subject.

In bed that night, wild ideas tumbled through Bruce's head. Gone was the remote bronze goddess of his dream, the imaginary wood nymph. He had met the real Melanie, seeing in her another kind of dream, unpossessable, yet something he'd craved for a long time. Had she suspected this dream when she looked at him? It wasn't at all the sort of emotion he'd felt in Boston when he had caused his family such pain.

How could he make this dream a reality? He saw no way. Yorkville might as well be a continent away. The die was already cast to keep Green Bay and Yorkville apart, two enemy camps that could never make peace. But even if peace were possible, Melanie could never be his. And this wasn't Boston snobbery speaking. It was the simple truth of vast differences between two people. Melanie was a mystery woman who talked to Black Deer in his own language. Amazing. He hadn't even guessed that Black Deer knew her, but he must.

Bruce didn't sleep until well past midnight and awoke before dawn to the memory of Melanie Cloud on the white beach, her firm, voluptuous body swaying as she walked down the sand toward the mare. Out of his life, leaving his sharp hunger unappeased. He would not forget her easily, and he dared to hope that he would meet her again . . . and soon.

8

THE WINTER OF 1853 was one of the wettest that the Green Bay community would ever see. Instead of heavy snow that fell in the higher reaches of the land, there was a steady onslaught of sleet, slush, heavy rains, and plain misery.

Even with more mill machinery and personnel, along with the gradual erection of buildings in Green Bay, work did not go too well. Bruce was glad that he had a backlog of lumber to ship out in the spring, as well as money in San Francisco from which Guy Kelsey could draw for his supply trips north.

Yorkville and Green Bay seemed to enjoy a period of truce, mostly enforced by the weather. If York had plans to destroy Bruce's operation,

these were suspended during the cold season.
Even though only a few miles separated the lumber
camps, and despite Black Deer's well-defined forest
trails between the two enclaves, there was still no
official communication between the owners themselves.

Some of Bruce's and Alan's loggers did take
occasional trips down to Yorkville, where they
were allowed to gamble, see the girls, and involve
themselves in a brawl now and then. But nothing
serious; no bludgeonings or knifings. It was almost
as if Henry York and Connelly were biding their
time for bigger things than scuffles and skirmishes,
Bruce thought.

This proved to be fact in April when the cold
weather seemed to dissolve and the sun emerged
from the pearly mists, warming the land that lay
steaming and ready to blossom beneath it.

Green Bay became a hive of activity. The loggers
went cheerfully into the forest once more to begin
full-time operations, and Janet had her baby at
dawn one clear, crystal morning. They named the
boy Guy after his pleased grandfather, who, with
Marian and a shipful of supplies, had just dropped
anchor at Green Bay.

Alan's pride in his first child, especially since it
was a boy, made him suddenly more ambitious
than he had ever been. He went out into the
forest each day with the advance crew, working
alongside the men, urging them on, returning each
night to his wife and child, exhausted but pleased
with the progress that Territorial Mills was beginning to make after a long period of virtual inac-
tivity.

If a logger was reluctant to act as high climber,

to top a spar tree in preparation for high-lead logging, Alan would volunteer for the job. He and Janet had tense arguments over just how much Alan should be doing out in the field, but Alan couldn't be deterred—not even by Bruce, to whom Janet went after one fierce set-to on the subject.

"You owe it to Janet and little Guy to stay on the ground," Bruce told Alan. "What does it take to make you realize that I need you as much as Janet and the boy do? You're too valuable to be doing the job of the timber beasts. They're paid for risks. You aren't."

"But I haven't come up with any new ideas," Alan protested. "I'm not earning my salt and I owe you so much."

"You owe me nothing," Bruce continued firmly, recalling what Melanie had said about people who save other people's lives. "Tell you what, if I double your salary, will you stay out of tree tops and spend more time thinking about ways to get our timber from the interior to the bay?"

"Certainly. But you're far too generous," Alan objected.

"No, you're the one who's too generous. All I do is sit back and make money. Now, no more climbing trees—promise?"

"If you say so," Alan promised, reserving the right to go back on it in case of an emergency.

One soon arose. There was a large Douglas fir that needed the proper high rigging. It was standing in the way of the drag route used by the oxen teams to pull saw lengths of peeled logs down to the bay. Because of its canted position on a hillside, no high rigger would touch it. So, the morning after Alan's talk with Bruce he was out inspecting the tree and decided that it would be his last job of topping.

Alan was dug in two hundred feet above the earth when a sudden squall swept in from the bay and beat against the tops of the tall fir grove. The top of the tree snapped and fell, and Alan's arm was broken; he had to be helped down to the ground.

Bruce said nothing to Alan when he was brought in to be treated by the camp medic, feeling that Janet would give her husband a lecture he would never forget. That night, Janet rattled through her household duties.

"You're mad at me, I can tell," Alan said from his bunk. "You're going at your chores with a vengeance."

"No, dearest, I'm not mad, I'm perplexed," Janet replied. "Why you'd want to deprive little Guy of a father—which could easily happen if you go on being a daredevil—is beyond me. It really is."

"I hadn't thought of it that way."

"Well, please do. If you keep on being a logger, you'll be depriving your son of a father and make me a widow. The loneliest, saddest widow in Washington Territory."

"Come here, darling," Alan said, holding out his good right arm, a mischievous smile on his face.

Janet put down the pot she was scrubbing, glanced at their sleeping son in his trundle bed, and sat beside Alan. He slipped his right hand beneath the folds of her dressing robe and touched her bare flesh. She shivered slightly.

"Stop it!" she whispered, and he knew he'd won her back. She wouldn't scold him anymore.

Janet lay on the roomy bunk beside her husband while he explored her as best he could with one hand. She moaned softly as he entered her, and the baby stirred in its bed. Yes, she thought, they would soon need an addition to the cabin or their son would be watching them make love, and that would never do. Then she abandoned herself to Alan completely.

Alan's splinted, bandaged arm kept him in the house and inactive for the better part of a week. During his convalescence he busied himself with reading, but he soon tired of that and began making sketches for the planned expansion of Green Bay into a model community. From there his natural inventiveness took over. Thinking about ways to increase production by making it easier, he sought some method other than depending on Green River to float logs downstream to make log booms. By chance, he hit upon a crude but helpful idea, what would amount to an innovative transport system.

Why not build a sled railroad, all of it inclined, starting from whatever point the loggers worked and ending up at the sawmill? The rails would be slick wood, the sled cars would have grooved runners that fitted over the rails, and the cars would be flat-bedded. The cars would possess clamp brakes, also made of wood, so that they could be ridden down from the logging site to the bayshore by a brakeman. They would be hauled back up the incline empty by oxen. The more pronounced the incline, the more easily the sled cars would move. There was some danger if they broke loose, but with good brakes, maybe with sets on both the front and the rear of the sleds, they would be safe enough.

Metal rails were out of the question, of course; so were standard gauge metal wheels. Both items would have to come from California, be specially manufactured there, and would not only be expensive but not immediately available. It could be another year before a real railroad could be set up, if not longer. Time was precious if they wanted to turn it into money. The makings of an effective sled railroad with wooden tracks were right there in the forest!

Excited, Alan completed his drawings, then made a scale model sled car with a length of sample tracks. He sent Janet over to tell Bruce he'd made a discovery.

Bruce arrived, still irritated at Alan for topping the fir, but willing to listen to him.

"What would you say," Alan asked, "if I told you I'd come up with an idea that may revolutionize our whole logging operation? It'll make the skidroad obsolete, I promise you."

"I'd say your confinement's getting to you. That fir must have broken your head as well as your arm."

Alan grimaced. "I guess I deserved that. But you'll change your tune when you see what I've dreamed up."

"I hope it doesn't involve climbing," Bruce said pointedly.

"Wait and see. It's crude, but the idea's workable."

Alan whisked the red and white checkered tablecloth off the railroad model, then sat back, smiling.

"It looks like some kind of a railroad," said Bruce.

"It is," Alan said, and began to explain his idea and how it would work.

In less than a minute Bruce was as excited as Alan. Two weeks later, a trial sled was sent down wooden rails from the logging site to the mill, with no problems at all. Four strong oxen hauled the car back up to the work site, the car was loaded once more and sent down with only one braker aboard.

The long and laborious system of having oxen drag single logs down the inclined route to the mill twenty times a day was finally eliminated. The new method even made it easier for the over-worked oxen. Now the transport time could be measured in minutes, not half-hours.

"Your invention's fantastic, Alan," Bruce congratulated his camp boss. "You see, you're able to use your education after all, even if you're not teaching school."

"Don't tempt me," Alan said playfully, his arm just out of the sling, "I might go back to school-teaching and leave you alone up here."

Bruce looked startled. "You're not serious? You mean you'd take Janet and little Guy and go back to California?"

Alan laughed, realizing he had gone too far. "No, no, I was only joking. Janet and I were saying last night, this is where we want to be for a long time to come. It's exciting to be in on the beginning of something, to get to know the woods, to see our operation grow. It won't be long before we'll have a regular township here, with a church and everything. Then, of course, I might consider

9

ALAN WAS RIGHT; Bruce had needed a vacation badly. The voyage down the west coast with Guy Kelsey was a pleasant one, the weather holding fair with a nice breeze. As soon as the brig left the Strait of Juan de Fuca, Bruce breathed an automatic sigh of relief that his cares and worries, for the time being, at least, were behind him. He swore he wouldn't concern himself about what happened back at Green Bay, because now it was out of his hands.

Guy Kelsey was in fine spirits on the voyage. The captain and Bruce had recently entered into an agreement whereby Kelsey would act as lumber agent for Territorial Mills, a most felicitous arrangement for Bruce. With Kelsey's extensive contacts, he was able to secure markets where even York couldn't. Kelsey was respected as a captain and a businessman, other men trusted him, and soon Bruce's lumber was in great demand. With the help of schooners that traded between China and California, Kelsey had found a whole new market for lumber: the Chinese. This trade would increase enormously during the next few decades, becoming one of the steadier markets for Territorial Mills.

Bruce stayed at the Pacific Hotel, a small but elite hostelry close to the waterfront business district. He made arrangements for more mill equipment, did his banking, and after two days was ready to return to Green Bay, having concluded all matters to his satisfaction. But Kelsey was still waiting for supplies and the *Rupert* wouldn't sail for another three to four days, leaving Bruce free to do as he wished.

"Why not go down the peninsula?" Kelsey suggested. "Take a coach ride to San Jose, see the countryside."

Bruce reacted indifferently to Kelsey's proposal.

"I need another kind of a change, and it isn't open countryside. I really need a woman," Bruce admitted. He'd been chaste entirely too long. The tension was beginning to fray his nerves, especially in San Francisco, where beautiful women were in bountiful supply and smiled at you on nearly every corner, in every saloon, from every whorehouse window.

Guy Kelsey understood Bruce's need perhaps even better than Bruce himself did. Any woman Randall took would have to be exceptional—not only proficient but in good taste.

...ewd of her, he thought, but then, the art of
...was her business.

...m thinking about my mill in the Northwest,
...ce improvised.

...Oh dear!" Estelle sprang lightly from the bed,
...y and nubile in her nakedness, as vibrant as a
...noir model. She reached for a filmy white dress-
...g gown. "No need to fib to a lady," she said
...rchly. "I declare! Somethin's distractin' you, and
...t's not your pesky old sawmill. Now tell me the
...truth."

"You're on target," Bruce admitted.

"I thought so. I know my men, darlin', and what
causes their minds to wander. Either you have a
wife at home up in those north woods—"

"I'm not married. I wouldn't be here if I were."

"Glad to hear it. Or a mistress?"

"I don't have one," Bruce said flatly.

Estelle laughed playfully. "It's not a *man*, is it?"

"Damn!" Bruce threw back the covers and got
out of bed. "Now you've gone too far!"

"Oh dear," Estelle said, amused. "Anyway, the
afternoon's done, I'm afraid. Shall we meet again
during your stay in San Francisco?"

"I wonder if we should?"

...e eyed him indifferently, still smiling.

"...s entirely up to you, darlin'."

...she wasn't Melanie Cloud, not by the width
...ocean. Melanie would have handled the en-
...ation with tact. Alert, self-protective, but
...nd sensitive beneath her hard-bitten fa-
...knew that Melanie would have told him
...just what she thought. But then, why was
...y such comparisons? They were unfair
...men.

"Well," said Kelsey, "Marian's having luncheon
with some ladies, so that leaves us alone. Give me
an hour and I'll meet you at the Niantic for a
meal."

Bruce agreed to the rendezvous. Without Bruce's
knowledge, Guy arranged for a woman to satisfy
Bruce's needs. This was no ordinary prostitute. She
was one of the most sought-after sporting women
in San Francisco, a charming, well-spoken demi-
mondaine from New Orleans, just recently introduced to San Francisco through Madame Flora's
discreet salon at the Hotel Splendide, and presently
available for a rendezvous. Kelsey got vicarious
enjoyment out of making the arrangement for
Randall, and went to the Niantic feeling com-
placent.

The two men were just finishing their luncheon
when a stunning woman in white entered the
restaurant, settled regally at a table close to them,
and ordered tea alone while she studied the menu.

"My God," Bruce said to Guy, "what a magnificent woman! Is she an actress?"

"Let's say she's excellent at portraying passion."

"You know her?"

Kelsey shrugged his shoulders. "I know *of* her.
Does she meet with your approval?"

"I think she's as lovely as any woman I've seen
in San Francisco," Bruce acknowledged.

"Yes, she is attractive," Guy agreed. "Now,
about the question of the mill parts, Friedman tells
me he can't have them ready for our departure."
Kelsey was enjoying his game.

"To hell with the parts! How do I meet that
woman over there? Do I dare walk up to her and
introduce myself?"

"If you don't have the courage, I'll do it for you."

"She's probably waiting for her husband," said Bruce.

"She has no husband," Kelsey said. "I know, because I'm acquainted with her."

"You?"

Kelsey nodded. "She's Madame Flora's choicest flower from the Splendide. Her name's Estelle Windsor."

"Ah, so you do indeed know her," said Bruce.

Guy Kelsey lifted his heavy eyebrows. "Now, Bruce, I don't 'know' the lady in any carnal sense. How could I get away with such behavior while Marian's around? I just happened to meet the lady the other day drinking with friends at Madame Flora's salon at the Hotel Splendide."

"The Splendide? It's a whorehouse."

"Not quite. It's a house of illusion, old boy, a place where the exhausted tycoon goes to renew his ego and test his manly skills. Surely it's about time for you to. . . ."

"You're a sneak, Guy Kelsey," Bruce said under his breath. "A wily old salt. You've maneuvered me into a corner."

"She doesn't look like she has any corners," Kelsey said. "I may be married, but I've still enough red blood in my veins to respond to beauty, even so."

And the lovely Estelle was a feast for the eyes, Bruce observed, with her own pale blue eyes, and dark hair nearly the texture of Melanie's. She had perfect poise, acting every inch the proud lady as she sipped her tea. His heart stuttered, desire stirred in his groin, and he realized that he had

denied himself pleasure entirely
a fool to bypass what was obviou
uation.

"I ought to lecture you," he told (

"Nonsense! That's not you speakin
stuffy Boston Brahmin background.
some bills on the waiter's silver tray
"Come, I'll introduce you two. Oh, one t
there's to be no talk of money."

"But I . . ."

"Whatever you *thought*, its all been tak
of. Enjoy yourself."

Kelsey walked over to Estelle Windsor's
and introduced Bruce to her. He left the two
gether. Bruce sat while Estelle finished her tea a
paid the small check; then they departed . . .

An hour later Bruce found himself in bed with
Estelle Windsor in a comfortable room at the Hotel Splendide, making love to this delectable creature, velvety and rose-scented. Estelle proved to
be as artful a lover as she was beautiful, and it wa
easy for Bruce to abandon himself to a joy he h
thought he'd forgotten, but had only put as
more than a year.

There was something about F
minded him of Melanie Cloud
he thought of Melanie made
had not been long from
first meeting on the b

"You have somet'
told him as they lay t
second time. "Your body
isn't."

After dressing quickly he took a note from his wallet, a large one. He folded and pressed it into Estelle's hand at the door. She glanced at it, and back at him with barely concealed distaste as she opened the door.

"There was no need for that, darlin'. I was bought and paid for in advance," she said with irony. "But thanks all the same . . ."

He left the Splendide with a bad taste in his mouth, with a sense of frustration. It seemed ridiculous, but while he was making love to Estelle he had actually felt that he was entering Melanie, that it was Melanie's fiery tongue eagerly meeting his own. An outrageous assumption, damned stupid. But it was a situation that he hoped for, because he was in love with Melanie Cloud. Or at least, in love with a dream, an image that she'd left him with after that one brief meeting. It was almost as if she'd cast a spell upon him.

And maybe she had. After all, she was half-Indian. It could be that the Indian blood in her veins was seeking out vengeance for the treatment of her people by the American government —in 1838 the Supreme Court and President Andrew Jackson—when the Cherokees were forced out of their homelands in Georgia and marched west of the Mississippi. Thousands had died on that trail of tears. Melanie had been a mere girl at the time, but who knew what she may have seen and remembered?

Well, Bruce reflected, on his way to his hotel, he would have to see Melanie Cloud again, and soon, upon his return to Green Bay. He didn't give a damn that she might be York's mistress, al-

though after meeting her he couldn't believe this
to be true. And yet . . .

There were so many things to sort out. He was
grateful to Alan for making him take the ship to
San Francisco. It had cleared his head, brought
him closer to the Northwest, which was now un-
questionably becoming home to him—a place to
live for, to struggle and fight for, perhaps even to
die for. The trip had also brought him closer to a
woman he did not know at all, as unreachable as
a dream, and for many reasons, as tantalizing . . .

The last night in San Francisco, Bruce took Marian and Guy Kelsey to a new restaurant for dinner.
The Oyster House specialized in seafood, but there
were many other dishes just as satisfying, especially for Guy Kelsey, who was a meat and potatoes man, having enough of the sea when he was
working. The captain ate beef.

Marian was full of news from her stay in San
Francisco and regaled both men with gossip about
the nouveau riche that was beginning to form San
Francisco social life. In fact, Marian wanted nothing more than to settle permanently in this fast-
growing city, get Guy to sell the *Rupert* and settle
down and open a ship chandlery handling marine
hardware at the port.

As they were taking coffee in the restaurant's
outer lounge, a couple entered the Oyster House
that made Marian clutch Bruce's coat sleeve.

Leaning slightly forward she whispered, "The
woman in violet, she's Beryl York, Henry York's
separated wife. I thought she'd left San Francisco,
but apparently she's still around."

Bruce studied the handsome, young, fair-haired

woman in lavender velvet that almost matched her eyes. Figure, features, bearing, all were quite proper and quite exceptional. He had expected that Henry York would choose a flashier type. Beryl York was anything but flashy, and perfectly at ease in her surroundings. She leaned casually on the arm of her escort, a tall man, impeccably dressed, about Bruce's age. She, however, was in her mid-twenties.

"Who's her escort?" Bruce asked.

"Phil Bennington," Marian said. "An attorney. I don't know their relationship, but since Mrs. York left her husband and came to San Francisco she's had no other escort."

"Dear me," Guy Kelsey chided, "the things you find out and never tell your husband."

"You don't expect me to lead you to pretty women, my dear," Marian said with a smile. "Seriously, as I said, I thought she had already left for the east coast."

"I've heard many tales about Bennington," Kelsey said.

"Good or bad?" Bruce enquired.

"Ambiguous," the captain replied. "An opportunist, always looking for the fast dollar, whether it's closing an estate or making off with one. From what I've heard through reliable sources, even Henry York would do well to steer clear of him.

Was Beryl York also an opportunist? Bruce wondered. It seemed unfair to ask such a question of the Kelseys.

"Do you think York and Bennington know one another?" Bruce asked, and the captain immediately caught his meaning and grinned.

"It's a small world out here on the west coast,"

Kelsey replied. "If they aren't acquainted yet, their paths will probably cross one day. Or their fortunes."

At this point, Beryl York glanced in Marian's direction, caught her eyes and smiled, then said something to Bennington. The couple rose and approached Bruce's table.

Bennington bowed to the men and Marian, introducing himself.

"I assume that Mrs. Kelsey and Mrs. York have met," Bennington said in his grating baritone, quite at odds with his suave appearance, "so there's no need to introduce them."

Kelsey introduced Bruce Randall. "Mr. Randall's the owner of Territorial Mills, the property close to Henry York's holdings at Green Bay near Puget Sound," the captain explained.

Beryl scrutinized Bruce slowly. "I imagine you've met Henry?" Beryl said in a surprisingly gentle alto voice.

"No, I haven't," Bruce replied.

"Well, you undoubtedly will at some time or other."

"Are you staying on permanently?" Marian asked, plunging right in. "I thought you'd gone east."

"For the time being I've taken a house."

"That's nice," said Marian. "We're leaving on my husband's brig the *Prince Rupert* tomorrow at noon for the Puget Sound area."

"Interesting," said Bennington, exchanging glances with Beryl. "Would it be possible for you to carry some legal papers north for us?" the attorney asked.

"What kind of legal papers?" the captain said.

"Oh, claim papers. We could wait until a ship goes directly to Yorkville, but if you took them along it might save some time," Bennington explained.

If there was one thing Bruce didn't want, it was unnecessary involvement with York and Yorkville. What in God's name was the man trying to do, make him and Kelsey intermediaries in some vicious game that raged between York and his attractive wife? The woman was obviously the friend and possibly the mistress of a lawyer with an unsavory reputation.

Glancing at Kelsey momentarily, Bruce said, "I think the captain and I have enough responsibilities as it is without assuming any more."

"Of course," said Bennington, and let the matter drop.

After a minute or two of idle chatter about the weather, city matters, and the quality of the Oyster House menu, Beryl York and Bennington retired to their table.

"Comely creature," Guy Kelsey observed.

"You're as predictable as summer fog in August," said Marian.

"Well, she's attractive, all the same."

"She is indeed," Bruce agreed. He wasn't impressed with Bennington and wondered if perhaps Beryl York happened to be using the man. Surely if she were serious about Bennington she would be in the process of divorcing York, unless, of course, York wouldn't give her a divorce.

Anyway, he'd done the right thing in refusing to carry any legal papers. Kelsey had seemed relieved when he'd spoken up. Still, Beryl York looked like a woman who would not have taken his rejection without a discussion. Bruce dismissed Beryl York from his mind. She didn't come to mind again until just before sailing time the following day . . .

As Kelsey was giving orders to cast off, Beryl York came hurrying down the dock. She looked stunning in a soft blue ensemble with a feathery hat to match. She called to Bruce on deck from the wharf, and Bruce went down the gangplank to greet her.

"Mr. Randall," she said breathlessly, "I really do need your help. Mr. Bennington spoke of some papers to be sent to Henry. These need to be signed and returned before the month is out or I shan't be able to sell some property that's mine, but under Henry's guardianship."

"Sounds complicated."

"It isn't. The property is a ranch south on the San Francisco peninsula. It's a family property but Henry's involved, as I said. Will you be so kind as to deliver the papers? You can send them over to him by messenger. There's no need for you to get involved personally. I know that things haven't been the easiest between you two."

Was the woman lying? Was he getting himself into something he'd feel sorry for later on, Bruce wondered?

"I know you refused Mr. Bennington last night, and I can understand your reluctance. All the same, there won't be any trouble. The papers are what I say they are. You must believe me."

And then again, why shouldn't he take Beryl York's word? Bennington was obviously hanging around her for two reasons: she was an attractive woman, and she was also probably a wealthy one in her own right. Well, that was her business, not his.

"All right," Bruce said, "I'll deliver your papers —taking your word, of course, that I won't be involved in some kind of vendetta. It may give me that long-awaited chance to meet Henry York." He took the thick packet of papers she held out to him.

Beryl rewarded him with a bright smile of gratitude.

"I'm glad you didn't say 'long-awaited pleasure'," she declared. "Henry isn't always pleasant."

"So I've heard."

"Will you be down again this way soon?" she asked with what appeared to be more than polite interest.

"I doubt it. We're going into our heaviest season now before the rains really begin, trying to build up a backlog for winter shipment. But then, you know what the weather is like up there. Any chance of you going back?"

"I see no reason to while Henry's still there," she said abruptly, which seemed to close the subject.

Captain Kelsey called down to Bruce at that moment.

"I mustn't keep you," Beryl said, "since you're about to sail. Have a pleasant voyage. You needn't give my regard to Henry. The papers will do that for me. And thank you so much again for taking them up with you."

Beryl extended her hand to Bruce, who took it and smiled at her. There was a sparkle of warmth behind those violet eyes that was frankly inviting. He said goodbye and went aboard thinking about her.

If the trip to San Francisco had done nothing else, it had renewed his self-esteem. He hadn't lost his charm for lovely women, nor was he entirely indifferent to them, as he'd thought before he'd met Melanie Cloud. But still, none of them intrigued him as Melanie did. He was determined to see her again.

"You may not have helped your situation up at Green Bay by taking the papers," Kelsey told Bruce as the captain put the parchment envelope into the ship's safe for the voyage.

"Oh, I don't know. Somehow I have a feeling that Mrs. York wants me to meet Henry," Bruce said.

"It's not Mrs. York who bothers me," Kelsey said, "it's that Bennington. I didn't want to tell you this last night in front of Marian, but Bennington bilked a sea captain friend of mine out of his life savings with some kind of paper-processing plant he was going to build in the San Francisco area. The money simply evaporated. Oh, it was all very legal and above-board, there was a statute of limitations on the investors' money, so the law couldn't get at the knave. But it was a damned rotten fraud, all the same."

"Well, so be it. I've involved myself in the delivery of the papers," Bruce said, "whatever they are. We're already under sail"—they were passing through the Golden Gate at that moment—"and I can't very well swim ashore to return them. I'll just have to hope that I'm not already in hot water with York."

"Let us hope so," the captain observed, and locked the safe.

10

THE SITUATION AT GREEN BAY community was far from peaceful when the *Rupert* dropped anchor there on its return voyage to the Northwest.

Alan was waiting at the wharf for Bruce, but there was little joy in his welcome. He took Alan aside immediately.

"Lord, I'm so glad to see you," he said, embracing him. "You look splendid. The trip was just what you needed, wasn't it?"

"It was good. You look worried, Alan. Anything wrong?"

Alan's expression was grim, as though something were troubling him.

"The mill's just fine," he replied. "We're way ahead on our production schedule. The men worked well under my overall supervision, I'm happy to report. That is, all was smooth as silk until Saturday night."

Bruce began to feel an icy knot forming in his gut.

"Then what?" he said.

"That was four days ago, when a bunch of loggers went down to Yorkville to have some Saturday night fun. Black Deer was telling me that there was some trouble at Yorkville over money."

"Go on," said Alan.

I asked Bill Dexter to tell his men to stay in camp. I didn't want to do it myself, thinking they'd listen to him. Well, they didn't. A group of them set off after a few drinks, led by a newcomer who came up from California redwood country while you were away. A real grizzly bear of a man named Tulsa."

Alan paused and shook his head, smacking his right fist into the palm of his left hand. "I wish I'd talked to the men myself," he muttered. "Shouldn't have left it up to Bill. Maybe they'd have listened to me and not gone off to Yorkville. I don't know."

"Go on, Alan. Tell me the rest."

"Tulsa got into a roaring fight with one of Connelly's bullies. Knives were pulled. I have to give Connelly credit. He broke it up before anybody got stabbed."

Bruce was relieved. "Well, that's not too bad."

"Wait. There's more. Coming back alone through the forest after visiting the whorehouse, Tulsa was shot in the back. He died on the trail. Black Deer and his men found him and brought him in."

"Oh Christ!" Bruce exclaimed, anticipating a vicious feud between the two camps. This time it wouldn't stop with logging nets. "What about the logger who fought with Tulsa? Where was he when Tulsa got it?"

"Just coincidentally he was playing a hot poker game in plain sight of our men in York's saloon at the time Tulsa was shot. So anybody could have done it. Maybe even Connelly himself."

"I don't think you should draw conclusions, Alan. It's dangerous."

"It's murder, that's what it is, and it *could* be Connelly. Our boys say he wasn't playing poker."

"How's the general reaction?"

"Shock, first off. Morale's been mighty low. Even if Tulsa was a growler and a bitcher, he was a fine worker and popular with the other loggers. He made no enemies here."

Alan pressed his hands to his temples.

"I feel terrible about it, absolutely awful. The death was pointless."

Bruce agree. "And worse than that, nobody will swing for it. We'll never identify the murderer."

"Our men are about ready to go down to Yorkville and wipe out the whole gang, York included."

"A shooting war won't bring back Tulsa," Bruce said. "Did you give him a decent funeral?"

"Of course. Bill Dexter made quite an emotional speech. Janet left, crying."

"Where did you bury him?"

"Just north of the houses in that new clearing. It seemed as good a place as any to establish a cemetery."

"Good thinking. Well, what's our next move?"

"I've given it a lot of thought, Bruce. I asked the men to stay in camp until you came back. The only solution I see is to issue a permanent order forbidding loggers from going down to Yorkville again."

"That isn't going to be easy. The boys get restless toward the end of the week. They need a safety valve."

"We could open our own saloon," Alan suggested, "but that wouldn't solve anything either."

"Not unless we opened a whorehouse. And I refuse to allow that. Dammit," Bruce exploded, "we're not in competition with York's circus, or with anybody. Green Bay is a solid, peaceful, hardworking community and we're going to stay that way, even if yours is the only familiy here."

Alan sighed with relief. "I'm glad you feel the way I do. I thought maybe San Francisco might have gone to your senses."

"There was precious little chance of that."

"Anyway, what can be done about Tulsa's murder?"

"I shall go down to see York tomorrow. It's too late to make the trip today."

"It might be wiser to send York a letter, telling him you've put his place off-limits for your loggers."

"I'll tell him in person at our meeting," Bruce promised. "Besides, I'm carrying some papers for him from his wife, Beryl. She handed them to me on the dock in San Francisco. I was reluctant to take them at first. Now I'm glad I did. They give me the perfect excuse to meet him."

"Maybe you can make York see your point of view," Alan said.

"If I can't then we're going to have real trouble next spring."

"Or sooner," said Alan.

"Or sooner," Bruce agreed and went to his cabin with Alan to see what progress had been made.

Later, toward midnight, still studying papers by lamplight, Bruce decided that he was being too trusting about Beryl York's papers; they might mean trouble for him.

He opened the brown parchment envelope Beryl York had entrusted to him, expecting to find a sealed envelope inside, bearing York's name. Instead he found a plain white linen bond envelope sealed only at the point of the flap, and easily opened by simply slipping his index finger beneath the seal.

He drew out a sheaf of papers. One was a document of sale on a large number of acres south of San Francisco. Another concerned a property in San Francisco. Covering both was a formal letter on Bennington's stationery asking York, as the legal guardian of his wife, Beryl, to please sign the release so she could sell property that had always been hers. This, said the letter, was all she'd ask of York, except for a statement that he would allow her a divorce; if not that, at least a legal separation, for which she would ask no support.

Beryl's requests looked reasonable enough, the papers in order. It seemed unlikely, however, from what Bruce had heard about York, that he'd grant his departed wife a divorce on any grounds, even infidelity. He wanted to keep her tied to him, rumor said, for her money, like it or not. As for the releases, he knew nothing about those.

What puzzled him most was that Beryl York hadn't fully sealed the envelope, making it simple for him to examine its contents. Was this a deliberate move on her part and not an oversight? Maybe she wanted to provide him with information about a common enemy. If so, he liked her better for it. However, facing York was another matter. He put the papers back into their envelope, sealing the flap with hot wax for delivery to York the following day.

Bruce didn't look forward to the meeting; it would be thorny. Instinct told him to make the trip only with Black Deer. Alan and Bill Dexter would just increase tension at the meeting, especially so soon after Tulsa's death. Neither camp could afford open warfare. A couple more murders and the loggers might desert altogether, and that could put him out of the logging business. It was one thing to have Saturday night brawls—that was almost the loggers' inalienable right—but ambush killings would only lead to a whole chain of ugly reprisals on both sides. And this wouldn't be the end of it. It would involve the Siwash Indians too. Most of these lived south of Yorkville on land that York had leased from them with the right to log it out. Because of Black Deer, the Siwash were bound to place their loyalties with the scout's, with Green Bay, in the event there was trouble.

Bruce had a difficult time sleeping that night. He ran through his trip to San Francisco once more, thinking only in passing of the beautiful Estelle Windsor, wondering more about the effect that Melanie Cloud would have on him next day if he should see her. He wasn't going to stir up things any more than they were by asking for her.

But word would get around camp that he had come for his first visit and perhaps she would be there.

Next year, he promised himself, he would have to think about getting married and raising a family. What he really would like was a woman who combined the qualities of Estelle, Melanie and Beryl York in one delectable package. But where on God's green earth was he going to find a woman like that? Thinking how ridiculous his fantasies were, he fell asleep.

It took Bruce and Black Deer nearly three hours to make the trip from Green Bay to Yorkville by forest trail.

A light rain was falling and Black Deer rode slowly, talking occasionally to Bruce.

"My people having trouble with York's men," the Indian told him. "Nothing bad yet, but not friendly. They come as far as edge of our land and make threats. They get drunk, they say bad things."

"Just so long as they don't bother the village or cause physical violence," Bruce said.

"I worry. Not too many men there now, and very old. Can't defend women and children."

Perhaps it was a matter Bruce should bring up with York, if he had the chance.

"You might consider moving your people up to the north of us," Bruce suggested, "putting yourselves on the very tip of the peninsula. Then York's men would have to come through my land to get to you. I don't think they'd try."

"Maybe good idea," Black Deer agreed. "I talk to my people about it."

As the two men passed through the forest nearing Yorkville, they came upon a crew of York's loggers at work on a fresh stand of redcedar and hemlock. They had no sooner passed out of sight than they heard a horse's hooves galloping off through the dense timber, taking a shortcut to Yorkville and carrying word that the competition was approaching. Bruce was right about the alert; the place was deserted when they rode into Yorkville, except for a lone figure.

Henry York stood on the covered portico of his central office building in the muddy square as the two riders came into view. If York wasn't exactly making them welcome at least he was exhibiting curiosity, Bruce decided.

He and Black Deer dismounted and tethered their horses to the hitching rail. Black Deer disappeared around a corner of the building; he seemed to know where to go to get out of the rain.

Bruce took the steps with a slight smile. York stepped forward, hand outstretched.

"Mr. Randall," York murmured.

Henry York was a much smaller man than Bruce, but what he lacked in stature he made up for in presence. On this wet grey day, he projected a kind of musty malevolence. He struck Bruce as a man who was always one step ahead of you, whose schemes were not concerned with your survival. He wondered what the attraction had been for Beryl York. York may have managed a business deal for Beryl; she had indicated something of the sort.

"Mr. York," Bruce responded, shaking York's hand.

"Shall we go inside?" York bowed and led the

way into his office, waved Bruce into a chair and indicated a bottle of whiskey with two shot glasses on his desk.

"Drink?" asked York, pushing the bottle at him.

The last thing Bruce wanted was a drink, but instinct told him that York expected him to go through the ritual formality.

"It might be just the thing to counteract the cold rain," Bruce said, smiling. "Thank you . . ." He poured himself a shot. Still holding the bottle he said, "And you?"

"Of course," said York, nodding at his glass.

"To the forest, Mr. Randall, the source of our wealth!"

Bruce acknowledged the toast with a raised glass. Both men drank their shots straight down. York banged his glass on the desk, sat back, and hooked his fingers in his vest pockets.

"So," he said, scrutinizing Bruce, "you'd best shed your mackintosh, sir, and tell me what brings you here."

"Thank you." Bruce took off his coat and hat and sat down again, more relaxed. From his inner coat pocket he removed Beryl York's packet and laid it on the desk.

"I was commissioned to bring this envelope to you, Mr. York." Bruce pushed the packet toward York.

York's eyebrows shot up. He leaned forward and picked up the packet, took out the sealed envelope, and broke the seals. Without glancing up, he excused himself and began to read Beryl's letter. Moments later, he threw it down with a grunt and sat back in his chair again. His features showed no emotion, but Bruce was certain that the man was furious and was concealing it.

"I gather, Mr. Randall, that this envelope was given you by my wife's attorney?"

"On the contrary," Bruce said, "she came to the *Rupert* personally just before sailing time and asked me to see that you got it. I might not have delivered it myself, however, except for the death of one of our loggers, a man named Tulsa."

"Ah yes, the quarrelsome one with the knife."

"From what I heard, there were knives on both sides. But killing my man on the trail was uncalled for. And shooting him in the back was especially reprehensible."

"I've initiated an investigation," York said blandly. "The death is a mystery. Several times in the past, the Siwash have staged attacks to make it look as though the white man were responsible. In my opinion this is what happened to your man. We had several trail deaths of our own, just before you came to Green Bay."

If York were lying, there was no way Bruce could prove it now. Even Black Deer would be hard put to substantiate how the loggers had died; whether by a forest accident, illness, or bullets in their backs, was virtually unanswerable.

"My men won't be satisfied with your explanation," Bruce said. "Nor am I, I should add."

"Mr. Randall," York said evenly, "are you calling me a liar?"

"No, Mr. York. I'm simply saying that I'm not convinced the Siwash had anything to do with Tulsa's killing. His body wasn't robbed; there was no motive that the Indians would have for eliminating him. On the other hand, someone might have thought he'd come down again to Yorkville and be too much to handle."

"I'll continue to investigate, but I assure you, Mr. Randall, nothing new will turn up."

"Perhaps you're right," Bruce said. "By the way, I hope this won't start a rash of trouble between our camps. I feel we're all here principally to work, to make as much money as we can in the quickest, most peaceful way possible."

"What do you suggest we do to secure this peace you talk about?" York enquired mildly.

"I'll keep my men in my camp if I have to chain them to their bunks, and you keep your men down here. You've provided everything they need."

York smiled coldly. "You'd do well to provide entertainment for your men, Mr. Randall, as I do. Import some women, open a saloon."

"I'll do things in my own way, thank you."

"Satisfied workers are happy workers," York said. "Yours obviously aren't satisfied or they wouldn't be coming to Yorkville on Saturday nights. Be that as it may, we won't welcome your men in the future if you prefer it that way."

"It will be appreciated." Bruce stood up, deciding that the interview had gone on long enough. "Thank you for the hospitality."

"You're welcome to stay for dinner," York said expansively. "Overnight at the hotel, too, if you like."

"I think not," Bruce replied, aware of the implications. "We want to beat the dark back to Green Bay."

York nodded. "You have nothing to fear in the

dark from white men, Mr. Randall, only from the Siwash."

Bruce let the remark pass. "One more thing, Mr. York. If your crews want to work the territory that borders on mine, even they go over somewhat onto my land, I'm not going to start a war with you over it. Just as long as it doesn't become a habit."

"I was about to suggest the same thing to you," York replied. "I guess that's as near a truce as we're likely to get, is it not?"

"Apparently," said Bruce. He purposely decided not to shake hands again with York. Despite his outward civility, this pompous, self-centered bastard had managed to raise his normally placid nature to near-boiling.

"Goodbye, Mr. York," Bruce snapped, picking up his rain gear.

York opened the office door for him. Standing just outside it was a small man who fitted Dexter's description of York's lieutenant, Egan Connelly. No doubt Connelly had been eavesdropping, probably at York's orders.

Bruce swept past the man and out the front door, getting into his raincoat on the portico. The rain had tapered off to a fine chilly mist. The two horses were still tied up near the steps, but Black Deer was nowhere in sight. Then suddenly, to Bruce's relief, the Indian stepped out from the rear of the hotel and walked slowly across the square toward him: materialized was a better term. Black Deer's timing was uncanny.

As he watched Black Deer approach, Bruce realized that York hadn't stepped out on the portico

with him, and that the door to the office building
had swung shut behind him. He was standing by
himself. Then he noticed another thing: Melanie
Cloud was standing in the doorway of the hotel,
motionless as a statue, staring out across the rain-
misted square at him.

Black Deer mounted his horse, Bruce untied his
mount and took the saddle. He sensed that York
was watching him from his office window; he
didn't need to look to realize that York would
recognize if he acknowledged Melanie Cloud's
appearance. Did he know about their meeting?

It took all of Bruce's will power to avoid glancing in Melanie's direction. Anyway, it might not
be necessary. Black Deer had quite possibly spoken with her, Bruce hoped, remembering that she
understood Siwash.

The two men walked their mounts slowly out of
the Yorkville compound without looking back.
They didn't speak to one another until they were
beyond the point where the logging crew had been
felling trees.

"Cloud gave me word for you," Black Deer said
at last. Bruce was relieved.

"Is she all right?"

Black Deer shrugged; well-being was a relative
term.

"She said you must set up many guards. York
is ready to do battle. The other white man's death
was only the beginning."

"But why!" Bruce asked in surprise. "We're not
at war."

"York wants to frighten you away. He wants the
whole peninsula."

"I made concessions. I told him he could cut on

my holdings, if his men couldn't help getting over the line sometimes. He agreed to it."

"York is not a very agreeable man. Watch out when he is," said Black Deer.

"Why in God's name does she stay there then?" Bruce asked in bewilderment. "She's not tied to York."

"She is one of us."

"Is she spying for us?"

Black Deer nodded. "If something is wrong, we will know through her."

"But how?"

"We have ways," said Black Deer. "And we must prepare ourselves."

Maybe, thought Bruce, as they rode in silence he was going about building his empire the wrong way. Logging was a way to develop a healthy and thriving community, and establishing a true township would support its growth. But again, he had enough money now, profits plus his capital, to withdraw from competition with York, and buy peace by getting rid of the logging crews and shutting down the mill's commercial operations, and simply plan and build a community of Utopian design.

Damned if he'd knuckle under, Bruce decided! He owned his land; he didn't have to bow to York's villanous greed. He would continue to work as he had from the start of Green Bay. York wouldn't dare go too far. He might have Egan Connelly at his elbow, but Bruce had Alan and Bill Dexter, and a fair-sized crew of loggers just aching to settle the score of Tulsa's untimely death. And now that they knew York's intentions, they could plan accordingly.

* * *

Egan Connelly and one of his men brought Melanie to York's office shortly after Bruce and Black Deer departed.

When York was alone with Melanie he said, "You did the right thing, my dear, to show yourself to young Randall."

"It was your bidding," Melanie said sullenly. "Now, when can we leave?"

"When I fancy it," said York, feasting hungry eyes upon her. York's gaze pierced the core of her being, making her feel used and dirty.

"And when is that?" she said with as much hauteur as she could muster.

"When two things have happened. When the ship comes in with the new girls, and when you've decided to be friendly and grant me your favors. Of your own free will, of course. I am not a violent man, merely one with normal desires."

York didn't have to tell her what he was; Melanie knew. He was a devil incarnate, a sadist who enjoyed exercising his dangerous power with people's souls.

"I demand that you release us," Melanie said quietly, knowing better than to anger him.

"My dear, you are free to walk out of the hotel anytime," York declared. "To enter the forest and take the trail for Green Bay if you so choose. But there are many dangers in the woods. Someone could easily mistake you or your companions for deer and shoot you down. Someone, that is, who doesn't know the area as well as me and my men. One never knows with that Green Bay bunch. It's a chance you would have to take."

"I'll get out alive, I promise," said Melanie,

thinking of the note she had hidden in the shed behind the house, where Black Deer had pointedly lingered while Bruce Randall was having his interview with York.

"My way is easier than anything you could devise," York told her.

"You never give up, do you?"

York's smile was icy. "I never forget, my dear," he said softly. "Once you made a fool of me in a San Francisco saloon. But you shan't do it twice. So, make up your mind which it's to be. Indefinite detainment here, or freedom. I assure you, you'll remain here, even if your girls get away. After all, it shouldn't be so difficult for you to bend to my wishes. It *is* your business, isn't it?"

Melanie thought of many things she could say to Henry York at this moment, all of them devastating—and all of them detrimental to her physical welfare, and to the girls'. Especially the girls. He'd promised to put them aboard the ship that brought their replacements, but she had no guarantee that he would. Submitting to York was really a trifling matter; she was certainly no virgin. But on the other hand, she had her pride. She trusted her pride because it had always made her indomitable in the past. She was determined to hold out now, hoping blindly that help would come either from Bruce or even from the next sea captain to bring his vessel to Yorkville. She had always relied on fate. It had carried her through some dark and bitter days and had brought her to Bruce in the forest. Bruce, whom she owed her life to, and with whom she was not yet finished, she knew.

No! She simply refused to surrender to York, except as a last resort if the girls were endangered.

Then she would see the group safely aboard ship, promise York his night with her, and be prepared to yield. Maybe she would even kill him. But meanwhile she wouldn't give up hope.

"Please let me go back to the hotel," she said quietly. "I want to be by myself."

"You'd do well to reconsider. I would even settle for an hour or so with you now. There's fresh linen on my bed, a fire is burning cozily in the stove, the wine can be ready in a moment. Dinner for two, a gracious evening together . . . Think about it," York said. "I might even build you a small house of your own if you pleased me. You could stay in Yorkville for as long as you care to in comfort . . ."

Melanie tried to keep the repugnance for him from her features and her voice as she said, "I'll think about it."

York held up his finger, his face drawn with anger. "You think about it," he said in a choked voice. "Think quickly. My patience is nearly ended. When I come to you at the hotel, you had better be prepared for me. I have made my offer, my proud lady. We both have our limits. Mine are nearly reached . . ."

York turned away from her and flung open the door.

"Take her back, Egan," he growled.

Egan Connelly and his man stood aside to let Melanie leave the building.

Melanie did not glance at York but drew her shawl over her head and walked straight and proud through the slushy square to the hotel.

She saw the pinched white faces of her girls with

out their business make-up looking out of one upstairs window frame. She hated herself for continuing the duel of wills with York, but some deep
stubborn wellspring born of her Indian heritage
controlled her behavior. She was powerless to
brush it aside. It was her fate to move as she was
moving, to hope even if it were hopeless. Whether
or not she yielded to York—and she had no plan
there except to act as she was already acting—she
had the feeling that she wouldn't get out of the
Northwest without first experiencing great ec-
stasy and great anguish. Meanwhile, she must live
her life, moment to moment, a prisoner more of
herself than Henry York. . .

As Bruce and Black Deer dismounted at Green
Bay, Black Deer handed Bruce a folded piece of
paper.

"What's this?"

"Message from Cloud. She leave after warn me
about York. I forget until now."

Bruce felt his hands tremble as he touched the
paper. It was like touching her, he thought.

"I go," Black said, and led the horses away.

Bruce hurried to his cabin. He shed his wet
clothes, got into dry ones, lit the oil lamp and sat
down on his bunk to read the note. It was written
in a fine, spidery hand, and read:

> Mr. Randall: You must be very careful in the
> future. I write this to you at risk of being
> found out by York. I will stay for a time to
> see my girls out, and because there is nowhere
> else to go. It is like prison. If things get worse

you will hear from me somehow. If I am all right, you will hear nothing.

Melanie Cloud

The message told him no more than he already suspected. Or maybe it did. Melanie was expressing fear and she didn't know what in hell to do about her situation. He couldn't invite her to come to Green Bay with her girls, and naturally, she wouldn't desert them. She would probably be loyal to them under even the most trying circumstances, unless they chose to leave there without her.

He folded the piece of paper, tucked it underneath his mattress of pine needles and went to see Alan and Janet. The Travers were eager to hear Bruce's impression of York.

"Sounds like a proper rogue to me," said Alan. "I'm afraid I wouldn't have been as polite as you were."

"I couldn't very well pick a fight with him on his own territory," Bruce replied. "I think he knew that I thought he was lying. I also got a very eerie feeling about Yorkville. It is obviously ruled by strong wills. York, Connelly, and whatever they use for a strong-arm force, are keeping things under tight control."

Bruce went on to tell Alan about the truce he and York had agreed to. "*If* he'll observe it. I have the feeling that he's going to cut wherever he likes, and dare us to do something to stop him. That will give him an excuse to use any kind of retaliation he wishes."

"All we can do is carry guns to our felling sites and keep our men out of Yorkville."

"Talk to Dexter about it," Bruce said. "He understands Connelly."

Bill Dexter heard Alan out next morning. "Tell you how to prevent the whole shooting match," Dexter advised Alan. "I'll ambush the bastard in the woods and that'll be the end of it. He's the one who does all of York's dirty work."

"No, Bill," said Bruce. "York would just hire someone else and it would be the start of a nasty little war. I won't have it."

"Mr. Randall, I've worked twenty years in lumber camps, from Minnesota to the West Coast. Ain't never seen a meaner cuss than Egan Connelly," Dexter declared. "He'll stop at nothing. I'll bet my bottom dollar that he shot Tulsa."

"We'd best forget that unfortunate incident," said Bruce. "We've plenty of rifles and ammunition. Let's go armed into the forest, and protect ourselves. Alan and I will fire anyone who visits Yorkville. If they do, let them stay south and work for York. We'll tighten up our night security around the community, too. That's imperative."

"We could go to Yorkville," Dexter suggested. "Sneak in at night, foul up some of their machinery. I like night raids. We've got the men rarin' to go."

"No!" Bruce said firmly. "None of that. I'm trying my best to keep the situation calm and peaceful."

"So we just sit and wait?" Dexter asked. "Let them come at us?"

"Yes," said Alan. "But we'll be prepared for them."

"All right, gents," said Dexter, "we'll do as you say. But I don't like it. Things been too quiet lately. You didn't settle nothin' with York, Mr. Randall, mark my words. We're in for trouble. Real trouble."

"All the more reason to be ready for it when it comes," Bruce pointed out. "We can't spend all our energy on hate. We've a business to run."

Bruce turned to Alan. "Are you behind me?"

"Of course," Alan responded.

"And you, Bill?"

Dexter hunched his shoulders. "Do I have a choice?"

Bruce grinned and shook his head. "Well, I guess we're all in agreement. Now, about that new spur for the sled railroad . . ."

11

FOR ALMOST A MONTH after Bruce's visit to York-ville, a gentle peace settled over the two logging communities.

Bill Dexter somehow managed to contain his crews at Green Bay on Saturday nights. How he did it was a wonder to both Bruce and Alan, but since the system was working they asked no questions. Bruce suspected that heavy poker games raged ceaselessly through the bunkhouses from early Saturday night until midnight Sunday. They probably were not even slowed down by a Sunday morning hymn-sing in the large meeting hall next to Bruce's office, but that was all right with him if it kept the men in camp. Bill Dexter's authority also helped to keep the men in line. He

exercised his power sparingly, through fair play,
candor, and never going back on his word, and it
prevailed as camp law.

During this period of uneasy peace, Dexter was
organizing his troops. Those who knew nothing
about arms were learning fast from those who did.
Black Deer had lessons in pathfinding techniques
for the men and taught his skills to the leaders of
different units. If Bruce and Alan felt that the
calm would continue indefinitely, Dexter reasoned
skeptically that it was always quietest just before
the storm, as he told Alan again and again.

"With Egan Connelly behind York, it won't be
long before we see some activity," Dexter pro-
phesied, and he was right.

When war finally came, however, it was in an
unexpected fashion. The heavy snowfall had just
begun to melt, when a letter was delivered by a
mounted messenger from Yorkville directly into
Bruce's hands. It came enclosed in a white envelope, scarcely a harbinger of peace, Bruce thought
wryly as he opened it, more likely a sign of trouble to come. The letter read:

> *Dear Mr. Randall:*
> *I have been mulling over the kind offer
> you made on your visit here some weeks ago.*
> *It concerned, as you will no doubt recall,
> your permission to cut timber inside your ter-
> ritory to a reasonable but unspecified degree.*
> *At this time I would like to make a specific
> request regarding your stated generosity.*
> *We are closer to the southeast end of your
> property than you are. So why not allow me
> to log off the Douglas fir there? Certainly it's*

*not possible for you to do so at this time, con-
sidering the distance from your mill. In return, you may log off an equal number of trees
from the lake down to the bay, but taking
only the red cedar?*

*I shall await your reply to this proposal wth
great interest.*

*Your obedient servant,
Henry York*

Bruce went immediately to the office and
showed Alan and Dexter York's request.

"I especially like the "obedient servant," said
Alan.

"Rotten son of a bitch," Dexter growled. "He
knows the value of timber as well as we do. He'd
be getting twice as rich a yield, Mr. Randall, if
you agree to his proposition."

"And what if I don't agree?" Bruce asked.

"He'll damned well do what he pleases anyway."

"Exactly," Bruce said. "So what must our response be?"

"Why not propose a ratio agreement?" suggested Alan.

"That's more like it," Dexter agreed.

"It seems fair, since York will probably steal the
timber if we don't agree to something," Alan declared.

That afternoon, Bruce wrote a sober document
that authorized Henry York of Yorkville to cut
25 Douglas firs from the designated area through
the end of June 1854, in exchange for Bruce's right
to cut 50 red cedars on his land, to be boomed
down Green River for tally by York's crew. The
ratio of 2 to 1 was predicated on the fact that the

fir trees were not only larger than the red cedars—which were used for shingles, but brought better prices, being light, strong and ideal for construction. York would, in fact, still be getting the best of the bargain.

York readily agreed to Bruce's proposal by return courier. It appeared, Bruce thought as he sent off his acknowledgment of York's consent, that problems between the two camps would thereafter cease. Peace, to his relief continued.

By late spring, the Green Bay crew had logged off the red cedar agreed upon and floated it down to the sawmill on the bay. York sent two men to tally the logs, which was done in a quick and orderly manner.

Following that, a party consisting of Bruce, Alan, Dexter and Black Deer made a one-day survey of the forest to check on York's Douglas fir cuttings. By actual count, the men tallied 42 giant trees felled and dragged from Bruce's land through the forest to the Yorkville mills.

"Connelly must have put the whole damned crew on the job," Dexter observed.

"He knew he was going to overcut, he did it quickly," said Alan.

"He didn't leave much," Bruce agreed. Most of the grove was gone. York had made a rich haul, all in the name of a fair and friendly exchange of goods.

"Well, the next move is up to us," Dexter said. "I'm all for burning out the bastards."

"Absolutely not," said Bruce. "I'll write a letter first."

He did this as soon as the party returned to

Green Bay and sent it off by Black Deer, with instructions that he should wait for a reply.

Black Deer returned empty handed.

"They tell me to go," he said. "Quickly or else . . . " He drew his index finger across his throat.

"All right," Bruce said, "that's it!"

"Can we burn him out?" Dexter asked when the men met at Bruce's office that night.

"Bill, forget about sabotage. We'd get it too, you know."

"Not with our guards," Dexter retorted. "They're sharp."

"I'm telling you to forget it," Bruce said flatly, and for the time being Dexter shut up, biding his time.

Three nights later a red glow lit up the southern skies. Black Deer reported the next morning that York's northernmost lumber yard had gone up in flames during the night. By the time the fire was discovered, it was too late for York's crews to extinguish it, and the neatly processed, stacked supply of Douglas fire burned to the ground.

Bruce went immediately to Bill Dexter and mentioned the yard fire. Dexter's innocent smile was all he needed to convince him that Dexter had planned the conflagration. It had to be Bill and his small core of diehards, who also knew Connelly and shared the foreman's hatred.

"I'm not going to ask if you were involved in the arson," Bruce told Dexter. "But if anything like this ever happens again, I may have to think about letting you go."

Dexter shrugged nonchalantly. It was quite apparent that evening up scores with Connelly was far more important to Dexter than the consequences of his act.

"You've let us in for some real trouble," Bruce went on. "I suppose you know that."

"Don't you worry, Mr. Randall," Dexter said. "We'll have guards night and day all over Green Bay, waiting for Egan."

"This isn't a vendetta, for God's sake, Bill," Bruce exploded. "I'm trying to conduct a decent, honest business operation, not border warfare."

"It's out of your hands now, Mr. Randall," Dexter said, and that seemed to conclude the subject, for indeed it was.

The first retaliation came a few nights later. Every evening after work, the sled railroad cars were secured at the top of the line, ready for loading the following morning. Or in some cases, where lodgepole pines were involved, the loading was done before the shift shut down.

Somehow, probably because of a dozing guard, a band of York's men got through to the sled car, doused it with turpentine, set it afire, released its brakes and sent it hurtling down the incline. It went like a blazing rocket, holding the track almost to the end. Then, about seventy feet before the track came alongside the sawmill platform, the car rose and flew through the air, a flaming ramrod that battered in the whole side of the mill structure with a crash that woke everyone in camp.

Thanks to quick thinking on Dexter's part, the blazing outer wall of the mill building was poled away from the machinery, so that no damage was done to the actual operating portions of the mill.

By dawn the next morning, carpenters were re-building the loading platform, a crew was checking out and repairing the sled track, and Bruce was grim with foreboding.

"What will they do next?" he asked Alan as the two men drank their morning coffee in Bruce's office.

"The important question is," Alan replied, "what in hell can we do to them? We can't let those devils get away with this. We're just lucky we weren't put out of commission."

"It's Dexter's fault," Bruce said.

"Come on, Bruce. If that fire hadn't been set to the Douglas fir, York still would have done something to us. He wants us out. I don't think you quite understand that. I didn't either for a long time, but working with the men in the field has taught me about the ethics, or lack of it, that make up the whole system. It's grab as grab can, and the man who turns coward might as well run away and leave the spoils to the victor."

"I'm not afraid of what might happen," Bruce protested.

"I didn't say you were. I only said that trouble is inevitable when someone as greedy as York is your next-door neighbor."

"I wish the man would quietly drop dead."

"I second that, but in the meantime, I vote to leave Bill Dexter alone. Right now he's our strongest ally. Let him work out our destiny for us."

"But Green Bay won't be a safe place with raids back and forth. I'm thinking of your wife and little Guy. Maybe you ought to send them away when Captain Kelsey comes up next time."

"Nonsense. They'll be all right. These incidents

happen upon and down the entire west coast every week, in all lumber operations where there's fierce competition and unscrupulous operators like York," Alan pointed out. "It's an occupational hazard. We might as well accept it as a fact of life for the time being."

"I'd just as soon sell out, pack up and move off," Bruce said, suddenly depressed. "I should have settled in the West Indies and bought a sugar plantation."

"One day a great wave of settlers will move in and the Northwest will calm down and become civilized, then it no longer will be a wilderness. But until then, we'll make money and put up with the trouble."

"All right," Bruce said quietly, "you have a point. Go ahead, work with Dexter to protect our community. Do whatever you have to do to guard it."

"Good! I'm relieved to hear you say that. You know, we could do with more carrier vessels and increased operations. Let the captain plan a new supply line for us. We're way ahead of York there. Our carriers don't have to sail all around the peninsula to load and return."

"Still," said Bruce, "the grudge with Dexter and Connelly makes me nervous. There's so much hate between them they're hardly rational. I'm disgusted with the violence and sabotage. We could be annihilated."

"Dexter will protect us as best he can. We're not going to burn up in our bunks," said Alan.

"Very well, let Bill do what he has to," Bruce declared. "Although I don't like the idea of retaliation."

'What do you mean?" Bruce recalled Melanie's
te: *"It is like a prison . . ."* But he didn't think
the time that she meant this literally, but rather
t she felt hemmed in and was simply biding
contracted time until she and her girls could
art. But now he realized that there might be
e explanation for Melanie staying on alone.
urely York's not keeping her there against her
"

le is," said Black Deer. "He makes her offer."
k Deer's expression was dour.
Vhat kind of offer?" Bruce asked.
ie must become his squaw, then he will re-
her," Black Deer explained. "York is evil

ather thought she was already his mistress."
t so," said Black Deer emphatically. "Cloud
strong."
just how strong? How long could a woman
it in an armed camp against its strongman?
speculated. Not too long. York might not
above torturing her, he imagined, perhaps
death. The thought that made him nau-
nd angry.
t can we do?" Bruce asked. "Should we go
d demand her release?"
ll cause war," said Black Deer. "Not help

what can we do?"
r will take care of itself," said Black Deer.
strong woman. She will find her way."
had known the Siwash long enough now
tand that this meant fate would step in.
ns' gods had reasons for every event, no
w cruel or joyous. He had learned not

"I don't either. But without fighting back we
might as well leave."

The following day a note came from York via
one of Black Deer's men. It spoke of the two fires
as acts "perpetrated by enemies who want to see
us both out of business in the Puget Sound area."
York made no intimation that the lumber fire was
set by Bruce's lieutenants, anymore than he suggested that the sled railroad fire was set by Connelly and his gang. "Acts of God often occur in
lumber camps," York's note continued. "We will
pray that fires in the future will be confined to
domestic stoves in both camps. Let bygones be
bygones."

Bruce read the message with grim objectivity,
wondering how York could be such a bold-faced
liar. Was York actually hoping the sabotage would
end with the railroad fire? Or was he already covering his next move in advance?

The latter turned out to be true.

Connelly's men sneaked into Green Bay from
the water a few nights later, made holes in the
three rowboats beached near the wharf. The next
day when one of the chefs went out in a boat to
catch some fish, he was too far out to get back by
the time he discovered the leaks. He couldn't swim
well and his shouts for help went unheard. Panick-
ing, he left the swamped vessel and he drowned.
If fires were tacitly outlawed, sabotage of any
other sort apparently was not, Bruce decided, as
they buried the second victim of the mill wars in
the new cemetery.

Bill Dexter planned a reprisal and made a commando raid on Yorkville one rainy night, taking metal-cutting saws and cutting all the logging cable that lay exposed around the Yorkville saw-mills into short sections. In the morning York's men under Connelly would be unable to drag any whole logs to the mill. They would be reduced to the slow and arduous method of cutting up the lumber at the logging site and then dragging it piece by piece to the mill.

York's retaliation came several days later. A dry sawdust pile leaped into flame at Green Bay one midnight. The orange glow that lit up Alan's cabin brought him awake and the first to reach the sawdust pile. By the time several men joined him, he had the fire already contained. But then another blaze, at the logging site's end of the rail-road, burst into flame. The logging crew with Bruce and Alan spent half the night battling and extinguishing several small fires throughout the site. Houses and the mill were left untouched, for which Bruce was grateful. This consideration was probably self-serving: York didn't want his fine new buildings razed in retaliation.

Bill Dexter's raiders did, however, set fire to the pier at Yorkville harbor. Liberally doused with turpentine, and the fire aided by a stiff breeze off the Sound, York's pier sustained major damage and would have to be torn down and rebuilt.

"That's the last straw," Bruce said angrily when he heard Alan's report of the wharf fire at York-ville. "I don't particularly like York, but I don't mean to destroy him. This is becoming more and more a personal vendetta between Dexter and Connelly, and a vicious one at that."

"It looks as if it's a two-man war
it's making all of us suffer," Alan ag
"I know what I'm going to do.
and suggest we call a truce, here a
"He's not much of a respecter c
said.
"Well, in that case we'll just ha
Henry York either moves out of t
dead," said Bruce.
"I hope the latter," Alan re
would be just too much luck
afraid the son of a bitch is goir
give us trouble for a long, lon
"I'm inclined to think you'r
ought to send Janet away when
Bruce advised. "I'd feel a lot
the baby gone."
"*I* wouldn't. She won't go
"Well, I've made the sug
"You're not bound to follow i
rest easier if you did."
"We'll take our chances, j
Alan said, and the subject
Bruce wrote his letter t
reply. The silence betwee
ened into weeks. Captain
unable to persuade Janet
cisco. Marian was now li
the Kelseys had bought
News reached Bruce
Melanie Cloud's girls h
San Francisco, but wi
"She remains at th
Bruce. "It is not good

to enquire too closely into any prediction of Black Deer's; these had a way of coming to pass. The Indian had uncanny psychic powers of precognition. Often his most casual generalizations would turn disturbingly specific. If only Bruce knew she were safe . . .

Melanie had waited in the hotel room until her patience had given out, expecting at any moment that knock on the door that meant Henry York had arrived for his confrontation.

Since Dolly and the girls had sailed away two days earlier, she had continued to hold out stubbornly against York's proposal that she present herself at his house and become his mistress. There were new girls in the hotel now, girls presided over by a woman named Rita who was old and ugly and hated Melanie on sight. This woman would have gladly changed places with her, Melanie knew, but York wasn't after old and worn-out flesh, only vibrant young bodies like hers.

The longer Melanie postponed the meeting with York, the more cantankerous and violent he might become. She was prepared for this possibility.

Rita knew what was going on and said, "Honey, you'd be a smart girl to go give him what he wants and with smiles and sweetness. I don't know where you get off being so high-minded and proper. You're in the same business I am."

"I have my principles," Melanie told the old woman, who laughed coarsely and said, "Principles don't buy groceries, and they can get you dead, honey, in a hurry. Straighten up, show some sense. Go to the man before he comes and gets you."

But Melanie wouldn't, until finally one night she

began thinking about Bruce Randall. The only way she was ever going to see him again was to submit to York. She was sitting in her room, depressed, staring out across the square and seeing the frosted, rosy glow of the lamp in York's parlor window. It was always lit at night. A reminder of her obligation. All York wanted at this time was her public humiliation and her servility. And ultimately, what did it matter after all, if York took his pleasure? This was the wilderness, and besides, she was already considered a low woman as a madam. She couldn't sink much lower if she became known as a whore. Was that so horrible? And then she would be free to go north. Very well, she would do it. Now!

She went out into the parlor where Rita was sitting chatting with one of her girls.

"Call Connelly or one of his men to come and get me," she told Rita. "I've decided to go to York."

She marched across the square, stiffly and proudly, and into York's quarters. He wasn't there, but she was told to wait in his parlor, which she did, sitting on the edge of the red damask chair, ready to faint with anxiety and fear. She was terrified of what York might decide to do with her. She had taken a long time to make up her mind, and York was probably going to make her suffer for it.

An hour went by. No York. Then another hour. It was midnight, her brooch timepiece told her, but still she sat primly and stiffly on the same chair, willing herself to be silent and controlled.

She dozed. Then she leaned her head against the chair's high back and fell into a deep sleep. Next thing it was daylight; sun streamed in through the window, making a bright pool on the Turkish carpet, she awoke, stiff and sore. York hadn't come. At eight o'clock, when she thought her bladder would burst, Connelly walked in, grinning.

"Your client changed his mind for now," he said with a leer. "You can go back to the hotel."

She was too proud to ask any questions. She rose from the chair and marched out of York's quarters and across the square to the hotel.

She found out later from Rita that York had intentionally spent the night on his office couch. The attempt to make her uncomfortable had worked. York had scored another point for himself as the complete master of Yorkville.

Two days after the first incident, Melanie was summoned a second time to York's quarters. Again York failed to appear. Connelly came for her when her vigil was up in the morning.

Crossing the square with her he muttered, "Sure wish you was my whore for an hour. You wouldn't have a stitch on your back after two minutes. I'd wipe that proud look off your face fast, once and for all."

It took all of Melanie's strength to keep her features calm and unreadable, her hands at her sides when her fingers fairly itched to dig into his loathsome face, then choke him to death. He and York were a pair. Without a qualm, she wished them both very short lives.

12

THE SUMMER OF 1853 was an exceptionally dry one, forcing Bruce and Alan to resort to building boom dams along the Green River, for there was no other way to raise the water level in the channel. Bruce used Dexter's experience and expertise on the project.

Bill Dexter knew everything there was to know about river dams. The ones he supervised for Bruce Randall were sturdy and durable, but they were not the entire answer to moving logs from the deep forest to the mill. Bruce dreamed of a time when railroad tracks could be brought into the forest, when logs could be transported by flat car down to the mill for processing.

Bruce knew that the reality of the railroads was

a long way off: in fact, they did not come until 1890. In the meantime, Captain Kelsey arrived from San Francisco periodically with some new gadget, a saw or a tool, that helped to make the loggers' difficult task in the field that much easier.

Among Dexter's crew were twins, Tim and Toby Moore, who arrived on the scene during that first dry summer of Territorial Mills' operation and were Dexter's right-hand men in the construction of the splash dams. They had worked with Dexter several years earlier in the Minnesota forests. Tough young men in their early twenties, close as fraternal twins could be, one was dark-complexioned, black-haired, the other was fair and straw-blond. Their minds, however, functioned like two parts of a single brain. What one did, the other could also be counted to do.

If Tim decided to get drunk on a mid-week night, Toby managed to find the liquor somewhere. If Toby decided to spend Sunday morning washing clothes, Tim heated the water, got the soap and hung up the clothesline. When Tim read the Bible, Toby listened.

There was talk around the bunkhouses that the men would have slept in one bed if given the chance, and this was probably true, they were that close. There was no evidence that this closeness was incestuous, however. All the loggers knew better than to voice such an opinion in earshot of the Moore brothers. They might not have lived to repeat it again.

Tim and Toby were surprisingly law-abiding for lumberjacks and while they were as scrappy and foul-mouthed as any other loggers, they possessed an exaggerated respect for American womanhood.

This made them courteous to all women, to the point of shyness, preferring to admire them from afar. The Moore twins were one of the few men in the camp who didn't frequent Melanie's girls while they were in residence at Yorkville. They went there ostensibly to drink and scrap, but more often they were there to spy for Dexter. They particularly liked Melanie Cloud, and the information they gathered for Bill Dexter usually included news about the beautiful half-breed.

Curious as to what had happened since the change of girls, the Moore twins decided to visit Yorkville, although Dexter had given them express orders to stay home. One week before the Moore twins planned to leave, however, something occurred in Yorkville to alter their plans . . .

York summoned Melanie next at twelve o'clock one night when she had already retired. Rita's raucous voice woke her up through the locked door: "Get your ass moving, honey, the boss wants you now. Connelly will come for you in five minutes . . ."

Melanie rose, washed and dressed carefully, bound up her hair, applied perfume and was ready and waiting for Connelly in the parlor when he arrived twenty minutes later. She sat with folded hands, calm and neat in her best dark blue silk dress, demure enough for church.

She was escorted across the square to York's quarters. This time York was waiting for her, in a bright red tailored floor-length velvet dressing robe, an ascot scarf at his throat. Champagne cooled in a silver urn and the fire was crackling and warm. Through the open door leading into the bedroom, Melanie saw that the sheets were already turned down. There was no escaping the inevitable this time, she knew. She forced a smile as the lord and master of Yorkville closed the door behind her, locked it and pocketed the key.

"Make yourself comfortable, my dear," York purred. "Glad to see you looking so fresh. It was sensible of you not to try running away."

"How could I?" said Melanie, with a forced smile. "Your men would only catch me."

York nodded. "Very wise of you."

He poured two glasses of champagne, offering one to Melanie. She accepted it calmly. The more she composed herself, the more she could draw on this control, and the easier it would be when he made his move with her.

"Why, my dear, you're trembling," York said with mock concern. "Be careful not to spill your champagne."

"I'm sorry."

"Just don't get it on the Turkish carpet. This one came around the Horn. You've been dreading this meeting with me, haven't you, my dear?"

"No," Melanie said. "Not dreading it exactly. But I have been waiting."

"Ah yes, that. You must excuse me. Sometimes I can barely call my time my own."

York picked up a heavy gold watch from the table at his elbow. The elk's tooth fob on his gold watch chain was set with a huge solitaire diamond that sparkled in the firelight as he twirled it in his fingers.

"Half after midnight," he observed. "We have until dawn together. That should be sufficient time in which to get to know one another. Then I must get back to work. Business after pleasure, so to speak."

He shifted slightly, setting his dead-cold eyes on her, penetrating her flesh. She tried not to shiver.

"You have pride," York told her. "An admirable mark of character. But sometimes pride gets in the way of obedience and then, of course, the prideful one must be humbled."

"I am only a woman, Mr. York," said Melanie. "All I ask of life is to be let alone to survive."

"You're a good business woman," said York, "with charm and beauty to boot. There were no complaints about how you managed your girls. The pity is, you're not respectful. It's one virtue that you will have to learn."

York sipped his champagne, put it down thoughtfully.

"I've devised a little game for us tonight. The design is to encourage humility in the female player. The male, me of course, will play the dominant role."

Melanie felt her hands growing cold from the tone of his voice. She had an idea that whatever York had in mind would be extremely unpleasant for her.

Suddenly York put down his champagne glass and stood up.

"Come," he said, holding out his hand to her. "We might as well begin our little diversion."

She had barely sipped her champagne, but she was relieved, at least, that he wasn't going to string out the preliminaries until her nerves screamed.

His hand was warm. She could feel the brutish

life in him, and the viciousness, and she knew it
wouldn't be easy.

"I'd like to have some place to undress," she
protested meekly. "If I could be alone . . ."

"Oh, that won't be necessary," said York, leading her into the bed chamber. "Stand over there,
please . . ." He nodded toward the right side of
the bed where the covers and linen were turned
down.

Melanie moved to the position indicated.

Then, in one quick, convulsive movement, York
ripped off his neck scarf and the robe. Standing
naked before her in a profound state of excitement, abruptly he stepped forward. Before she
could protest, he had seized the top of her dress
and ripped it to her waist. He did the same with
her undergarments, so that her dusky breasts with
their delicate pink nipples were exposed.

She continued to stand motionless, expression-
less, trying desperately not to move a muscle. Inside she was screaming in loathing and terror, but
she let none of this show. In fact, a faint smile
trembled on her lips as she threw her head back,
her chin thrust bravely forward.

York reached out and gripped her dress at the
waist, ripping it entirely away, tearing off the
lower undergarments. Now she stood as naked as
he, except for her stockings and shoes.

York scrutinized her taut, trembling body for a
long minute, and ran a tongue over his dry lips.
When he had inspected her to his satisfaction, he
pushed her roughly backward, so that she fell unexpectedly across the bed, feet dangling over its
edge.

York moved toward her, spread her thighs, drove

himself into her so violently that for a moment she thought she would faint from the pain of his brutal thrust. But she kept her body under control, giving no hint of her agony. She willed herself to ignore what was happening. She blanked her mind of all thoughts except the promise that one day she would even the score. She would have her revenge even if it meant her life.

York rutted until his sweat fell onto her and his heavy breathing brought her to the panic of suffocation. Then before climaxing he withdrew, stepped back, said in a deadly chilling voice, "Sit up."

Melanie struggled vainly to obey.

"Sit up!" York screamed, and Melanie found the strength to do as she was ordered.

"Now, kneel before me!"

Not that, she prayed, no, never that. She knelt before him. He held himself out to her, took her head and thrust his throbbing member into her mouth. She gagged as he climaxed.

It was all over in seconds; she fell back away from him and threw up into a towel. Meanwhile, York walked over to clean himself up at the wash basin.

He stood gloating over her. Then he dressed quickly and turned to her as she lay crumbled on the sheets. "Rita will send you some clothes. This is only the beginning of the lessons. Be ready. I may want you here again tonight." He grinned at her. "You'll never make a successful whore, my dear. A madam, yes, but not one of the girls."

She heard the key turn in the outside door as he left. She collapsed on the carpet and lay there sobbing.

Presently one of Rita's girls named Esther came and brought her a dressing gown.

Esther eyed the stricken girl curiously as she put on the dressing gown and folded her ruined silk dress and undergarments into a pocket. Then Melanie pulled herself together.

"I'm ready," she told Esther.

Esther patted her hand. "He's a full-fledged bastard, dearie," she whispered. "Ought to have his cock cut off and stuffed up his ass. Christ, the minute my time's up here I'm heading out to spread the word about this place. Come on, let's get out of here. Gives me the shivers just to be here."

As Melanie walked across the square with Esther, one of Connelly's men fell in behind them. She made herself a promise as she walked to the hotel. She swore she wouldn't go through another night of humiliation as a pawn in York's perverted game.

She had no idea what she could do to avoid going to him another night, but she would think of something. Meanwhile she would pray both to the Christian god and the gods of her people for her release. If that didn't work, then she would just have to find a way to kill York before he destroyed her. It was one or the other.

Bruce received a letter from Beryl York while Melanie was being held captive at Yorkville. She expressed deep gratitude to him for delivering her papers to Henry York, and for confirming the delivery by ship's mail.

"I suppose," she wrote him, "you're no more anxious to see Henry again than I am. Once is usually enough. He is ruthless and brutal, Mr. Randall. I say this on the basis of personal experience. He will stop at nothing to gain his own ends. I shouldn't be surprised, however, if he continues to prosper. With Connelly around to handle his dirty work, he can pretty much do as he pleases. But sooner or later his misdeeds will catch up with him . . ."

Bruce was surprised at the vehemence of Beryl's letter, but had to agree with her that York was indeed a slippery, dangerous man.

"I think of you often," Beryl went on. "Perhaps we shall meet again. Meanwhile, I shall remain in San Francisco. Again, my thanks go out to you. Henry has agreed to follow my instructions. Otherwise he would have to risk involvement with the military and the United States Marshal's office."

She concluded: "I trust that you are in good health. Mr. Bennington sends his regards . . . Sincerely, Beryl York . . ."

Bruce rather doubted that Bennington wished anyone well besides himself. The attorney didn't seem to him on short acquaintance to be the kind of man who would go out of his way to do anyone a favor without expecting one in return. But Beryl probably felt obliged to add this civility as a courtesy.

Yes, he *did* want to see her again, but she was obviously involved somehow with Bennington, and unless he sailed down to San Francisco there was small likelihood that he would see her for a long time. Then there was Melanie. It was frustrating. He had little chance of a future with either woman. He wrote Beryl a simple note of thanks and sent it off to San Francisco when the *Rupert* departed.

York called for Melanie two nights after their first encounter. As Melanie prepared herself for the ordeal she wished she could get hold of a hunting knife; she would rejoice in plunging it into York's repulsive body, and watching his blood drain out all over his precious Turkish carpet.

She walked across the square to York's quarters. He was waiting for her, as before, in the same red velvet dressing gown and the same ice bucket cooling a bottle of champagne.

This time she found it almost impossible to mask her loathing. But she knew that any manifestation of resistance or repulsion would simply prod him on to greater brutality than the last time.

"You're looking very well, my dear," York observed. "Either our last session did you some good, or all the sleep you've been getting has refreshed you."

"I am here," Melanie replied simply.

"Docility," York declared, in the savage parody of gentility that he affected on these occasions, "is a quality that I much admire. Women should always be submissive. Some forget this. They rebel and it eventually becomes necessary to discipline them. Don't you agree that the first law of Nature decrees that the male is to be dominant?"

She refused to look at him. She could almost feel his gaze bore into her. She deliberately sipped her champagne slowly, trying to concentrate on its excellent taste and on the flickering fire in the grate.

"Tonight," York said, "I thought we might change our pace and have a lesson in behavior. Do you understand me?"

She nodded, not trusting speech for the moment. Whatever he had in mind, it could only be degrading, she thought, and possibly worse than the last time. She tried not to let her panic overcome her, at least not show in her eyes.

York stood up. "Come," he said, "let us begin." He led her into the bed chamber.

"Undress," he ordered sharply.

She did so as slowly as she dared until she stood naked once again in front of him.

He walked over to the high mahogany cabinet in the corner, opened a door and took out a scaled-down bullwhip of black rawhide, a plaited lash about five feet long.

Holding it looped in one hand, he advanced on her with a tight smile.

"No," she breathed, backing away. "Please don't!"

"You are still too haughty to suit me, my dear," York said. "There's still a lesson or two you must learn."

"Please put down the whip," Melanie begged him. "I'll do anything you want. Anything . . ."

"This is what I want." York pointed to a blank section of wall next to the bed. "Stand facing the wall. Put out your hands and lean against it."

"I won't," she said firmly.

York uncoiled the whip. "Do as I say!"

Melanie moved into position. She raised her hands, leaned forward and braced herself against the wall with the palms of her hands. After two

or three strokes she hoped she would faint, and
then maybe it would all be over.

She bit her lower lip until she tasted blood. The
first lash came suddenly, across the buttocks, a
light flick of the whip that was over fast, but stung
horribly. She could feel her flesh swell and she
emitted a soft moan of pain.

The lash came again, but the stroke was softer
and much lighter. He was trying to lull her into
believing that it would be easier now.

Melanie bit her lip again, rested her forehead
against the wall, hoping for the strength to endure,
so she could kill York when she had the chance.

The third lash was unbelievably savage. She
could hear York grunt as he brought the whip
down.

Suddenly the wave of pain that burst over her
was so bad that she could stand it no longer. She
turned, seeing the upraised whip and gathered her
strength to lunge for him.

The whip caught her across the cheek, but her
fingers found York's throat as the momentum of
her unexpected move threw him off-balance. He
fell heavily against the corner of the cabinet with
Melanie's weight on top of him. There was a
sickening thud as his head smashed into the wood,
then he lay still as she rolled away from him and
sat up.

She held her breath, hoping that no one in the
corridor outside the parlor had heard the commotion. She slowly let it out as she gazed down
at the inert figure of York. He lay crumpled, un-
naturally still, his features waxen. The left side of
his head was covered with blood. She realized

without emotion that she probably had killed him.

She knelt beside him and took his pulse. She felt nothing. He didn't seem to be breathing. She got to her feet. She found her clothes and dressed quickly. The wall clock said one. Three more hours of darkness, more or less. But how would she get away? Where would she go? She couldn't walk out through the building with the guard standing out there.

The bed chamber window! She could open it, she thought, and the drop to the ground was only a few feet. But the area all across the square was open, and there were frequent patrols through the community at night since the raids between Green Bay and Yorkville began. So she would keep to the back of the buildings.

Thankfully she was wearing a dark brown dress and a black scarf. They would help to conceal her in the darkness. And the sky was overcast, so the brilliant half-moon wouldn't give her away.

She raised the bed chamber window carefully, propped it open with a clothes rod from the dresser and slipped through the window. She reached up and removed the rod when she was though the window and let it down quietly.

Now she would have to depend on sheer good luck, for the passage through Yorkville to the edge of the concealing forest was going to be dangerous.

She took a deep breath and began to move along the back of the building. She was thanking the gods for her good luck when she heard footsteps and realized that a patrol of camp guards was approaching at that very moment. She flattened herself on the ground, trying to become as much a part of the deep shadows as she could. The guard marched by less than two yards away, totally unaware of her.

When the guard's steps had faded into silence, Melanie stood up and began to creep stealthily across the edge of the square. She reached the safety of the hotel shadow and found herself just below the window of the room where she had been kept prisoner. She was about to move on when two loggers staggered out of the parlor, stumbled down the porch steps and emerged to the side of the building where she was stretched out on her stomach.

The men stood no more than ten feet from her and urinated in the short grass. They were men she knew.

"Pretty good, that ole Jenny," said one.

"Pretty good. I like Flossie best."

"Got your black wool socks on tonight, Jeff?" the first one said.

"What you mean by that?"

"You ain't never gonna catch the clap wearing black socks, boy. Didn't you know that?"

"You're daft, man."

"Nope. Just depends what you put the socks on. Come on, let's go bunk down . . ."

They shook themselves, buttoned up and left.

Melanie stood up, shaken by the close call and what her next move would be. Of course. The woodshed.

She crept toward the small shack that lay some twenty feet behind the hotel. She had almost reached the shack when someone threw open the rear door of the hotel and sent a shaft of light across the ground just ahead of her. She froze, then moved off in the direction of shadows and crouched down motionlessly to wait.

It was one of Rita's girls, Flossie, heading off to the outdoor commode. The minute the outhouse door banged shut, Melanie slipped into the woodshed, climbed nimbly over a pile of cordwood and settled down. She heard Flossie return to the hotel a few minutes later.

Feeling secure for the moment, she thought furiously about what to do next. Probably she had three more hours before first light, but she had to be out of the camp before then or she would be discovered. On the other hand, she wouldn't be able to see her way through the forest, until it was light. If no one discovered York's body until then, she would be able to lose herself among the trees. She might just be able to elude the pursuit squad that would surely come after her.

Escape meant going north. She wondered how Bruce Randall would feel about harboring her if he knew that she was a murderess. Could she convince him to give her sanctuary? She'd go to Green Bay anyway. She would go through the forest to the path that she'd taken with Dolly on horseback that day. Once she found the beach north of Yorkville, she could probably reach Green Bay without being caught by York's men. Maybe she'd leave Randall out of this and hide in the forest until night. There must be ships in port at Green Bay, to load lumber. She'd plead with the captain, bribe him to take her to San Francisco. With her body, if necessary.

This was all she could think of right now. There was no doubt in her mind that she'd killed York and had to get away fast. She tried to relax. Eventually she dozed off, came to with a start, then drifted off again. Finally she fell soundly asleep.

Melanie awakened as the first light of day was beginning to turn the sky grey, filtering through the chinks in the woodshed's walls.

Opening the door cautiously, she stepped out of the shed. All was quiet. The edge of the forest loomed darkly about sixty yards away across the cleared land. The daylight was growing brighter with each passing second. She had no concealment between the shed and the tree line.

It was now or never. She picked up her skirts and ran, swift as a young doe. She expected at any moment to be spotted by someone, to hear shouts and hear bullets whistling around her. Nothing happened.

She reached the thick gloom of the forest in seconds and entered its sheltering canopy. No trail existed where she had entered, but she knew where to find one and worked her way through the trees until she came to it.

As she caught sight of the trail, she paused to catch her breath, wondering why Yorkville hadn't been alive with pre-dawn activity. Then she remembered that this was Sunday morning. The only activity would be at the hotel where the girls might still be taking on some late customers, or at the saloon with its endless poker games. One of the cooks might be rattling pots and pans in the cookhouse, preparing Sunday morning breakfast, but that would be all.

Melanie pressed on along the trail for about half an hour. Then she left the path and took a

parallel route that led her north to the wide white
beach. In clear morning sunshine, the breezy,
white-capped bay water sparkled. The snow-
crested peaks of the Olympic Peninsula loomed
in the distance against a bright blue sky.

In another forty minutes, Melanie reached the
fallen log where she and Dolly had tethered their
horse. She sat down on it to catch her breath, remembering Bruce Randall and Black Deer as they
rescued her from the grizzly. But she didn't stay
exposed long, knowing she dared not linger. Surely
by now someone would have discovered York.
That prospect set her shivering. She jumped up
and ran to the cover of the forest, moving north
under its protective camouflage.

She had gone no more than half a mile into the
dense stand of spruce, hemlock and red cedar
when she heard voices. Instead of standing still,
she panicked and began to run through the under-
brush. She scratched herself, twigs tore at her
dress. She fell several times, but each time she
struggled to her feet and ran on.

Finally she caught her foot in a deep hole and
fell, twisting her ankle. Stifling a cry of pain, she
tried to rise but couldn't, and lay helpless sobbing
on the ground.

"Get up!" she heard a voice behind her say.

It was all over, she thought.

She turned on her side, brushing a lock of hair
from her eyes, expecting to see the muzzle of a gun
pointed at her. Instead, she saw the heads of two
young men peering through the foliage at her.
One was blond, the other had dark hair. Except
for their coloring, they looked remarkably alike.

Melanie breathed a sigh of relief. She knew

every face in Yorkville: these men weren't familiar.

"Who are you?" she asked them.

"Toby Moore," the blond one spoke up, as they both stepped closer. "That's my brother Tim. You're Miss Melanie from Yorkville. We've seen you there. What're you doing in these parts?"

The men helped Melanie to her feet. She tried to stand on her bad ankle, but when she put pressure on it the pain was so great that she fainted in the arms of Tim. Or was it Toby . . .

The men made a litter for her from saplings and carried her back to Green Bay. Bruce Randall put her in a newly finished cabin and Janet came by to look after her.

Fortunately the ankle wasn't broken, only a bad sprain with a torn ligament. Her ankle bound and splinted, Melanie was given a headache powder. She slept through the day and into the evening. Bruce came to look in on her later and get her story.

Melanie apologized for the inconvenience she caused and thanked him for letting her stay. "I'll leave for San Francisco on the first ship out," she promised. "I'll get right aboard. I've no money, but I'll arrange passage with the skipper."

"That will be Captain Kelsey on the *Rupert*," said Bruce. "It's due in tomorrow or the next day. I wouldn't put you on any other vessel. I trust the captains, but not the crews. It was different when you and your girls were under York's management."

Henry York. For the past few hours since the Moore twins had found her in the forest, Melanie had purposely avoided thinking of Henry York, concentrating on her rescue. Green Bay was a heaven of safety, but she couldn't put reality aside indefinitely. She would have to tell Randall the truth.

"Henry York is dead," Melanie said.

Bruce's jaw dropped open, shocked.

"Dead? How? When did it happen?"

"Last night," she replied, "when I went to see him. When he made me come to him."

"I thought you and he already were . . ."

She shook her head. "No, Mr. Randall, Henry York and I were never lovers. I remained at York-ville because he kept me there. It was the only way my girls could get back to San Francisco."

Her words made Bruce miserable. He should have done something about her the minute he read the note; turned back with Black Deer and demanded York release her into his custody. He'd been a coward.

"How did York die?" he asked.

"I killed him," she said.

"*You* killed him?"

She nodded. "It was an accident. I might as well tell you the whole story," she said, and proceeded to give him the outline of York's abusive behavior, omitting the details she couldn't bring herself to repeat. When she was finished the sordid story, there were tears in her eyes and she lay back on the bunk, staring at the rafters. A heavy silence settled between Bruce and her.

At length she said, "I don't know what to do."

"You realize that keeping you here puts all of us in jeopardy? Especially you. I'm thinking of Connelly. He's probably mad as a bull and ready for blood."

"You're right. Can't you put me aboard the schooner that's loading now?"

"It's not going to San Francisco," he said. "The *Raven's* next port of all is Shanghai."

"I'll go there, and take my chances," Melanie said.

Thinking of the alternatives, Bruce finally settled on a plan.

"What we'll do is this," he said. "We'll have Tim and Toby carry a litter aboard just before sailing time. It will go to the captain's cabin, but you won't be on it. It will be the body of a deer we're planning to shoot for the captain. We'll put out word that you're leaving, so in case Connelly comes looking for you, he'll think you're aboard. Black Deer is establishing a camp to the north of Green Valley. So far there are no women in it; he hasn't brought any of his tribesmen up from the south yet. They'll come later. You'll be the only female there so no one will suspect you're there. No one except me. How does that sound?"

"You're letting yourself more trouble than you've bargained for when you're discovered, and you will be soon enough."

"I'll take that chance," Bruce said calmly. He believed absolutely in the truth of Melanie's story, and the fact that she had caused York's death didn't change his feelings toward her one iota. He still cared for her, even though one part of him said that this was a dangerous and thankless position to take. He might come to regret it.

"Then it's all arranged," he said. "You'll go to the Siwash camp. The deer will go aboard the *Raven.*"

"Maybe I'd better go to Shanghai after all," she said.

"I won't let you. Our little ruse will work, wait and see. And while you're hidden in the camp we'll work out what else must be done."

"I'm nothing but bad luck," Melanie said morosely. "Wait and see."

"I don't believe it," Bruce said, taking her hand. "I've trusted you since the moment I first saw you."

It was on his mind to tell her about his own experience in Boston, and the trouble that had changed his life, but for the time being he decided to keep the story to himself.

He released her hand and said, "We'll move you early in the morning, before dawn. I'll come for you then, so be ready."

Bruce took Melanie on his horse to the Siwash camp about half a mile north of the Green Bay settlement, an area that he and Alan had declared out-of-bounds for their logging crew, since they anticipated the arrival of Siwash women and children eventually. That morning Alan shot a white-tailed deer some distance from Green Bay and brought it to a rendezvous where the Moore twins waited with a litter. The lumbermen were ordered to keep their mouths shut about what they were carrying and took the covered litter aboard the *Raven* just before sailing time.

The *Raven* cast off at noon. All day Bruce waited on edge for a visit from Connelly and his men. He let Alan and Janet in on what had actually happened at Yorkville and briefed them on the subterfuge of smuggling Melanie out of camp instead of taking her aboard the *Raven*.

Under the watchful eyes of Black Deer, Melanie reached the Indian camp, where she would remain until Bruce chose to see her.

That evening Bill Dexter paid Bruce a visit, bursting with self-confidence. "Good thing you got rid of that woman," Dexter told him. "It would only mean more trouble with York."

"You mean Connelly, don't you? York's dead."

"Not the way I heard it from one of Black Deer's guides an hour ago. He had just come back from Yorkville. The woman knocked him out, but she didn't kill him. Just a bad gash in the head, and he's mad as hell."

"Oh my God," Bruce groaned, not knowing if he were relieved or upset, "now we'll have to get her out of here or we'll have a war on our hands for sure."

Bill Dexter's jaw dropped open. "You mean to say she's still here? Who the hell went aboard the *Raven* then?"

"A dead deer," Bruce explained.

"Christ, Mr. Randall, you should've sent her away. When the word gets out—" He shook his head dolefully. Dexter didn't want to state the obvious; his boss was stuck on the half-caste, and he couldn't blame Randall. The woman was beautiful.

"I suppose you're right," Bruce agreed. "What do you suggest we do?"

"Don't do nothing until you can put her aboard the *Rupert*. It won't be ready to sail to San Francisco for another two days, if Kelsey's on schedule, and he usually is. How many people know where she is?"

"Alan, Janet, you, myself, the Indians and I suspect the Moore twins know too."

"That's already too many. It only takes one to spill the beans. Well, the damage is done. We'll just have to hope York and his men don't come gunning for us. I'll see to it that we have weapons handy at all times, in the forest and in camp."

"Personally," said Bruce, "I'm going to say a prayer for Green Bay." And he meant it.

13

HENRY YORK DID NOT come looking for Melanie
Cloud. In fact, it was a week before he was seen
up and around again and inspecting the Yorkville
logging operations, giving all but Connelly an extra
dose of his venom.

On a visit to the mill, York severely cursed out
several of the millhands for laying down on the
job. Two of the millhands, independent and hot-
tempered, weren't used to York's blunt speech.
They quit summarily, and another worker, trying
to speed up operations beyond the safety point
after York left, lost the fingers of his right hand up
to the second knuckle in one of the saws. York sent
him off on the next ship to San Francisco.

The millhands who quit York's operation came north to Green Bay looking for work. Aware that they could be spies for York, Alan and Bruce took extra precautions to keep the newcomers ignorant of the Indian camp. But they couldn't keep Melanie hidden forever, and they knew it. Sooner or later it would get to York that she was on the peninsula. Bruce hadn't any idea how he would deal with the consequences, but he planned to meet that challenge when it came.

Whatever the source of his suspicions were, York suddenly learned that Melanie hadn't left the peninsula and was living in the forest, hidden from all but a few people, and that Bruce Randall and his associates were among them. This so infuriated York that he called in Connelly and revealed this information to his manager.

"The halfbreed whore's gone for good," Connelly argued. "Our spies up there saw her loaded aboard the *Raven*, bound for Shanghai."

York wasn't buying this story anymore, since he knew it wasn't true.

"Set a trap," he ordered his henchman. "Get one of those slimy Siwash and bring him in. Be sure it's one of Black Deer's favorites. We'll make the bugger talk if we have to brand him with a hot iron."

An Indian, Red Sun, was brought in. He refused to tell York anything, although Connelly branded him several times for his silence. Finally Connelly became so enraged that he hit Red Sun a vicious blow on one temple with a crowbar and killed him instantly. The body was taken to the trail where Black Deer was known to ride and dumped there, a warning to the Indians that York was at war with Green Bay and all its allies.

Red Sun's death was the first Indian fatality in some time that could be blamed on the white man. Its savagery caused such anger among the Siwash that retaliation was inevitable. Even though Bruce begged Black Deer in the name of continuing peace, to do nothing in revenge, Black Deer merely nodded his head in silence and went about the business of evening the score.

First, a party of Siwash set fire to the central sawmill in Yorkville early one morning before dawn, and then the saloon. The saloon burned to the ground; the fire at the sawmill was extinguished before it could render the machinery inoperable.

Then a lone logger was ambushed on his way back to Yorkville from work one afternoon at dusk and scalped. Another hapless logger going to the outhouse behind one of the bunkhouses the same night was stabbed to death. Yet another man had his throat cut and was left to bleed his life away on the steps of York's office.

Black Deer and his people considered the death of Red Sun now properly avenged, the ratio of slayings in their eyes was only just. They did not think that York would strike back as he did.

The night after the logger's throat was cut, York asked Connelly to organize a small, handpicked gang of toughs who were out for blood. Connelly brought his men to York's office, with the idea that he would personally be leading them wherever York directed. York had other ideas.

"Egan Connelly," he told them all, "is going to stay here and patrol the camp while we're gone. You men are coming with me to the Siwash camp. You'll get your instructions on the way."

"But boss," Connelly protested, "I thought I was going to be in charge."

"It's time I got in my licks," York said, savoring the moment. "Besides I need some target practice. That treacherous half-breed bitch is probably long gone by now, but this will help pay her back for trying to kill me."

York rode south with his men to the Siwash camp, two hours before dawn. The party was well-armed, carrying guns, bush knives and axes.

The Siwash camp was located on a stream at the edge of the forest, a semi-circle of tents facing a wide beach. The area was so tranquil that the Indians had left their southern community virtually unguarded except for a couple of old braves who dozed on token sentry duty. There was never any trouble down this way, nothing like the difficulties at Eureka, California, where whole communities were wiped out, or, in some cases, only the young girls were left alive and forced into sexual slavery or sold as slaves.

Originally, York had shown no interest in attacking the women and children; only young braves were the white boss's targets. But the young Siwash braves were temporarily away in the northern camp near Green Bay, employed as hunters, loggers or guides for Territorial Mills.

With their faces blackened, except for York who held such tactics in contempt, and all armed to the teeth, the raiding party set upon the encampment in the small hours of the morning.

One of the old braves had his throat slit before he could sound the alarm. The other shouted and ran for his weapon but got no further than the last

tent before one of York's men disemboweled him
with a bush knife.

The men dismounted and set about systemat-
ically slaughtering all the terrified, screaming
women, children and old men in the village, until
there was not a single soul left alive.

Except, that is, for a young boy. Unknown to
York and his men, the boy had gone to the toilet
away from the camp, and made it safely into the
forest, hiding until the raiding party had done
their terrible work. It took him two days to get
to Green Bay and find Black Deer to deliver the
sad news.

Black Deer's first question was, "Who led the
party?"

The boy hunched his shoulders. "A small man,"
he said, "heavy in the belly. I remember his face.
It was like a demon's."

Black Deer nodded. "That is Henry York."

"I think so," said the boy. "Someone called him
mister. His face wasn't painted."

"You did a good thing," he told the boy. "You
will live here now."

Black Deer formed a party of braves, and Bruce
furnished a boat without protest to carry the party
down past Yorkville to the southern Siwash camp.
Black Deer was tempted to go even further south
and recruit a hundred or so of Siwash from a
nearby community, but these men wouldn't stop
to single out victims; they would go into Yorkville and kill everybody indiscriminately, as the
raiding party had done with the Siwash. They
might even be tempted to go north and attack
Green Bay. Black Deer had promised Bruce to

stop with the death of York and his marauders.

"See the whore Esther," Melanie advised when she learned of Black Deer's plan. "She'll know who the raiders are."

Black Deer spent a long and dangerous night hidden by the woodshed where Melanie once took refuge. He pounced upon Esther as she was walking to the outhouse, and clamped a hand over her mouth to stifle her screams.

"It's Black Deer," he said. "I come from Melanie. Don't yell."

Esther nodded and he released her.

"What does Melanie want?" Esther asked. "What're you doing here? York's men will kill you on sight. Do you know what happened?"

"Yes," said Black Deer, "I am here to find out who the men were with York. Once I know . . ."

Esther wanted no part of the quarrel but she had no choice. In fact she had felt helpless ever since she'd come to Yorkville.

"I can tell you," she said. "These bastards have bragged about killing thirty people."

"Where are they?"

"I don't know where they are now, but they work together on the far edge of York's holdings. They're Egan Connelly's toughest crew and they all wear black hats. Vilest customers we have, and mean as mule shit," said Esther. "I hate the nights they come in."

"You don't worry after today," said Black Deer pointedly. "They won't bother you again. I promise."

He let Esther go and slipped back into the forest, hiding out with his small band of braves. When the sun had risen and York's crews had

gone to work, Black Deer and his men worked
their way along the easternmost skidroad to the
logging site where Connelly's men worked.

Each brave took a man. Their deaths were quick
and quiet, each throat neatly cut, then all laid out
side by side with their hats over their faces for
Connelly, or possibly York, to discover their bodies. When the men didn't show up for evening
mess, a rider would be sent out with a lantern to
investigate.

This was about what happened. A rider came
by at two o'clock in the afternoon and found the
four raiders. He didn't stay around longer than to
make sure that all the men were dead, then he
galloped down to Yorkville to give the alarm.

That night the camp was in a turmoil. Most of
the loggers felt that a bloody raid on Yorkville was
inevitable. They sat up all night in the bunkhouses,
most of them, discussing the massacre and playing
cards. No one left their quarters; the saloon and
hotel were without customers.

Community patrols were armed and tripled.
Fires were lit at the four corners of the main
square and lamps kept burning in ground floor
windows all night. Paired guards made fifteen-
minute inspections throughout the camp.

York stationed patrols outside the door to his
quarters, and the main square guards watched the
outside of the building. This presented no problem
for Black Deer; he could make himself practically
invisible at night, even in the flicker of the camp-
fires.

York's mistake was Black Deer's opportunity.
Unable to sleep, stifling from sweats of fear, Henry
York propped open his bedroom window, feeling

safe enough in doing so. The patrols went by
regularly—he had timed them—and it seemed impossible anyone could enter the square without
being seen, not even an Indian.

It took Black Deer fifteen minutes to move
around the building to York's window, but only a
moment to slip like a shadow through the same
opening that Melanie had used for her escape.

York sat before the crackling fire in his red velvet dressing gown, slumped down, his chin on his
chest. He never knew what happened. His throat
was cut from behind by Black Deer so swiftly that
there was no time for York to cry out. His vocal
cords were severed and Black Deer held him for
the few seconds it took him to bleed to death.
Black Deer surveyed the room for some memento
to carry back to Melanie. It took him only a few
moments to decide on the heavy gold watch and
elk's-tooth fob with the inset solitaire. Then, smiling, he grimly unsheathed his knife and took his
own trophy.

Slipping the watch into his waist belt, Black
Deer left by the same window as quietly as he'd
entered. He crept stealthily out of camp only a
few seconds ahead of the patrol guards. They
weren't even aware of his visit.

When Henry York didn't answer the usual knock
that announced his breakfast tray the next morning, Connelly was called over. He broke the door
down, thus becoming the first to see the drained-
out, emasculated corpse.

Henry York had written two specifics into his
recently revised will. More to anger his wife than
out of any real consideration for Egan Connelly,

York had left three-quarters of his estate to his manager, the remaining one-quarter to Beryl. She'd have to fight for more.

"I expect to outlive both of you," York had told Connelly a month earlier, "and don't try killing me off for my estate, if by any chance the thought crosses your mind."

"You know me better than that, Henry," Connelly protested, pleased that York had remembered him, although not quite believing that his good fortune would hold up. York was a man of changeable moods. Tomorrow it was quite possible that he'd leave everything to some total stranger, cutting out both Beryl York and himself.

"Frankly, I don't trust anybody completely, not even you, Egan. Just don't try to hurry me on. I'll reach out from the grave if you do."

"Don't worry, Henry. If you feel that way, leave me out of it. Will it all to your wife."

"I wouldn't give her the satisfaction. Let her fight with you for everything she gets beyond 25 per cent."

"You're sure the will is legal?"

"Of course it is. All proper and legal. It'll be honored by any U.S. court anywhere. I can already see Beryl's face when she gets the news."

"Don't tempt fate by talking about it," said Connelly. "Gives me the shivers."

"I'm not afraid of death," said York. "Are you?"

Connelly shrugged. "Don't know, boss. Been too busy living to think much about it."

"You'd do well to consider your mortality, old boy. None of us has very long in this hard world."

Now, of course, York was dead and his will lay in the office safe, a huge iron affair sitting in a corner of the room and as impregnable as any bank safe in America. And the combination to the safe was a secret that went with York to his death. That is, except for Beryl York.

Connelly thought of blowing the safe apart with a charge of gunpowder outside in the square. But what was the sense in doing that? He could very well destroy the document, and where would he be then? Beryl York would get everything.

So, with a loaded schooner sailing for San Francisco that noon, Connelly sat down and composed a blunt letter to the new widow.

"Dear Mrs. York," he wrote. "Henry York died yesterday. He was murdered. His throat was slit. Only his watch is missing. We think it was Indians but we have no proof. You better come up here right away and help me settle the estate. We are both heirs. Perhaps we should consolidate our holdings. Respectfully, Egan Connelly."

They were partners, whether Beryl liked it or not. Unless he had misjudged the woman York had married, she wouldn't do more than buy a single modest black silk dress for her arrival at Yorkville and then she'd be on the first ship heading north. And who could tell, thought Connelly, she might consider marrying him, as he implied in the letter. After all, nobody else could run Yorkville the way he could. If Beryl York didn't know he was the power behind the throne, she'd find out when she arrived.

The five-man funeral brought the entire community to the cemetery at the edge of the clearing. Nobody cried. There may even have been a few sighs of relief. Everybody felt, even if they didn't say so, that the troubles that had plagued the camp for some months were finally over. This was somewhat premature, of course. There were others besides Connelly who wanted a hand in the affairs of Yorkville. This would become clear to the loggers and everyone else at the camp soon enough.

Before returning to Green Bay, Black Deer and his men built burial platforms in the trees at the edge of the beach near the southern camp. There they placed the remains of their massacred people in preparation for the spirit world.

The news of York's death reached Green Bay before Black Deer's return. It threw a pall over the entire community, but it also brought a sense of relief.

"Well," said Janet, "at least Melanie can come out of hiding now."

"You don't bear her any ill-will for doing what she does for a living?" Alan said.

Janet stared at him. "She's a woman, isn't she? And she hasn't had an easy life. I don't care what she's done, what she is is more important. You forget where I was brought up. I've seen just about everything aboard ship, nothing much surprises me. Bring Melanie down here now, Alan. That Indian camp's no place for her."

"But she's half Indian."

"Yes, and she's also half-Irish! But she's all human—let her stay in the guest cabin where you put up the captains and I'll have some company. Don't you think I get bored seeing men all the time? And carrying this second child around is no picnic without another woman to share it with. I'm big as a house and need someone to cheer me up."

Alan went to the Indian camp and brought Melanie to Green Bay. She was relieved to be out of confinement. Now she was at least free to roam Green Bay. It seemed unlikely that Connelly would chance annihilation by mounting another attack, and especially since his four cohorts were murdered so easily.

Alan met with Bruce in his office after he had brought Melanie into camp and settled her.

"I put her in the captain's cabin," Alan said. "You don't mind?"

"No, of course not." Bruce was delighted but wouldn't say so. "I hope there won't be any reprisals. The possibility frightens me."

"Scares me too," said Alan. "But we have the Indians on our side. While I was at the Siwash camp Black Deer came in from the bay. I'm sure the ambush of Connelly's men and York's death were his responsibility. One can hardly blame him if it's true, and he'll certainly never tell us."

"Is there any chance he could turn on us?"

"He has no reason to. We're on his side," said Alan. "He knew that when we lent him the boat; it was the smartest move we could have made. That was your inspiration, not mine."

"Don't be silly, Alan. You gave the order. Now let's get down to business. I've been thinking a lot lately about our relationship. I'm not satisfied with it."

Alan looked suddenly confused. "What's wrong? What have I done?"

"It's nothing like that. It concerns my position as owner of Territorial Mills. I'm unmarried and childless, I'll never leave one red cent to my family in Boston. I need a substantial partner and heir.

Who better than you, Alan? You're m
sponsible, a father who's expecting

child. You want to make a permanent life here at Green Bay and watch the place grow and prosper. Well, what better way than this?"

"I'm overwhelmed," said Alan after a long silence.

"Don't be, old boy. You're like a brother to me, the one I never had. I'm telling you all this just in case the situation gets grim and something happens to me. I felt you should know that I sent off a document to my San Francisco bank with Guy Kelsey as witness. It names you as an equal partner in Territorial Mills. You'll be rich even before I'm gone. And when I am, all of it will be yours."

"I'd rather have you around, if you don't mind," said Alan. "Besides, it's bad luck to talk like that. May I tell Janet?"

"Certainly. In the meantime, increase our guards. Be sure our field crews are constantly armed, and send out the Indian hunters on field patrol day and night. We don't want to be murdered in our beds some dark night by misguided admirers of Henry York."

"I think Yorkville has simmered down with his death if you ask me," Alan said. "Rest your mind and think of happier matters."

Bruce knew Alan was referring to Melanie, and smiled. "Yes it's about time," he said. His feelings about Melanie hadn't changed. He really must do something about it.

14

MELANIE AND JANET had many mutual interests to occupy them. Melanie adored little Guy who had never seen another woman besides his mother and grandmother. She tried at once to teach the child to count. Quick with needle and thread, she made Guy a blanket from one of Janet's old coats and a pair of riding pants from a skirt Janet no longer wore for herself. Black Deer brought buckskin at Melanie's request and in two days she had cut and stitched together a buckskin suit similar to the one she had left behind at Yorkville's hotel. Then she fashioned a cape for Janet.

Janet was having a difficult time with her pregnancy. Melanie treated her with massages and also with root herbs she gathered in the forest and

from which she made poultices and brewed medic-
inal tea. The two women cooked, and read Jane
Austen together: Janet loved the story, Melanie
the ironic style. They found many hours of pleasure in each other's company as the rains began
to fall, signalling the approach of winter.

There were some unanswered questions burning in Janet's mind about Melanie. She was intently
curious as to the reason Melanie had associated
herself with prostitutes. Melanie was a handsome,
strong-willed person, neither slatternly nor dis-
honest. She could read and write. Had she accepted customers herself at Yorkville, or before?
Finally Janet found the courage to discuss the
matter with Melanie by posing the question
bluntly, "How did you ever get into the strange
business that brought you to Yorkville?"

Melanie laughed, seeing Janet's crimson flush
at her response, and not in the least intimidated.

"Two reasons," she said promptly. "To go way
back, I was sold into marriage when I was only
a child. There was no love in it. I saw life raw; I
looked at everything in a hard and practical way.
Then my husband was killed. I was taken in by a
family of good, poor people who didn't mind my
mixed blood or what my life had been before. I
lived and worked with them for my keep, and
when they decided to come West, I came along.
I had nowhere else to go. No one who cared what I
did. The family and I eventually drifted apart.
They stayed in Arizona. I needed all the tough-
ness I could muster to go on to California, and
once there, to keep from being destroyed. I knew
how to handle men, and they liked my looks. I
learned all the tricks early."

"You must have been very strong," Janet reflected. "I was totally protected by my parents."

"You were lucky," said Melanie without envy. "By the way, I only use my talents to keep men supplied with their need. I'm not a whore. I've not met many men I would offer myself to. I can measure a man the moment I lay eyes on him. I trust my brain, not my heart."

. "How did you happen to meet Henry York?"

"As a dance-hall girl in San Francisco. It was a disaster. Later I answered an advertisement for working girls in the north woods; I thought it would be a good chance to make some money. I didn't know it was Henry York."

"As a madam you—"

"I managed the girls, that was all. And I could have managed York too, anywhere else, but not up here."

She broke off, her face impassive. She admitted, "I didn't know how monstrously evil the man truly was, that he cared for nothing in the world but exercising his will on people. I learned. But I survived . . ." She shook her head, her full lower lip quivered. "I guess," she continued almost inaudibly, "there's nothing more I can say. I don't have much hate left, only regret at my stupidity in coming up here. Of course, there has been some good to come of it all. One thing in particular . . ."

Janet understood Melanie's reluctance to say more. She regretted bringing up the subject but was gratified that Melanie thought enough of her to discuss it. As for that one good thing, did Melanie mean Bruce? Possibly.

"Do you think you'll be staying here long?"

"That would depend on Mr. Randall."

"I think he wants you here."

"He hasn't said so, just that I am welcome. I think I make him uncomfortable. He's always so formal when we meet."

"He can be made to relax," Janet said. "There are ways. You must know some of them."

"Oh yes, some. I shall at least stay around long enough to know him better," Melanie promised, and the two women smiled conspiratorially, like two small girls over a shared secret.

A week later the weather turned unseasonably warm. Bruce had wanted to make a trip to the lake hoping eventually, when security was better, to build some cabins for summer use. He suggested the idea to Alan, who mentioned it to Janet, who in turn told Melanie.

"He shouldn't go alone," said Melanie.

"Then why don't you accompany him?" Janet suggested.

"I don't know the woods well enough," she protested.

"Bruce knows the way. He'll jump at the chance."

He did indeed. Bruce was overjoyed that Melanie had asked. They were taking something of a chance going as a pair; on the other hand, the lake was an area where no loggers from either settlement had ever worked. The only humans in the vicinity were Siwash, and the only animals to worry about were grizzly bears.

The day was cloudless and balmy, the forest fragrant with the pitch of the great pine trees and the carpets of needles over which their mounts carried them.

Once or twice as they rode through dense forest and passed through patches of brilliant sunlight, Melanie wondered why she had come along with Bruce. His conversation was impersonal; small talk about the mill, production figures, the community he intended to build on the bay some day, eventually a real city to rival San Francisco, he explained. Yet nothing of his talk indicated that there was any rapport between them. She was disappointed, but she told herself to be philosophical about whatever occurred. She tried not to hope for dreams to become reality. Her life had never held that much promise.

They came out of the forest into an open meadow. The hill ahead of them blocked the view, but when they climbed to the crest, there was the lake. It lay no more than thirty yards away, about half a mile across, a backdrop of low, thickly forested mountains behind it. Blue and inviting and beautiful.

They dismounted and Bruce spread an Indian blanket on a fallen hemlock log facing the lake. The sapphire water glittered brilliantly as a gentle breeze ruffled the surface.

The sun warmed their backs. Bruce poured out two cups of black coffee from his canteen into enameled mess hall mugs. Later they would sample the cold venison sandwiches that Janet had prepared for them, and some apples one of the captains had brought from northern California.

"It's such a lovely day," Melanie observed, drawing desperately on the Irish in her. An Indian would simply absorb the beauty surrounding them in silence, with no compulsion to comment on what was obvious to the senses. But she was determined to make this Bruce's moment. "A rare and beautiful day, in fact," she added.

"It is indeed," Bruce agreed. "We couldn't have picked a more ideal time of year." He turned toward Melanie. "Would you like to stay here?" he asked.

"Here? You mean here by the lake?" she teased, knowing full well what he meant, though this was an odd way of expressing it. No, it wasn't a proposal, but more like offering her a situation, a job, she thought, disappointed.

"You know what I mean, Melanie. You're a complicated woman," he said gently. "I have a feeling you've known my innermost thoughts since we met. Or before. Stay here with me at Green Bay."

"You haven't said why," she replied, "or for how long."

"Do I need to say it?"

"I would like very much to know your feelings."

"Very well then. I care very deeply for you. I've purposely not said anything to you about it before. I wanted you to have some time to get over the shock of everything that happened at Yorkville."

She fixed him with her clear, steady gaze. "Do you have any idea of what really happened?"

"No, but I can assume most of it."

"That isn't the same thing. I want to tell you, but please don't interrupt—" And she proceeded to recite the entire chilling story from the moment the ship brought her and the girls to Yorkville and tied up at the wharf.

When she had finished a thick silence lay between them. She felt drained, distant from him; he would never accept her now. Even at this moment he was weighing and judging her. She wondered how she had managed to tell him everything without breaking into tears.

Then Bruce turned to her and broke the suspense by taking her hands in his, as he had done once before by the bay.

"What you've said only makes me love you more, Melanie," he murmured softly, tenderness in his eyes. "I'm not much on emotions. I find it difficult to express even my deepest feelings. All the same, I think I knew you long before I met you. I know I dreamed about you. I realized that when we met. I'm not quite sure what it is I feel for you, but I know that my heart is yours."

"And mine yours, Bruce," she replied without a trace of coyness. "It is not something that happened by chance. It has always been there, waiting for us to recognize it."

"You're right," Bruce said, and took her in his arms and kissed her. And kissed her.

They remained locked together for several minutes, drawing nourishment from each other. Then, gently, Melanie disengaged herself, stood up and said, "I think I shall go for a swim."

"But the water's probably near freezing," he protested.

She smiled and walked down to the lake, shedding her buckskin suit as she went. By the time she arrived at the lake shore she was naked, her perfect body drinking in the sunshine. She tested the water with one toe and waved back to him.

"Come," she called out. "Join me!" She put a foot in the water. "It's really not cold."

A goddess, he thought. It was the most natural act in the world for her to undress, just as it was perfectly natural for him to follow her. He rose and walked down to the lake side, dropping his clothes as he moved. Gone was all thought of the enemy in the forest, of hostile eyes watching them. Or even that a rampant grizzly might have picked up their horses' scent and come charging out of the forest over the hill. Bruce forgot all about his rifle and the two pistols back by the log.

As he reached her she stepped further into the clear water and then plunged in, swimming in a lazy circle beyond his reach.

"Come in," she urged. "It's wonderful!"

"It looks awfully cold."

"You won't know until you've tried it."

He was obliged to play the game. He stepped into the water, warm at the shoreline, and waded out to his waist. He immersed himself in the chilly water and swam toward Melanie who waited for him. He put out his arms, stood on the bottom, and encircled her waist. Her soft flesh burned against his, exciting him beyond control. His teeth started to chatter and he shivered violently.

Melanie laughed, released herself from his grasp and climbed out of the lake. She shook herself, making a shower of droplets, then moved swiftly up the low hill, retrieving her discarded clothing as she ran.

Bruce followed. By the time he reached her she lay on the blanket holding out her arms, an enigmatic smile on her lips. She was like a glistening wood nymph, he decided, her long hair tangled about her shoulders, ends wet from the lake. A beguiling and bewitching water nymph, making the invitation to love as natural as their surroundings.

He'd never made love out-of-doors before, but he thought it a perfect time and place to start learning. He lay down beside her, kissed her damp throat, her small, hard breasts. She lay back with a soft sigh, drawing him down upon her. The fear that the touch of a man's hands might repel her was gone with Bruce's tender caresses. She felt only joy and warmth and gentleness. She brought her expectant moistness up toward him. He entered her, trembling, and she gave him her strength as she partook of his.

They feasted on each other, making ardent love under the bright, hot sun, with only heaven to witness their boundless joy.

They lay lovingly together for more than an hour, secure in their happiness. If he were to die at this moment, Bruce mused, he could not ask for more from life.

Presently a breeze sprang up, and dark clouds moved in from the Strait of Juan de Fuca. Rain was coming and their moment of exquisite Indian summer was over.

They dressed reluctantly, embraced and kissed again, then mounted their horses and rode halfway around the lake so Bruce could determine where the cabins might eventually be placed. He picked two sites, both lovely, and decided to let the matter rest for the time being.

"We can't build her until we've cut a trail through," he said, "and until we have a real railroad."

"You're looking to the future, aren't you?"

"I think it's wise," Bruce said, "if I'm going to raise a city on the peninsula. But there's more to the whole matter of settling down than my personal wishes alone. I'm not greedy like York. There's Black Deer's people to take care of. I want them to have a permanent settlement, bring the other Siwash up from further south and mark out the land they'll need. No exploitation, no logging and no white men to cheat them."

"You'd actually do that, set aside land for a reservation?" Melanie asked, deeply impressed. Whatever she had expected from Bruce, it certainly wasn't this sort of concern. "The Siwash will owe you their lives."

"I'm not doing this for personal aggrandizement," said Bruce. "It has to be done. I want them to be as free as possible when the territory is finally settled by white Americans. I'm here to profit, not to plunder."

"You make me want to stay a while," said Melanie, as they rode through the forest. "At least I'll be here for the birth of Janet's child. I can help there, certainly."

"As far as I'm concerned, you can stay here forever," Bruce said. "I leave the matter entirely up to you."

That night Bruce came to Melanie's cabin after the camp was asleep. By the flickering orange glow of the small stone fireplace, they made gentle love again. Afterwards Bruce said, "Today at the lake you had the courage to tell me everything about yourself that could possibly concern me. I'm grateful."

"But I had to tell you."

"Now it's your turn to know about my life."

Melanie put a finger to his lips. "No need to tell me anything," she whispered. "I accept you as you are. That is all I need from you."

"Melanie, I need to tell you—"

"Very well," she agreed, "but no regrets afterward."

"There won't be," he promised, and began.

"It all happened a long time ago, or so it seems. My Boston background was a very proper one, my education was typical for my social class. My mother died when I was about to enter Harvard. I was inconsolable for almost a year, and for that reason my father sent me off to an uncle in New Haven for an indefinite stay. I remained on to attend Yale rather than return to Harvard. I was the one and only man in my family who broke the tradition of a Harvard education.

"My father took a dim view of my defection but he finally came to accept it. He had inherited the family business and a great deal of money. He was a shrewd, industrious man who made a fortune for himself in shipbiulding. When I returned from Yale after graduation I went immediately into the business. It was a sinecure, but I saw no alternative.

"Things had changed at home. During my senior year, my father had met a woman he intended to marry. I'd expected that if my father married again, it would be a woman near his own age, perhaps a widow. Not so. She was young, no more than two years older than I was, exquisitely beautiful . . ." Bruce paused a moment and gazed at Melanie. "In fact, she was exactly the kind of woman I would have chosen to be my wife."

"And what did you do?" Melanie asked.

Bruce took a deep breath and continued his reminiscence. "What could I do? I behaved like a proper Bostonian. I stood by silently while my father got married."

"Then what happened?"

"Louise came to live with us. The big house on the river suddenly became quite small. I told my father that I wanted to live in a separate building—one has to go through special channels in Boston for this sort of thing, especially when he is an only child, and unmarried. My father refused to listen to me. 'The house is big enough for a dozen people,' he told me. 'Let's not argue the point, son, you're staying. And besides Louise will be offended if you go. You can leave when you marry . . .'

"So I stayed on for a while, exposed each day to Louise's charms, careful to maintain a neutral pose when I was alone with my stepmother, so she wouldn't know the passion I was concealing from her.

"Finally I could stand it no longer. I begged my father to send me to Jamaica where we were opening a branch office, and at last he granted my request. I stayed away five years, not returning until I was in my late twenties. My father had wanted another child by Louise, but so far there were none. One of them was apparently barren, but my father wouldn't entertain such thoughts, so on my visit home, Louise turned to me. Eventually she broached this very subject.

"'I don't want your father's child,' she told me, 'I want yours. I love you, Bruce, I've loved you since the day we met . . .'

"Well, you could have knocked me over with a feather. The passion I'd always held in check spilled over and we consummated our affair one spring night when my father was in New York on a business trip. Unfortunately, he concluded his transactions in one day and didn't stay away overnight as planned. He returned late that evening to Boston.

"We didn't hear him enter the house or mount the stairs. He surprised us in his own bed. I think he would have killed us both on the spot if he had a weapon handy. Instead he turned without a word and walked out of the bedroom.

"I found him downstairs in the drawing room an hour later, when I worked up the courage to go looking for him. He was sitting in his favorite chair with a glass of brandy beside him, untouched. He was slumped over dead. His heart couldn't stand the shock of what he'd seen upstairs.

"Naturally, I called our family physician, my father's older brother, Clive Randall. Uncle Clive came in the middle of the night to pronounce my father dead of heart failure. He said he'd sign the death certificate, but the way he looked at me made me suspect he knew. Perhaps my father had said something to him about Louise and me. I'd never been his favorite nephew. He had his own son, my cousin James.

"Louise and I talked until dawn about what to do, knowing our relationship could not survive this tragic blow. Even going away, meeting where we were unknown, the incident would always be with us.

"The next morning I went to the office, accepting the sympathy from my staff and from the

Boston social set. I felt like a murderer. I came home that evening to pack a suitcase—I had decided to move into a hotel. But Louise had locked herself in the master bedroom and no amount of knocking by the servants could make her open the door. When I finally broke it down she was already unconscious. She had taken poison. There was nothing I could do to save her.

"My Uncle Clive came quickly, but Louise was already dead by the time he arrived. To Uncle Clive, Louise's suicide was a transparent admission of guilt, not grief. He told me, 'I shall protect the Randall name only because you are your father's son. On one other condition. You must turn over your share of the family business to James . . .'

"I started to protest but I realized that I had no choice but to agree to his demands. It was more like blackmail and left me expelled from the firm and virtually penniless. I went to New York to find work, while Louise's share of the estate—the house and some stock—went to her sister. I stayed in New York until my uncle from New Haven died. He left me the money that brought me to Green Bay and set me up in business here. That's all there is to tell."

"You shouldn't feel any guilt," said Melanie. "You have paid for your mistake, and paid dearly. Better for you to pay it than suffer remorse for years."

"I don't believe I've paid for anything," Bruce said. "It's something I can never forget. It's as though I've been carrying the guilt on my back."

Melanie kissed his eyes and said, "Poor Bruce, life is painful—but you have to learn to live with it. Cherish the moments that are precious and forget the rest. You'll always bear scars but eventually they'll stop hurting."

"I wish I could," Bruce sighed. "Then you're not shocked by what I've told you?"

"How could I be? Life is cruel to everyone. Even Henry York."

Bruce took her face in his hands and gazed into her eyes. "Will you marry me? Guy Kelsey can perform the ceremony when he arrives."

"No, Bruce," Melanie said sadly, pulling away from him. "I'm a product of two races, and I don't belong to either one. Marriage didn't work for me once, and won't again. The best I can do is survive."

"We are both victims," Bruce said. "But I believe we're both survivors. We match up . . . think about it."

He got out of bed, dressed and said, "I would like to have a child and I'd like you to have it, Melanie. I think it would be a remarkable baby, with our special heritage. It would be a girl, beautiful like her mother. The first one, that is. We could have as many children as you like. Up here in this perfect country, they couldn't have a better place to grow up in. Please, Melanie, at least give it some thought."

"I can't marry again, Bruce. Not me."

"Think about it," he repeated. "Then let me know."

15

BERYL YORK read Egan Connelly's letter several times, becoming more enraged with each reading.

How dare that rotten swine presume to claim any portion of Henry's estate, she fumed; much less the three-quarters that Henry had incredibly willed him. The will would never stand up in Federal court. What was worse, Connelly had the temerity to hint at marriage if she interpreted the letter correctly. No doubt he thought that in the north woods she'd be at a disadvantage. He might even be stupid enough to try to hold her in Yorkville against her will if she refused to submit to him. It was a ridiculous situation—and just the kind of thing that had delighted Henry. He spoke many times of reaching out from the grave for her, if he died first. Well, he ought to be satisfied, Beryl thought, for he had certainly thrown a monkey wrench into her life.

There was another complication in the person of Philip Bennington, her attorney. Phil expected to marry her, too, and for the lucrative San Francisco holdings she had inherited some years ago, not for love. Not that she had any illusions at her age. But he'd been pressing her relentlessly to file for a divorce, promising that it could be done through bribery. She had resisted, and now she was glad she did.

Beryl wanted independence at any cost. Yet this was a hard world for an independent woman and it looked as though she might have to strike a compromise if she were to successfully settle Henry's estate. That meant taking Phil along with her. Although she wasn't sure she could count on Phil for protection. He had become soft from too much sybaritic living. Not that he was above using violence if he thought it would make him rich. Yet who else could she trust? It would be sheer folly to take off for Puget Sound alone.

When Phil called at Beryl's modest house in San Francisco early that evening Beryl was still furious. She announced bluntly, "Henry's dead. I just got a letter from Connelly."

"Are you sure?"

"Not only is he dead, but somebody cut his throat." She held out the letter. "Here, read it for yourself."

"Well, well." Phil sat down on a plum velvet sofa. "That simplifies a lot of things."

"You won't think so if you read the letter."

Phil sat back and scanned the page quickly.

"Son of a bitch!" he muttered. "He won't get away with a trick like that."

"I don't imagine it's a trick. Henry and I are the only people who had the combination to the office safe. There's no way Connelly could get at the will to fiddle with it."

"What makes you so sure that letter is accurate? Connelly could be lying to lure you up there."

"The thought occurred to me, but Connelly knows that I wouldn't set foot off the ship until I learned the truth."

"What if York is still alive? He could have put Connelly up to it for some reason of his own."

"I thought of that too, and it doesn't make sense. No, Phil, you never knew Henry so you can't really understand him. I do. He was capable of any excess. No cruelty was too great, so long as he could exercise his personal tyranny over the vulnerable. What worries me is that there might be other clauses in the will. Henry never did anything simple when he could make it complex."

"It seems unlikely that York would leave Connelly the bulk of his estate," Phil observed. "He must have known you'd immediately go into litigation."

"Yes, and everything would be tied up for years and years. Don't you see, Henry wants me humiliated? I think he'd have died gladly to see me down on my knees and helpless."

"Come now," Phil objected, "that's putting it a bit strongly."

Beryl glared at Phil. He was being unusually obtuse; time and again she had told him about

York's diabolic character, but in his urbane, un-ruffled manner, he merely pooh-poohed her.

"It is not," Beryl insisted, slightly hysterical. "Henry's going to have his own way, dead or alive. After all, Yorkville has an unlimited potential, it's going to make millions of dollars. At the price lumber's bringing in the American market, not to mention the rich trade overseas, the potential is staggering. Henry knew I'd fight to hang on to it."

"Of course he did," said Phil wearily. "I've heard it often enough from you."

"Well then, what makes you think that Henry wouldn't love to dangle it in front of me, then make it impossible for me or anyone else to lay hands on Yorkville for years?"

"Possibly," Phil conceded. "Anyway, everyone knows you left him because you wanted to be independent."

"There's no sin in wanting that," Beryl snapped. "I left him, Phil, in order to stay alive. If he hadn't killed me one day, I'd have killed him. He used me financially to set up the Yorkville community. And then he refused to release my holdings. Now I have them, even if he's cheated me on Yorkville."

Phil regarded Beryl thoughtfully. She was quite sensual when she became angry; it gave her features passion that her normally cool demeanor did not reveal. What a shame that she refused his advances. It didn't seem to bother her that he slept with other women. He only wondered if it were possible for them. And marriage was something else. In one sense she truly needed him; she might marry him out of that need alone.

"You know," he told her, "you may be an independent woman, but sometimes you're rather frightening."

"Why? Because I won't bend to your will?"

Phil shrugged his shoulders. "All the same, one day, I hope you may change."

"Yes, I may," she said evenly. "If you go north with me."

"Don't you know its unethical to offer a lawyer a bribe? Besides, how can I be sure you won't kill me when I've served your purpose?"

"Oh Phil, for heaven's sake, don't joke about things like that. Henry was the only man I've ever known who could have driven me to murder. I'm not at all sorry he's dead."

"You're going to have to pretend otherwise," he advised, "for formality's sake."

"I know how to behave," she snapped. "A new black ensemble, carefully applied rice powder and a melancholy expression when we land at Yorkville."

"Pour me a brandy, my dear," Phil requested. "I need one badly."

Beryl went to the crystal decanter and poured two small glasses of French cognac. She brought them over to the sofa and handed one to Phil.

Phil raised his glass. "Cheers, my dear."

"I suppose this means you'll go to Yorkville?"

"Of course," said Phil, and drained his brandy. There was no need to hurry their departure.

Beryl took a sip from her glass and set it down.

"You seem almost happy that we're going. You're so damned optimistic I wonder how you became such a successful lawyer. Lawyers are supposed to be cynical."

"An attorney's job is to listen, to let clients do

his work for him, then fit the pieces together. There's very little in the world that challenges my ability. Other than you, my dear."

"A pretty speech," said Beryl. "Better have another drink." She rose and poured one for him. "Tomorrow you have your work cut out for you."

"How so?"

"Tomorrow we leave for the Northwest."

"Why so soon?" Phil asked, surprised.

"By an odd coincidence, I visited Henry's shipping agent today to find out precisely when Henry proposed to visit San Francisco. I wanted to be out of town when he came. Connelly's letter had just arrived. I found out there was a ship sailing for Yorkville with supplies tomorrow noon."

"Now wait a minute. I can't just take off on a moment's notice. I've a million things to do before I go."

"Phil," Beryl said sternly, "don't try my patience. There won't be another ship sailing there for a while, and you promised to go. I could hire bodyguards if I wanted, but I'm not letting you off the hook. After all, you *are* my lawyer; you get a whopping ten per cent of my profits for being my business manager, when I do all the work. Too many of your clients do that for you already. You'd damned well better come along or it's the end of our relationship."

Phil sighed. "I guess you mean business."

"You bet your soul I do! We're sailing up to Yorkville together. We're going to get to the bottom of this mess right away, or Egan Connelly will—"

She broke off, and picked up her brandy and drained it.

"Or what, my dear?" Phil asked, wondering if he wanted to know.

"Connelly wants to marry me."

"That's preposterous!"

"I can read between the lines. Anyway, I've seen the way he looks at me."

"That's only natural," Phil speculated. "At that time, you were by far the prettiest woman at Yorkville. And the only one, if I may remind you."

"Damn you!" Beryl said. "You're impossible."

"No more than you are," Phil replied nonchalantly.

Beryl paid no attention, and pressed on. "I'm a free woman now, and a very rich one, or will be once the details are sorted out. Don't you want to be in on the grand lottery, Phil? Correct me if I'm wrong, but I thought that's what you had in mind ever since we met."

"My dear, I love you," Phil said, and in his own way he did, despite her remoteness.

"Nobody's talking about love," Beryl said. "We're discussing a civilized arrangement between two people. If a physical attraction arises, so much the better. But first things first."

Phil perked up slightly at this speech. "Is it possible the human glacier might melt? Are you proposing marriage?" he asked playfully.

Beryl tossed her head. "You'll know when Yorkville is completely mine, and only then. But marriage isn't out of the question," she teased. "Everyone in San Francisco thinks we're lovers now, and we don't even live together. Henry thought so. I'm sure that's one reason why he was such a stubborn bastard about signing the papers. So, we *are* going to Yorkville together, aren't we?"

"Yes, my dear, at great inconvenience," Phil said, surrendering. "What about your mourning clothes?"

"I know a dressmaker who specializes in such occasions. I'll see her this evening. She'll stitch up something subdued for me by tomorrow morning, even if she has to stay up all night. I only need one outfit for my arrival at Yorkville."

"Sounds reasonable."

"I'll send word that we'll arrive at the dock after ten o'clock. There's room aboard ship for us. I took the liberty of reserving cabins as soon as I read Connelly's letter and a messenger confirmed it an hour ago. You're not going to let me down, are you?"

"No, Beryl, I said I'd go. Even though it's a whole month out of my very busy life."

"Your busy life! Ha!" Beryl's laughter was sardonic. "I'd like to have a silver dollar for all the hours you wasted around town, not to mention your . . . socializing."

"All right, all right," Phil replied, "enough sarcasm. I promise to call for you at ten. Be sure you're ready."

"I started packing as soon as I read Connelly's letter," Beryl said. "I'm ready now except for the black dress."

"Sometimes you astonish me," Phil declared, "though perhaps 'intimidate' would be more accurate."

"Oh, I often astonish myself," Beryl replied. "And the nice thing is that it makes life very interesting."

"You're a remarkable woman, my dear."

"That's earned you one more drink," Beryl announced. "You see, Phil, flattery does get you somewhere, the old saying notwithstanding."

"I still don't like the idea of having to close my office," Phil complained.

"Now don't start that! You won't have to close. You have your new young legal assistant and your clerk. They can handle routine business for a month. If I have to listen to complaints all the way up to Yorkville, I'll get those bodyguards and go on my own."

"I'll be the perfect travelling companion," Phil promised. "Do you mind if I finish this drink in peace before I set off for home?"

"I don't mind, so long as you can find your way home, pack, and pick me up in the morning."

"Signed, sealed and delivered," said Phil. "On to Yorkville and fortune!"

"Yorkville," Beryl breathed softly, her eyes glittering with anticipation. "I can hardly wait."

True to his word, Phil Bennington called the next morning for Beryl York in a carriage at ten o'clock on the dot. His bags were packed and he was freshly shaven, cologned and splendidly overdressed for the sea voyage.

Surrounded by their luggage, far more than they would need in Yorkville, the pair was delivered to the schooner *Windfall*, which was tied up at the San Francisco docks.

The ship sailed promptly at noon under threatening skies into a wintry sea. Outside the Golden Gate the vessel headed for Point Reyes; the sea became turbulent almost immediately and remained rough for the entire northern coastal voyage until they sailed through the Strait of Juan de Fuca and down to the peninsula.

Beryl didn't have to worry about Phil pressing his marriage proposal on the voyage. The lawyer was far too seasick to be concerned with anything more than his own misery. He came up on deck only with the aid of a cabin boy, to sit quietly green with Beryl, huddling a steamer rug and taking the fresh air as the ship plunged into mountainous waves. After just a few minutes he usually begged to be taken back to his cabin, leaving Beryl on her own.

To pass the time, Beryl read voraciously and entered into spirited discussions with Captain Joseph Blount in the *Windfall*'s main salon. Blount filled her in on all the known details of Henry York's demise, for Blount had been anchored at Yorkville when the five murders were committed.

Blount was a gruff, no-nonsense skipper with some forty years' experience. There was very little he didn't know about sailing and the sea. Blount was also an excellent judge of men, but Beryl had a difficult time in getting him to talk about York's death without revealing her relief that she was now a widow. She thought it unseemly to let him observe her lack of emotion, so she feigned delicate sorrow.

"What makes you think it was the Indians who killed my husband?" she asked Blount one afternoon in the salon, hoping her bluntness would be interpreted as the distraction of grief.

"The style of murder, ma'am, and the manner in which four who worked for Connelly were ambushed. I understand that there was a massacre of

Indian women and children at the camp a few miles south of Yorkville, just before your husband died."

This was shocking news to Beryl. "I didn't know that. Are you absolutely sure this is true?"

"As sure as one can be with third-hand scuttlebutt. A sailor no longer sailing with the *Windfall* got the word from a logger who talked about it at the Yorkville saloon. He seemed to know the details, but it was still hearsay. I didn't go ashore myself but once, to sign papers in York's office, and then boarded again quickly. Too much monkey business was going on." Blount was referring to the hotel and its bawdy old madam; she had even tried to board the *Windfall* with her girls, and had offered Blount a large bribe, which the captain refused.

"But who led the massacre?" Beryl wanted to know.

"I didn't get that information. Perhaps you'll be able to find out at Yorkville. In any case, the whole affair was unfortunate. If it was a feud between the Indians and the whites, you can be sure that the trouble isn't over by a long shot. It'll go on and on."

"Who was responsible for the killing of my husband, I wonder?" Beryl reflected grimly. "Probably no one will ever be found guilty."

"Well, you can rest assured that it's probably tied in with the Siwash. They're usually peaceable, but they'd be capable of extracting retribution for the senseless massacre of their people."

"It's so dreadful," said Beryl. "I shudder to think of it." She wondered if Connelly had been involved. But the matter would sort itself out when she had a chance to conduct her own investigation.

"I promise you there'll be a full enquiry into the matter when I get to Yorkville," she said with feeling, partly for Blount's benefit—she couldn't sound callous about Henry—and partly because he was sincere. She usually detested violence and bloodshed, and the small vicious war that had been raging so long must be put down once and for all. She intended to take charge of all operations from now on. Connelly would be taking orders only from her. And if he refused, she would force him. Even now she couldn't bring herself to believe that he had actually received the bulk of the estate.

Blount regarded the trim, pretty little woman sitting opposite him with admiration. Despite her tragic loss—even if it was that mean-minded York—she was rallying fast.

"I see that you're going to be captain of your destiny, all right, Mrs. York," he observed warmly.

"I believe in a firm hand, Captain. By the way, how would you like to be in charge of my shipping operations? I've a few ideas about the transport of lumber and we'll need someone honest and dependable to recruit several sound schooners for charter in our service."

Blount chuckled. "Who says I'm trustworthy?"

"I checked you out the night before we sailed, Captain. I have my sources."

"Ah," said Blount. The widow was a shrewd article as well as pretty. "From what I've been hearing, a firm hand is just what Yorkville needs. York paid a bit more attention to his ego than to business; I saw that firsthand. He didn't run a tight ship by any means."

"That doesn't come as any surprise to me," Beryl

responded crisply. "And another thing. I don't suppose it will be a revelation to you to learn that I am not overwhelmed with grief by my late husband's demise, Captain."

"I was wondering," the captain admitted.

"Now you know. We were scarcely on the best of terms for some time. Separated, you might say. I wanted a divorce."

The captain nodded silently, waiting for Beryl to continue.

"In fact, I made the separation from him formal before you sailed for him. I begged him for a divorce but he stubbornly refused. I was even willing to sign away any claim to the Yorkville operation, even though it was my money that backed Henry in the first place. So you see how much I wanted my freedom."

"Dear lady," Captain Blount said, "you don't have to tell me all this."

"I do, Captain. I want the record clear. I know you didn't admire Henry. Few did. But I want you to understand my motives because I admire you. I would like to see Yorkville turn into a happy, hard-working, virtuous community. A model. No one is going to play politics if I have anything to say about it, and there'll be no more violence."

"With loggers and seamen there will always be violence," Blount pointed out. "This is new territory, as you know, and still virtually lawless. Even in upper California bloodshed and prejudice continues to be rife. Whites against all other races. Trying to control Man's prejudice and raw emotions is a tough battle. It's unpredictable."

"But once my policies are implemented there'll be a minimum of trouble around Yorkville, you have my guarantee."

"Well, that's a laudable goal. You have spunk, Mrs. York, I'll grant you that. My cap's off to you and I wish you luck."

Beryl shook a finger playfully at him. "Ah yes, I know what you're really saying. Can a helpless woman subdue a camp full of rough, undisciplined loggers and put her ideas into action? You don't believe it's possible."

"Possible, but not too probable."

"Well, I shall prove you wrong, sir. I think I can succeed. At least I shall give it a good try!"

Blount acknowledged her determination with a quick approving nod of his shaggy white head.

"Now," he said, "let's do some talking about ships while we're alone here and free from interruption. First of all, we have to discuss their availability for charter on the West Coast, and their skippers: we'll need to match that information against Yorkville's recent output. Once we're at the mill, we'll have a realistic notion about what we can accomplish."

"Exactly my thoughts." Beryl opened her reticule and drew forth a pad of paper and a lead pencil, ready to take notes.

"Shouldn't we include Mr. Bennington in all this, since he's your legal advisor?" the captain suggested.

"Phil?" Beryl shook her head. "I can discuss the matter with him later when he's not so ill. Too bad he can't sit in with us, but never mind. I'm ready, shoot away."

"You know something, Mrs. York, you're an extremely refreshing woman," the captain declared, and got down to business, thinking: the man who gets her for a wife will have a handful. Were he thirty years younger he wouldn't mind considering the challenge himself.

16

THE *Windfall* TIED UP at Yorkville's wharf a few minutes before noon on a cold November Sunday.

Egan Connelly was there to meet the schooner and greeted Captain Blount with a hearty hello as the gangplank was lowered.

"I come with passengers," Blount told Connelly as the manager stepped aboard to greet him.

Timing her appearance to that remark, Beryl York emerged on to the deck from the salon. She was attired in a handsome fur jacket with a matching fur shako. She looked stunning and had that effect upon Connelly, who hadn't really expected her to rush up to Yorkville on the first available ship. He was surprised she had come at all.

"Mr. Connelly," Beryl trilled, and a hush fell

over the rough crowd of lumbermen on the dock. Some had seen Beryl before, but most hadn't, and the spellbinding effect of her arrival was all she could have hoped for.

Then Phil Bennington behind her appeared, tall and dignified, impeccable in a tailored tweed topcoat and high-crowned hat, every inch the gentleman; one shade away from foppishness, which was Phil's exact intent.

"Mr. Connelly, meet my attorney, Mr. Bennington."

Beryl stepped down onto the dock. The loggers politely made way for her.

"Yorkville hasn't changed," she remarked to Connelly. "Will you take me to Henry's quarters, please? Oh, and you may send a couple of your men aboard for our luggage. We'll need a change of clothing right away."

"Is Mr. Bennington going to stay with you, Mrs. York?" Connelly asked, with just a suggestion of confusion. He was so surprised by Beryl's total command of the situation, by her use of *Mister* Connelly instead of Egan, that he hadn't allowed himself to address her as Beryl. He had always done so in the past, and long before she knew Henry York.

"No, of course not," Beryl replied firmly. "Isn't there a guest room available at the hotel?"

"Oh yes, but, well, old Rita and her girls are living there."

"I thought it was another woman, some half-breed." No one had bothered to discuss the hotel with her, nor to tell her that Melanie and company had been replaced by Rita and her soiled doves.

"Melanie's up at Bruce Randall's Territorial Mills in Green Bay," Connelly informed her. "She went there some time ago."

"Good." Beryl was relieved. She'd heard about Melanie's beauty, but with only "old Rita" to deal with, her intended changes might be easier to effect.

Beryl lifted the hem of her skirts and started across the muddy square toward the main building. She wiped her boots on the entrance door mat and entered the corridor, heading directly for York's quarters.

At her side Connelly said, "I should tell you, I've been living in Henry's room since he died."

Beryl stopped in her tracks and turned an icy gaze on the wiry little man. "You? How dare you do such a thing?" she demanded, enjoying her pose as the outraged widow.

"Well," said Connelly, "we wasn't expecting you. And somebody had to guard Henry's possessions."

"You could have simply locked the door and put a guard on it. Anyway, it's done. Now you'll have the goodness to strip the bed and take away your effects, and in the next half hour. Is that understood? Meanwhile, Mr. Bennington and I shall wait in the office. And don't forget," Beryl added, "to see that Mr. Bennington's hotel room is scrupulously clean."

Glowering at her, Connelly opened the door to York's office, ushering Beryl and Bennington inside. He stood hesitantly on the threshold as Beryl and Phil made themselves at home, Beryl at York's desk, Phil in the chair beside it.

The big office safe stood against the wall to Beryl's right. She was nervously aware of it.

"Well," she snapped at Connelly, "what are you waiting for?"

"Is—is there anything else, Mrs. York?" He'd like to rub her imperious face in the dirt, the way he felt.

"Just one more thing. Rita and the girls must be out of the hotel and aboard the *Windfall* by evening."

"Out?" Connelly stared at her in surprise. "You can't be serious!"

"You heard me. I've made arrangements with Captain Blount. He knows my wishes. We've arranged plenty of bunk and cabin space for them. Rita can either be put ashore at Eureka or go on to San Francisco, whichever she desires, I realize it doesn't leave her much choice, but those are my wishes."

"You'd better tell Rita yourself, Mrs. York. She's a tough old biddy." He gave Beryl a knowing, rather defiant look.

"It's your job, Connelly," Beryl said coldly. "That's why you're company manager. And don't send her over here. I'll refuse to talk with her."

Connelly's jaw tightened. "The men are going to be mighty stirred up," he declared.

"That's quite all right with me," she replied crisply. "Let them climb aboard with Rita and her staff if they can't bear to part company with them. We'll get more loggers. There are fifty applicants waiting now in San Francisco for transport north when the need comes. So do as I bid you, then come back and I'll open the safe in your presence."

Connelly cast Beryl a baleful glance and reluctantly closed the door to York's office. She had always been a stubborn bitch, but the way she'd grabbed control, it was like a different person, a real hellcat, not the quiet girl he'd formerly known. Angry, disturbed to the core, he stalked across the square to the hotel and knocked on Rita's door.

"Yeah, who is it?" the old woman snarled through the flimsy panel.

"It's me, Egan Connelly. Get your ass up, I gotta talk with you."

"For Christ's sake, man, it's barely noon. I'm just getting up. I worked until six o'clock this morning."

"Open up," said Connelly. "Got to talk to you. I have some bad news."

The door to Rita's room came open almost instantly. Rita stood there in her stained dressing robe, without her curly brown wig and make-up, a half-bald, grey-haired, toothless old witch, Connelly thought, grim enough to frighten small children.

"What bad news? Somebody else get kilt by the Siwash?"

"Worse, as far as you're concerned. You and the girls are sailing tomorrow on the *Windfall*. It arrived a while ago with Beryl York and her lawyer. She gave me the order just now."

"The widow York? Where's the whore? I'll make short work of her."

"Don't bother to try," Connelly advised. "She's a cold bitch and she means business."

"You gutless bastard!" Rita screeched in fury. "Where're your balls? You practically guaranteed I could stay here long as I liked. You said *you* was the new owner, you liar!"

"York says I'm the new owner. But York's dead, and we ain't read the will yet." Connelly neglected to tell Rita that Beryl had brought her lawyer along. He didn't need any more trouble; now he wondered if perhaps he had made a mistake after York's death by neglecting to tell Rita he hadn't seen the will.

"Well, listen to this! I'm not getting aboard any ship today. I'm waiting till I know who's top dog here. And meanwhile I'm giving that bitch a piece of my mind she'll never forget."

"I'm afraid not, Rita," said Connelly. "You better do what Mrs. York wants for now."

The old woman stared at him in disbelief. This was a poor imitation of the Connelly she'd known.

"I never thought you'd lose your nerve, Egan. You mean we're actually to be put out of Yorkville, just like that?"

Connelly nodded, beginning to enjoy the situation. He wasn't fond of the old cow. "Bag and baggage you got the option of debarking at Eureka on the trip south, or going on to San Francisco."

"Eureka!" the old woman shrieked. "That's worse than Yorkville. You don't leave us much choice."

"Mrs. York said the same thing."

"Oh she did, did she? Let me at her!" Rita raged, trying to claw her way past Connelly, who blocked her way. He clouted her across the cheek with the back of his hand and the blow sent her staggering backward into her room where she fell flat across the bed, unhurt but screaming loudly.

Her outburst brought the girls running. Connelly explained what had happened and there were mixed reactions.

Ester made a face and said, "Who cares? It's all been decided for us. Personally I'm glad to get out of this pigsty."

Connelly put a guard on the hotel and sent one of the bunkhouse men to clean up the guest room and put fresh linen on the bed to prepare it for Bennington's arrival.

When this was done, he brought the bunkhouse man over to York's quarters and left him there while he walked reluctantly back to the office to rejoin Beryl and her attorney.

After Connelly shut the door and they saw him leave the building and cross the square, Bennington said to Beryl, "You were magnificent, my dear. I'm truly proud of you." He took out a cigar, clipped off the end, lit it. "I've never seen you so impressive."

"You weren't any help," Beryl said.

"But I was. By my mere presence. Isn't that what you wanted from me?"

"Yes, it was," Beryl admitted, clasping her hands nervously together in her lap. "Oh Phil, I'm terrified. Supposing Henry's left everything to Connelly? Supposing we have to get right back on the *Windfall* and return to San Francisco? I won't have a chance to manage this place, I'll be the laughingstock of the whole camp."

"To enlarge upon your reservations, if your fears are justified, then perhaps Connelly shouldn't leave this room alive after the will is read. Or, perhaps your worries are groundless."

Phil opened the leather brief he had carried from the *Windfall* with him and produced a large, wicked-looking pistol.

"You don't know it, but I'm quite good with one of these. My defense will be that he came at me with intent to kill and I had to protect both of us. He carries a pistol, as you saw, but he won't have time to use it. Still, I doubt if we'll have to be so melodramatic. I've done my homework. I'm not entirely ineffectual."

"What are you trying to say?"

"Don't ask questions, Beryl. Just open that safe before Connelly returns."

Beryl hesitated. "But that's not proper. We should wait until Egan returns."

"Who says so? Dear, dead Henry? Don't be childish, Beryl, open it, and be quick."

Beryl leaned over and spun the safe's dial. The heavy door swung open moments later. The will lay in an envelope among some loose papers and a very large pile of Treasury notes. It was unsealed.

Beryl handed the document to Phil. "You read it."

Phil put down his cigar, unfolded the document and began to peruse it. "It's handwritten," he murmured. Then seconds later: "Well, well, just as I thought. York wasn't joking. This does indeed leave three-quarters of the estate to Egan Connelly. The old boy planned to make you fight for your fair share."

"Oh dear God!" Beryl moaned. "I'm ruined."

Casually Phil passed the document to Beryl with studied nonchalance. Beryl read it and looked up to see Phil's smug grin confronting her.

"You could at least wipe that I-told-you-so look off your face," she said. "What damnable, rotten luck! We're a pair of fools."

"Cheer up, my dear. Things aren't that bad."

Phil reached into his brief and pulled out an envelope, identical in size to the one that had held York's document. It was sealed with red wax. He tapped the envelope with his index finger.

"Here is the *real* will, my dear."

"I don't understand."

"For all intents and purposes it was made by Henry York himself on his last visit to San Francisco, the time that you wouldn't go back with him here. Written, signed and witnessed by persons long gone from my employ and resettled far from California. Conveniently untraceable. As it so happens, I have a copy of the will in my files back in San Francisco, just as this original shall be found in the safe when you open it in Connelly's presence. It seems that Henry York, bless him, employed me to put his last will and testament into legal order. Then he brought the original document back with him, teased Connelly about getting the major share of his estate and thereby caused much undue suffering to his bereaved widow. So, how does that strike you? I'd say it was adequate."

"It's brilliant, but there's just one difficulty. You were never Henry's lawyer, Phil. Ben McDougall was at that time. Now, of course, it's Hugh Digby."

"Correct. But in this one instance I have invented a convenient legal circumvention. If you'll think back, you will recall that Ben McDougall died in the fire that burned his office down. That's why Henry came from Yorkville to San Francisco in the first place, to see McDougall about some matters he and Henry were at odds on; it was well-known around town. The fire was suspicious but there was nothing to make Henry a suspect, naturally. Henry's will was burnt up in the fire, so it was perfectly natural for Henry to come to me and make out a substitute copy. After he saw Digby a few days later, he left town without doing any further business with me, anxious to get away before anyone decided he might be an arsonist. He never guessed that I would make a copy of my own."

Beryl fanned her flushed face with one hand.

"You marvelous charlatan," she said with admiration. "But why have you kept the whole devilish scheme a secret from me until now?"

"We all need our little games, my dear. Anyway, I wanted to be certain I chose exactly the right moment."

"I've underestimated you again, Phil. I apologize."

"Think nothing of it," he said, dropping the holographic will that York had written in his law office into his leather brief.

Phil glanced out the window.

"I see Connelly coming out of the hotel," he said. "Put the new will into the safe and lock it. Hurry! Unless I miss my guess, Connelly's going to be one surprised beneficiary when you open up that safe. And, Beryl—let him break the seal."

Connelly saw the pistol on the desk the moment he entered the office: one brief glance and he deliberately ignored it from then on. When he had settled in a chair opposite Bennington and Beryl, she leaned over and opened the safe. She made a brief pantomime of searching for the document, came up with it smiling, and said, pushing it across the desk to him, "We want you to open it, please!"

Connelly glanced at Bennington and Phil said, "It's all right. Go ahead, read it."

Connelly broke the seal, took out and unfolded the document. He read it slowly, mouthing each word in silence. Presently he looked up, a pinched expression on his face and said, "Henry said he'd hand-written the will himself. 'All proper and legal,' he said. This isn't the same."

"You mean a holographic will?" Phil asked.

"If that's what it means. Anyway, we talked a long time about it and I got the impression he'd just finished writing it that day when I came to see him."

"You may have thought so," Phil said, "but there it is, as you can see. It's dated the same time York last visited San Francisco. It's perfectly legal, I assure you."

"Yeah, I guess so," Connelly admitted. "At least you let me find out for myself what it says."

"We wanted you to be the first person to see the original document," Phil explained. "Normally, I'd be the one to do that, but in this case where there was some doubt about the contents, I wanted you to be the individual to handle the will and determine whether the seal was broken."

"Are you satisfied with the disposition of the estate?" Beryl wanted to know. "Not being an heir?"

"I guess I'd better be," Connelly said sullenly,

squinting at her. "Not much I can do if I'm not, is there?"

"Do you want to stay on as manager?"

"It depends," replied Connelly, "on the benefits."

"There'll be a substantial bonus for you for taking over when Henry died," Beryl explained. "I appreciate the fact that you've kept things together and the mills running smoothly."

"Everything's accounted for," said Connelly. "The shipment books are ready for your inspection. The office ledger accounts are all up-to-date."

"I'm sure they are. We'll know in due time," said Beryl. "There's an increase of salary you're entitled to, as well."

"Sounds fine to me," Connelly said without much enthusiasm.

"If you plan to stay on, I don't want you trying to contest the will."

"Not much chance of that happening up here. I have a feeling it would do even less good in San Francisco," said Connelly.

"Well then," Phil said briskly, "everything's settled."

"Sure," said Connelly, "all settled. The women will go aboard the *Windfall* tonight."

"Our little interview is over," said Beryl. "Tomorrow we'll begin to go over the books and discuss some of the changes I'll want made around here."

"Any time," Connelly said, anxious to be gone. There was something about the deadly efficiency of the pair that struck him as definitely creepy. They weren't a pair of lovebirds, he imagined, so much as two cold fish with a single aim: to get even more out of Yorkville than Henry had, and in just as ruthless a fashion. What bothered him most of all was that they made him feel extremely vulnerable.

"If you'll excuse me," he muttered, rising, still avoiding a second glance at the pistol, "I've got me some errands to do. Manager's job's never done."

"Of course," said Beryl, actually favoring him with a cool smile.

"Your room at the hotel's ready, Mr. Bennington. And your quarters, Mrs. York, they should be prepared by now."

"Thank you," said Beryl, and Connelly nodded and walked out of the office, closing the door softly behind him with a deep sigh of relief, wiping sweat from his brow.

Yes, there was a strangeness about those two. He didn't swallow for a moment that story about the will he read being the same one that Henry York had discussed with him. Stupid of him to go out obediently on errands and let Beryl York and the shyster remain alone with that safe, her with the combination in her head. Downright foolish of him. But it wouldn't help much to kick about it now. He'd been diddled good and proper and knew as sure as York was dead that he ought to have had three-fourths of Yorkville mills for himself. If only he'd been smarter, and quicker on the draw, but he hadn't been.

And speaking of quick on the draw, he got a strong feeling from the pair that he was a marked man. The pistol had made a strong impression on him. They both knew he hadn't swallowed their story; he hadn't been very convincing. The smartest thing he could do now would be to pull out of

Yorkville immediately, get on the *Windfall* with Rita and her girls and go to San Francisco. Or take a look-see around Eureka, have a go at the redwoods again. He could get a job anywhere with his experience. But goddammit, he refused to be threatened. Hell, he was letting his nerves take over, and that could be dangerous. He had lots of life in him and ahead. And besides, he still had a score to settle with Bill Dexter . . .

That night Beryl and Phil Bennington had their dinner brought over from the messhall. With the abrupt departure of Rita and her girls, and only saloon poker remaining for the lumberjacks as a leisure activity, both felt that it was a bad time for the new owner and her legal advisor to put in an appearance at the messhall and confront the indignant men.

The meal was unappetizing, and a heavy atmosphere hung between the two. Phil had been against sending Rita and the girls into exile.

"Well"—Beryl pushed her plate away—"I suppose I'm the villainess for the time being. Do you think I'm being roundly cursed tonight for my action on the whores?"

"I would imagine so," said Phil. "The men need some outlet, Beryl."

"Just as long as it doesn't concern the loggers' lusts," Beryl announced flatly. "Let them concentrate their energy on their work."

"They're human, my dear, and a long way from home. You'd better think of something else soon or they'll desert your camp in droves."

"Doesn't Green Bay get along without any whores?" Beryl said. "Except for that half-breed?"

"Her name is Melanie Cloud and she isn't a prostitute," Phil said, "not from what I learned in San Francisco. Just a madam. Anyway, she's supposedly Bruce Randall's mistress now."

"Where did you hear that? You never told me."

Phil grinned. "Lots of things I don't tell you, my dear. You're a smart woman, but you're still governed by feminine passions—jealousy and ambition foremost among them."

"Oh, don't give me one of your genial alcoholic lectures," Beryl snapped, not in the best of humor. She admitted to herself that sending away the prostitutes may have been a bad mistake, but she wouldn't acknowledge this to Phil.

"And don't expect me to accept your limited experience with men as gospel truth or pearls of wisdom. You've never known a man other than Henry York, my dear, and from what you've told me, you didn't know him very well."

"There are times when I could gladly strangle you," Beryl told him in a steely voice. "Really, I could."

"You'd have a hard time strangling me, I'm afraid. Why not use a pistol? Mine's right there in the briefcase. It's a lot quicker. Makes more noise, but for a woman it's more effective. Speaking of explosives, I think it's time we burnt Henry's will, don't you?"

"Oh my God, I forgot all about it. Get it."

While Phil retrieved the holographic will from his briefcase, Beryl brought a large crystal bowl from the parlor, one she had carried up to Yorkville when she first arrived with Henry.

"Here," she said, "you can burn it in this."

"I'd rather drop it into the fireplace," Phil said.

"You can after I've burned it a bit first. I want to see it go. It's like incinerating that miserable bastard, little by little. I'm going to enjoy the ritual."

"My, my," Phil observed mildly, "aren't we bloodthirsty tonight? And such a delicate little thing, too."

He crumpled up the will. Carrying it in the bowl to the fire, he lit the will, then brought the flaming bowl to the table and set it down in front of Beryl.

"There," he said, uncomfortable with the ghoulish procedure, "watch it burn."

And watch Beryl did, with her lips half open, quietly, almost as if she were sitting in prayer at a church. Her hands were pressed together, her eyes greedily fixed on the flame eating away at the paper, consuming it by process until it was finally no more than a crisp abstraction of black ashes.

Then she stood up, white and trembling. Her eyes were charged with an excitement that Phil had never seen there in the time he'd known her. She looked utterly exalted, as though she had just witnessed a voluptuous rite.

She smiled absently at him and said, "You know what I'd like now? A brandy. There's some in the office liquor cabinet. Will you get it?"

Phil went without comment to the office. By the time he returned with the brandy, Beryl had slipped out of her dress and into a robe, taken the combs from her bright hair and let it cascade to her waist. Phil had never seen her in such a mood, but he made no comment as he set down the brandy bottle and got out a couple of glasses. This was just another of her strange little games. He had nothing to lose by going along with her, however, and lots to gain.

"Pour one for each of us," she told him, curling up on the parlor sofa. "I peeked through the curtains while you were gone. It's starting to snow."

"Yes, my dear, a night in front of the fire won't do either of us any harm. It's nice to be settled on solid ground once more, even if I haven't regained my land legs quite yet . . . How are *you* feeling?" He handed her a brandy.

"So-so," she said, and put the brandy down untouched. She stretched, yawned politely behind the back of her hand. "Excuse me," she murmured, then took a sip of her brandy. "So much has happened today. You were truly wonderful, Phil. It took absolute genius to think up what you did. You handled that emergency perfectly."

"Not exactly perfectly, but at least sufficient for the time being so far as I can see."

"The will you wrote out in San Francisco was the smartest move you could have made. Truly, I'd be lost without you."

Her flattery pleased him, but where was she leading? "I'm an attorney," he said. "I'm trained to see all the angles. Besides," he pointed out, "I have a stake in this, too."

"I know you do. And I shan't be cruel to you any longer. After all, we're going to be married, aren't we?"

"Married!" Phil exclaimed, plunking himself down on the sofa beside her. Her matter-of-fact question hit him with the force of a physical blow. After holding him off in every way possible since they met, she was now suddenly proposing marriage. Phil didn't delude himself; Beryl had some devious scheme in mind and marriage figured in it. But what scheme? He could only guess; he probably wouldn't find the key to the puzzle until he knew Yorkville as well as she did.

"Isn't this somewhat impetuous of you, my dear?" he asked. "For a long time now it was the divorce from Henry that occupied your mind. Actually, *obsessed* is a more accurate word. Every time I brought up the subject of marriage after your divorce went through, you avoided giving me an answer."

"I know, Phil, I know. But I've changed my mind. I think we'd be perfect together. I never really thought so until today. Think of the possibilities of this place. We're already a much bigger operation than Green Bay. We'll import settlers, start to grow, and one day we may even buy out Bruce Randall. You and I need marriage if we're going to turn this camp into a real township. Getting rid of those whores was only the first step. The next is to put up a church, build houses and bring in a group of respectable young women who will contract to marry eligible loggers. That will take a couple of months or so. Meanwhile we'll organize a special detail to erect cabins for the couples, and we'll have a mass marriage when the women arrive to accept their grooms."

"Christ, Beryl, you're out of your mind! Why do you want to build a community?"

"It was Henry's dream."

"You don't give a damn about Henry's dream. What about yours?"

"I want to build an empire. And I'm not out of my mind. I'll have you know I'm being very practical. The more settlers we lure up here, the more business we'll do as a lumber company. Yorkville Mills can be the biggest operation in the entire Northwest."

"But a mass marriage, my God—"

"I'm looking ahead, Phil. We need warm bodies. The contract marriage ceremony has been per-

"But a mass marriage, my God—"

know."

"But that was during the Gold Rush, damn it, not today. And not in the north woods. This isn't a place where men are willing to settle down."

"That's where your vision fails, Phil. Do you mean you won't settle down here and marry me?"

"I don't know now. You surprise me. As for settling down here, hell no! My life and work are in San Francisco. I'm only here to help you get things organized, and then, much as I loathe the prospect of another sea voyage, I'll head back to San Francisco, and you'll come with me."

"I said, are you ready to marry me, Phil?"

He wasn't sure. He knew he had been, and now with the powerful lure of the Yorkville holdings, Beryl was the catch of a lifetime. But sailing with her to the northwest had opened his eyes. She was a woman of indomitable will and unswerving conviction: she was determined to get what she wanted from life. Obviously, Henry York had been more than her match. What he wanted from her estate, he had taken, whether she liked it or not. Had she stayed on at Yorkville, she might have engineered his death herself, or plotted it with some likely male, using herself—or a share in Yorkville's rich potential yield—as the prize for Henry's demise. The act, fortunately, had been

consummated by somebody else, either Connelly
or the Indians. It didn't matter much who. Now
she was offering him something he dared not refuse; she might withdraw the offer tomorrow if
he rejected it tonight. But should he go blindly
into marriage, he wondered? And did she genuinely care for him, deep down in some secret un-
revealed part of herself? Should he take a chance
and go along with her? He sensed danger, but the
rewards were great and they beckoned seductively.

"Phil! Answer me. Are you ready for marriage?"

"I suppose I'm as ready as I shall ever be," he
responded dully. "Is that what you want to hear?"

Beryl drained her brandy glass. "That's it." She
stood up. "Come to bed," she said.

"Now? But I thought—"

"*You* thought. Let *me* do the thinking, silly
man. Come here. Right this minute."

She untied the waist sash of her white dressing
robe and let it fall away. Beneath it she was naked.
The dark triangle of her sex was an indistinct
shadow in the dim lamplight. Her flesh caught the
ruddy tone of the firelight. She dropped the robe
from her shoulders, it fell around her ankles. Her
body was a golden glory in the dancing flames.
She was like some mythical creature brought forth
from the fire.

She held out her arms. "Stand up," she commanded.

Phil found himself on his feet, his groin aching.

"Take Henry's ashes and throw them into the
fire," she told him. "Bury him there for me, once
and for all time."

They weren't Henry's ashes but he would let
her have her way. He did as she ordered.

"Now, take off your clothes in here. Then come to me in the bedchamber."

She left him feeling like a fool. He wasn't used to women telling him how to act. His accomplishment was seduction. But here he was being seduced, and by a young woman who knew next to nothing about the art. Or did she?

He dropped his clothing piece by piece, ill-at-ease, which was out of character for him. He walked into the bedchamber, faintly apprehensive, as naked as Beryl. He stood over her as she lay across the bed, in the exact spot where Henry York had so brutally taken Melanie. He lay down beside her, caressed her soft body, fearful from the tautness of her flesh that she might suddenly change her mind and send him away.

Instead, she returned his kisses with burning ardor. After a few brief minutes she threw herself upon him, covering him, then slid down, her mouth everywhere, as if a trigger had been pressed that released her long pent-up emotions, and she could suddenly express herself with voluptuous abandon.

He mounted her as she moaned, and took her, screaming and kicking, to a level where he was certain she'd never been before. He stayed with her all night, thinking that he hadn't really expected to, even if she and the entire camp had.

With morning came the recollection that Beryl had indeed asked him to marry her, and the realization that, whatever he thought of the idea, he would do as she wished. Sooner or later—he hoped it was sooner—he would be able to persuade her to return with him to San Francisco. He wasn't cut out for a crude sinkhole like Yorkville, nor was she. But meanwhile he would humor her. What had seemed like the most fervent desire of his life for some time, marriage to Beryl, seemed less attractive in this primitive setting. The sooner things could be put in order here and he could leave with Beryl, the easier he'd feel. He wished they could leave on the *Windfall* and be rid of Yorkville. But how could he persuade her to sell such a lucrative set-up? He had absolutely no notion. He dressed himself and walked over to the hotel to his room to shave and prepare for the wedding. She wanted the ceremony to take place that day.

Captain Blount of the *Windfall*, his sea-blue eyes glazed over with surprise, married Beryl and Phil in the salon of his schooner shortly before sailing time. He would carry a wedding document to Bennington's San Francisco office, where the staff would announce the nuptials to the newspapers.

The ceremony was marred by a minor disturbance. Rita and her girls, barred from the salon, were making a tremendous racket in their cabins when word reached them of Beryl's marriage through an incensed Connelly.

"I'll put a curse on the marriage," Rita announced to Connelly when he came to bid her goodbye in her cabin. "That union will be doomed. I'll bring misery to both of them; mark my words."

"That goes for me, too," Connelly said darkly.

"Why should you give a damn?" Rita asked. "You still got a job. I got nothing. Hey"—she cocked her head at Connelly—"you sneaky bastard! You want her for yourself, don't you?"

"I almost had her," Connelly said, "but the goddamn lawyer fouled that one up. But never mind, I may get her yet."

Rita snorted. "Hell, I don't know which is worse, men or beasts."

"We're all beasts," said Connelly. "Only most folks are afraid to admit that's what they are."

17

BLACK DEER VISITED Bruce Randall on Monday morning early to tell him of Beryl York's arrival. "She comes with her lawman," was the way Black Deer expressed it. "The San Francisco man who makes business for her. They say Connelly was to get most of mill and town from York. But this is not so. York has left all to his squaw." Black Deer pulled a dour face. "I know her before. She is young and headstrong. She will rule. She is only for herself."

Bruce's impression was far more favorable, but he made no comment. Having seen Beryl only twice, once in the restaurant, once at the docks before the *Rupert* sailed, he was forced to respect her for being a self-assured and determined woman. Now he admired her all the more for her spirit in coming north to manage Yorkville after the murder. Quite a job for a man, much less a woman with no experience in the lumber business. At least, Bruce reflected, there might be an end to the violence and bloodshed, now that the cause was removed. He hoped that the feud between the white settlers and the Indians was now over for good, and that all would settle down to a peaceful existence.

"Will you let some of your people go to work for the widow York?" Bruce asked Black Deer.

The Indian shook his head. "No one will go, boss. No one trusts York woman. There is a bad spirit in her, we think. When York die it wait for her to come. Now it has her. When she walk first on this soil, the woman makes trouble."

Mumbo-jumbo nonsense, Bruce thought, superstitious humbug. He said, "While I honor your right to strong beliefs, Black Deer, I don't quite subscribe to magic myself. We must remember that Mrs. York is not the person her dead husband was. At least we must be charitable and allow for this. York got what he deserved. Mrs. York so far is blameless."

"Maybe," said Black Deer. "But many white women are poisoned with greed."

Bruce resisted a smile. "She can't help being a white woman. As for greed, ambition is a virtue, when it's well-directed, not a crime."

Black Deer folded his arms and blinked inscrutably at Bruce. "Be careful, boss," he admonished. "She walks with too bright a smile."

Melanie had nothing to say when Bruce told

her what Black Deer had reported; her features were unreadable.

"Please, Melanie," Bruce said impatiently to her in her cabin, "you don't have to be so impassive with me. Maybe I ought to ask what your Irish intuition tells you about Beryl York."

Lately he had come to rely on Melanie's strong precognitive perception. She had felt a strong premonition that an accident with the sled railroad would happen, and it did. One of the brakemen was run through by a large, jagged splinter of wood and died from loss of blood before they could get him to the Green Bay infirmary. Melanie had also pointed out that she thought there would be trouble between the jolly Moore twins and a couple of new loggers from Minnesota. Three days later, the twins were roundly beaten by the newcomers.

"My Irish sense tells me very little," said Melanie quietly. "It's the Indian side that I always listen to. I see only darkness and misery around Mrs. York. I am afraid for the men who approach her."

"You mean like me?" Bruce teased.

"I am not jealous! Anyway, it's just a feeling."

"Bad luck for men, eh?"

"She was bad luck for her husband."

"York made his own destiny."

"Perhaps, but bad luck all the same. There is another unlucky man close to her."

"Her lawyer, Phil Bennington?"

Melanie shrugged. "I see no names. It could be. She will marry again."

"Now you sound more like a gypsy fortune-teller."

"An Irish gypsy," said Melanie playfully, "with passion in my savage's heart."

Half an hour later news reached Bruce that Beryl and Phil Bennington were married aboard the *Windfall* just before sailing time. Black Deer's guide also carried the news that the old madam Rita and her girls had been aboard the ship when it sailed. It looked, from that initial gesture, that Beryl meant business about straightening out Yorkville and making it profitable again after York's erratic dictatorship. He told the story to Melanie who declared, "The marriage won't last. Something will happen to end it very soon."

"I hope not," said Bruce. "Beryl deserves some security and happiness after Henry York. Bennington's a reputable attorney, very highly thought of in San Francisco."

"She will change his life," Melanie persisted, "because she'll never be content. She is fated to be unhappy."

Bruce moved closer to Melanie as they lay in bed together. The camp outside was quiet as a painting under a blanket of fresh, powdery snow.

"All this talk doesn't mean that you're nervous because there's another pretty woman on the peninsula, does it?"

"I told you before, I am not jealous when I know what will happen. There are no worries in my heart."

"That's fine," said Bruce, "because there's no need to worry. You know I love you."

"I know," said Melanie, and kissed him.

Two days later, Janet had her child, a girl.
She woke up Alan at two-thirty in the morning

when the first pains began. In a few minutes Melanie arrived. She sent Alan over to Bruce's cabin with little Guy, who was too excited to sleep. Then she went to work stripping towels, boiling water, mopping Janet's feverish brow and generally watching over her.

Janet remained in difficult labor until noon that day and finally gave birth to an eight-pound baby girl whom Alan named Marian, after his mother-in-law.

Little Guy was allowed to see his sister as soon as she was bathed, and swaddled in a linen garment that Melanie had made. The boy was delighted with Marian and demanded to touch her cheek. Everyone agreed that the girl baby was a good omen for Christmas at Green Bay camp, and augured luck for the entire operation in the coming new year.

Many changes took place down at Yorkville directly after the arrival of Beryl and Phil Bennington. First of all, the marriage of the pair caused a disproportionate stir in the camp.

Egan Connelly was stunned. This wasn't how he dreamed of matters going ever since York was murdered and he was certain of inheriting most of the Yorkville operation. Connelly was a man who allowed a grudge to fester in him like an abscess. He had a long memory and the kind of smoldering patience that allowed him to wait his turn for revenge indefinitely, certain that in the end he would be rewarded by the opportunity for appropriate violence.

Biding the time when justice turned in his favor, Connelly decided to be cooperative with Beryl. He even offered her his hearty congratulations on her marriage. He sent Bennington a bottle of bourbon and Beryl a handsome leather saddle bag that he'd bought from one of the murdered Siwash squaws some time ago and had never used. Then he sat back, awaiting developments.

After her wedding, Beryl's first major act as an administrator was to summon all loggers after Sunday dinner to a meeting in the saloon, where she intended to issue a set of operational rules.

Before the meeting Phil said, "Don't you think I should be the one to announce the new procedures, my dear? After all, I'm not only your legal advisor and spokesman, I'm also your husband now."

"Phil, I know how you feel about wearing the trousers in the family," Beryl told him. "But you see, I still own the business. I want the men to get used to taking orders from a woman. They have to see me up in front of them and hear me talk like an owner. Not just this one time, but permanently. There'll be more meetings and more orders, so the sooner they get adjusted to my presence and stop grousing about me, the sooner they'll accept me as the logical successor to Henry, the smoother this operation will run. Change has to come gradually, you know. This is the way I think it should begin, with a meeting."

Phil could not deny her logic, but insisted gently, "We are both in the business together, my dear. As partners."

Beryl glanced at him sharply. "We're both equal in sharing profits," she amended. "We are *not* both in the business as a team. We are married, of course. But I haven't signed anything over to you that I recall. I'm in charge and you're my business advisor."

"Marriage," Phil continued, "transfers half of the ownership and responsibility for your various holdings to me automatically, my dear. That is the law. We mustn't lose sight of that."

"I know what you're saying, and there's no need for you to get tiresome about it, Phil. I'm going to talk to the men and that's final. You can come along if you wish. It would be nice to have your presence there, but I mean to go whether or not you choose to accompany me."

Beryl spent all of an hour deciding what she should wear for her rendezvous with the loggers in the big saloon. First she sent Connelly off to make sure that the place was cleaned up, that there were no poker games going on, and that the men were sober.

Phil decided at the last moment to accompany Beryl to the meeting and introduce her. She arrived in a bottle-green silk ensemble with a small perky hat and gloves and purse to match. Her urbane wardrobe was out-of-place in the rough, smoky saloon, but that was exactly the effect she desired to create. She wanted to be unique and lovely, set apart—attractive and sensual on one hand, a figure of authority on the other. Looking good would get the loggers' attention. Voice, manner and words would bind them to her, Beryl was certain. Speaking directly to the men was the right thing to do. They would only have half-listened to Phil, no matter how well he delivered his speech. On the contrary if she talked from a

table top so that all could see her full-length, she
would be certain to have the audience's undivided
ears and eyes.

When the smoky saloon was jam-packed with
humanity, Phil brought Beryl in and stepped up
on a chair, holding up his hands for silence. The
buzz in the room gradually died away.

"Gentlemen," Phil began in his best courtroom
voice, "my wife, Mrs. Bennington, wishes to address you regarding a few matters that concern us
all. We want to work together peaceably, we want
to work hard enough to secure our bonuses, and
we want to be the most productive sawmill in the
whole Northwest."

There were shouts and whistles at this, and
when Bennington raised his hands again for silence, remarkably enough the men quieted down
at once.

"The new regime under Mrs. Bennington can
best be explained by having her address you personally. Gentlemen, may I present my wife—"

Phil helped Beryl onto a chair, then onto the
table, as the loggers applauded wildly to a man.

Beryl waited with a warm smile, her cheeks
faintly flushed, until the applause died away. Then
she said in a small, perfectly inflected voice,
"Thank you for coming here tonight and giving me
your time."

"Any time!" someone shouted from the rear of
the hall. Beryl smiled, nodded, and waited until
the laughter that ensued had died down. When
she had silence she went on:

"We are serious, my husband and I, in having
a camp so well-run that all of you will be able to

bring your wives, mothers and sweethearts here in the near future."

New applause erupted; she waited for it to subside and then continued: "I know there've been some strong feelings about the way we handled the hotel situation—"

Silence ensued. Every man strained forward to hear Beryl's voice, which she had scaled down almost to a whisper at this point.

"Neither my husband nor I disapprove of the needs of a group of healthy working men in as isolated a situation as Yorkville," she said candidly. "This is a manifestation of Nature which sensible people accept. However, I don't believe that these needs should be gratified in the middle of a community that will soon have families abiding in its midst. Therefore, we have sent the women away."

"Nervy," said a voice in the crowd. Some clenched fists were raised in approval, someone hissed for quiet.

"We will immediately build a small group of abodes a mile to the south of Yorkville. Within a few weeks we will have poker games and women settled there. Recreation rooms, cottages for the women. Any Yorkville worker may feel free to go there on Saturday or any other night to relax and be entertained. That is the first change to be made that will interest most of you."

Beryl paused a moment, examining the men's faces. Some were puzzled by what she'd said, some looked pleased; but at this point no one voiced an objection.

"The second change," she continued, "will be made here in our camp. The building in which we are now congregated will be enlarged and remodeled into a chapel, a non-sectarian one. You are all free to hold any kind of religious services here that suit you. All meetings will be scheduled so as not to conflict with each other.

"Next we'll build a general store that will one day rival the great stores of the eastern seaboard of America. At first it will be a small operation, but as families settle and grow, so will the store.

"And now to the most important change: The women in your lives. Many of you young men want to marry—" Cheers and whistles greeted this remark. "And of course," Beryl explained, "there is no possibility of courtship here, as isolated as we are. But we shall change that. Many young women want to find good, hard-working partners, like many of you, so we're going to provide young women willing to marry you . . ."

At this point all hell broke loose. It was a full minute before Beryl, with Phil's help, could calm down the crowd.

"Exactly how we will bring in these young ladies, and where they'll be housed until they are married, is still in the tentative stage. But rest assured, we will have a system figured out before long. What we must first do to make this project a reality is to build a whole new tract of small cabins to house the newlywed couples. There will be no living together out of wedlock at Yorkville center. I want this clearly understood.

"It is my belief—and my husband's—that men who live in a comfortable, secure domestic environment will work harder and produce more than they do isolated in the wilderness. It will be our pleasure to prove this theory.

"And now," Beryl said in conclusion, "I shall be

glad to answer your questions. I hope you're satisfied with these new and, for the present, quite
general changes. Any men who do not care to
work for a woman owner and general manager
may feel free to pack up and leave on the first
schooner that puts into port, which will probably
be tomorrow or the next day. We will pay your
fares to San Francisco only. We have a large and
healthy working pool of skilled lumbermen anxious
to come to the site, so make up your minds now.
If you stay on, you'll be working harder than ever
but you'll also be making better wages, ten per
cent higher than before. So now, are there any
questions?"

There were quite a few, which Beryl handled
confidently. With Phil's assistance, Beryl had done
her homework on the quantity and quality of
lumber cut at Yorkville, how it was processed for
shipment, the optimum number of hours the men
could work each season, and their general needs.

It was thirty minutes before all questions were
answered and the crowd broke up. Many of the
loggers pressed forward to get a quick, closer look
at Beryl, ignoring Phil Bennington in the process.
They wanted to see the new owner up close, shake
her gloved hand and stare at her pretty face.

By the time Beryl and Phil returned to their
quarters, Phil was in an irritable mood and Beryl
was keyed up and taut as a coiled spring, flushed
from the success of her experience. She was beginning to wonder why she had been so timorous,
convinced only a few hours ago that she needed
Phil's protection and stewardship up here in the
north woods. If anything, it was the other way
around. She had married Phil impetuously when

it really wasn't necessary. The plain truth was, she could do very well without him. But of course, the marriage had already been consummated, she couldn't legally annul it at this point. She would just have to live with the fact that they were husband and wife, and hope that eventually she might come to love him as he so obviously loved her. Or claimed that he loved her . . .

Beryl had never visited the south flank of the Yorkville holdings before. In fact, she hadn't been interested until this moment, deciding that she must inspect all the lumbering sites in this part of the Northwest with Phil.

"Why not wait until spring, my dear?" he suggested, snug in their quarters. The last thing Bennington wanted was to leave his lovely heated cabin for a freezing trek on horseback through wilderness country. Besides, he rode poorly, disliked horses and was generally uncomfortable around the skittish animals.

"We are not waiting until spring," said Beryl decisively. "I've made a good first impression. If I'm to compete with Henry's legend, which means be a stronger master than he was, then I've got to show myself in the remotest spots of our domain just like he would have."

"But you're not Henry York," Phil pointed out. "You're a woman. And you take the work much too seriously, my dear."

"And *you* don't take it seriously enough!"

"I will when the schooners are loading again. Winter operations are practically at a standstill now."

"Nonetheless," said Beryl firmly, "you are going with me, whether you like it or not."

"Don't be tiresome, my dear. I've no intention of leaving home and hearth. In fact, I think I'll have a drink, sit back and enjoy the warmth of this lovely fire."

"Do you think I married you so you could sit around and get fat?" Beryl demanded.

Phil gazed at her for a moment, then said, "I'm beginning to wonder. First, you were a veritable tigress. Now you're cold and passionless and refuse my attentions. What's next? I can only hope that you'll strike a happy medium by the time we get to know each other better."

"The problem wouldn't exist if you'd cooperate," Beryl said. "We should work as a team."

"Does that mean we do what *you* want all the time?"

"I think I know what's best for Yorkville. You didn't object to whores in camp, then you changed your mind and agreed on a separate location. You didn't think the mail-order bride system was practical, but you saw how the men loved the idea. And now you won't go to the holdings with me because you don't want to be discomforted. You're not being very decisive, Phil. Nothing's forcing you to stay here, or forcing me to keep you. I may have to send you home on the *Columbia* when it brings up fresh supplies. If my exposure here has taught me anything, it's that I can survive quite nicely alone."

"Don't threaten me, my dear. I'm your husband."

"I'll do as I like," said Beryl. "I'm not one of

your paid women back in San Francisco, Phil. I'm Beryl, me, myself, a flesh-and-blood woman who knows her own mind and intends to use it."

"You're too headstrong, Beryl."

"Come with me," she coaxed. "Change into something warm. I'll dress in a nice riding outfit, and we'll go out together. The sun's broken through at last. It will be fun, you'll see. Better than sitting here all day."

"Get Egan Connelly to go with you. Or won't he do?"

"No, damn it, he won't! Besides, he's gone south to lay out the buildings for the recreation camp."

"Well then, you can wait until tomorrow when he's back."

"I don't want to wait. The weather's fair now. Tomorrow we could have a storm from the northwest or maybe even a blizzard. Then we couldn't go out for days, perhaps even weeks."

Phil stretched his long legs toward the fire.

"Jesus Christ," he muttered, "I suppose I'll have to give in or else listen to your abuse all day tomorrow. Go ahead, my dear, prepare yourself for the arctic expedition. I'll be along shortly."

He rose and put on his fur-lined jacket and walked across the square to the hotel where he still kept his clothes. The single room also served as his place of refuge from Beryl. He would probably be sleeping here every night if things kept on the way they were going. From an exciting hot-blooded hellcat, Beryl had suddenly been transformed into a boring, shrewish woman. He could not have guessed it would happen. What had looked like a money-making, easy-going marriage was beginning to turn into a tiresome massive liability.

The plain truth, Phil decided as he changed into heavy woolen trousers, a lumberjack shirt, a thick sweater and waterproof boots, was that he had made a bad error in judgment. He clapped a cap on his head, studying his lean face in the speckled bureau mirror. Might let his beard grow, he thought, to give himself a rather jaunty goatee to return with to San Francisco. This would surely charm the ladies. And there'd be more of them, he was confident. Charm and cunning had gotten him nowhere with Beryl, clever, conniving minx. Her sole interest was the exercise of power. Their first night together she had clawed him passionately; she had been worth waiting for. Now she slept with her legs locked together. He'd need a crowbar to pry them apart and he didn't have the energy to try. The thought of her rationing favors like currency depressed him.

So, what was the alternative? he wondered, walking back across the square. If he tried for an annulment or a divorce, he could still make substantial claim to Beryl's estate, both the San Francisco peninsula holdings and Yorkville. She wasn't going to cast him out in the cold and keep everything, he vowed, even if it meant a bitter court battle on his part. He had friends in high places; he'd bite off an impressive hunk of her tender ass, by God, make it hurt her. In face, she really didn't know how much pain he could inflict. She'd never seen him in action. He wasn't above beating a woman about if she needed a beating. Henry York must have been driven to such ends more than once, he imagined. She hadn't told him so, but this was probably the reason that she'd fled Yorkville for San Francisco in the first place. Maybe she had an idea York would eventually kill her if she stayed on.

Go ahead, admit it, Phil reflected. You're already entertaining the idea yourself. You'd be rich then.

Beryl was dressed and waiting when he returned to their quarters. She looked marvelous, Phil observed. A pity it was all show and no substance.

"I'm taking the pistol," she told him. "You can carry a rifle."

"I'd prefer it the other way around."

Beryl gave him a quick glance. "I don't weigh enough to shoot the rifle and it's too heavy. I feel more at ease with the pistol."

"We're not going to run into an ambush, are we?"

"I doubt it," said Beryl, "but there are foraging bears about at this time of year. They're vicious when they're hungry, especially the grizzlies. Don't tell me you're afraid!"

Phil held his hands out to the fire. "I'd just as soon stay where it's nice and warm. Let's put off the inspection, my dear, until Egan can go with you."

"No, Phil, it has to be now. Come along. We won't be out more than two or three hours. You won't freeze to death in that time."

"I just might."

"Well, you have to take a few chances, don't you?" she said with a hint of contempt. "Let's go."

The horses were brought around by the stable boy, reluctant to be taken from their comfortable barn stalls and forced to walk through the heavy forest snow. Beryl and Phil mounted and set off on the southern trail that led into the peninsula's thickest groves, as yet uncut, and capable of producing billions of board feet of lumber.

They rode in silence for twenty minutes or so before they left the dark forbidding forest and came out into a natural clearing where the sun shone brilliantly and the white cover of melting snow reflected the yellow glare of ice.

Beryl came to a halt in the center of the clearing. "Isn't it magnificent?" Beryl said.

"What're you trying to prove by this outing?" Bennington asked irritably, reining in his mount.

"The grove that Connelly wants to cut starts over there," Beryl told him. "I think I'll tell him to leave it alone. It's too remote without a line of communication. We can log off the land easier on the northwest shore close to Bruce Randall's boundary. We might even go over the line, as Henry did. I'm sure we can get away with it."

"Better be careful there," Phil advised. "No need to make enemies of people you might need for good neighbors. There's plenty of lumber for everybody. You needn't get greedy, so early in your new profession, my dear. Makes you sound like your late lamented."

"My, my," Beryl said with a smirk. "Aren't we brimming over with goodness and charity toward our fellow man!"

"I'm only being practical," said Phil.

"You disappoint me," Beryl declared. "I had expected that we'd make a real partnership out of the lumber business. The least you could do is show a little initiative."

"Beryl, look. You have substantial income from the San Francisco holdings. Even if you never came up here again, even if managers cheated you blind, you'd still have more money than you could spend in the rest of your life—and then some."

"I know that. It isn't the money, don't you see? It's the thought of being able to expand and grow, to make decisions that will affect the lives of people and govern their welfare. I want to start a city and develop it, own it. I like the idea of being a female tycoon, Phil. I like being able to wield power that will eventually be absolute within its own sphere of influence, in my own lifetime."

"That's not ambition," Phil observed, "that's obsession, and you'll get it at the expense of your personal happiness. Drop the idea. Let's leave this place and go back to San Francisco, have a real honeymoon, enjoy life. This is no place to settle down, Beryl. Why can't you be sensible?"

"I am being sensible," she insisted. "I thought you were adventurous and had some spirit. I could carve a better man out of a banana."

"Oh come now—"

They both heard the noise at the same time.

"What was that?" Phil said, lowering his voice. "It sounded like a horse, and came from the deep forest."

"It's your imagination," Beryl replied, though in fact she thought he was right. The sound struck fear in her heart. Could Indians be following them? This seemed unlikely, but who else could it be? Anyone from the camp would make himself known, not follow them unseen.

"It wasn't my imagination," said Phil. "I distinctly heard a horse."

He turned his mount in the direction of the sound which had issued from a solid wall of snow-laden trees. Someone could easily be hidden in the grove, screened from sight, and still be able to see them clearly. He took the rifle from the saddle, broke it and loaded it.

This wasn't at all the way Beryl had planned things, she thought, laying a nervous gloved hand on the percussion cap revolver in its saddle holster.

"Who's there?" Phil shouted toward the barrier of trees. When no answer came he turned his horse slowly to the left, describing a complete circle.

As Phil Bennington turned his back to the grove of red cedars, a shot rang out. The bullet struck him squarely in the middle of his back, piercing his clothes and entering his rib cage, tearing through his heart and chest, and exiting out the front of his jacket in a gout of bright red blood.

Bennington was propelled forward over the saddlehorn with a mangled scream. He rolled off the left side of his horse, his feet dragging free of the stirrups, fell face down in the soft snow with the rifle still gripped in his hands. He was dead by the time he hit the ground.

Beryl shrieked in terror and her horse took off. She had trouble bringing it under control when it reached the edge of the clearing, and even more difficulty in forcing it to remain there until she could be sure it was safe. Later Beryl rode back to the spot where Phil lay.

She climbed down off her mount and knelt beside him in the snow. She turned him over. His eyes were already staring blindly and beginning to glaze over. His jacket and the snow around it was drenched with gore. She didn't have to check his pulse to know that he was dead.

What had happened was incredible. But why? If this were an Indian attack, she wouldn't have

been spared. And if it wasn't, then what else
could it possibly be?

She wasn't strong enough to lift Phil's limp body
across the saddle and lash him to it. She would
have to leave his corpse where it lay. The body
would soon freeze in the bitter air. Let Connelly
and his men come for it.

Strange, she reflected, taking the reins of Phil's
mount and climbing onto her horse, she felt nothing over his death. Neither shock, grief nor even
regret. What she could recognize instead was a
welcome, heady feeling of relief, as if she'd just
awakened from an unpleasant, entangling dream to
find that it wasn't life.

She was free of Phil forever. What she had considered doing herself had been accomplished by
some unseen assassin with motives that were a
mystery to her, almost as though someone had read
her mind and fulfilled her wish for their own reasons. She had been saved from becoming a murderess, she told herself. She had been about to reach
for the pistol and shoot him herself when she was
relieved of committing the crime. Beyond that, she
refused to dwell on who the murderer might be.

Beryl rode back to camp from the clearing in
the forest, taking the rifle beside Phil's body with
her. She held her breath frequently as she rode,
fearful that at any moment she might be the next
victim of the unseen gunman.

Would she ever know why Phil was killed? she
wondered? Even more important, how would she
present herself at camp? She would have to summon tears and hysteria before she rode in.

A quarter of a mile from camp she began to
tremble violently as the shock of Phil's murder

wore off. All at once the tears came naturally and she began to sob. She rode her horse into the square, and seeing men about, she began to scream "Murder, murder!" at the top of her lungs, still clutching the reins of Phil's riderless horse.

As she reined in her horse to a stop in the center of the square, she slumped over in a dead faint across the mare's neck. Men ran toward her from all directions . . .

18

THE NEWS of Phil Bennington's murder reached
Green Bay the following morning via Black Deer's
trail scouts, who seemed to learn their news from
some source unknown to the white settlers.

Bruce and Alan were stunned by the news, coming as it did so soon after Beryl's marriage to Bennington. They called in Bill Dexter and Black Deer
for a meeting. Black Deer was quick to deny any
Indian participation in the shooting.

"Not one of my people," he insisted. "We have
no grudge with the Benningtons. Not yet."

When Bill Dexter was questioned, he said,
"Well, I could offer a theory, but I'm prejudiced
so I'll keep my yap shut."

Bruce finally decided somebody ought to go to Yorkville and offer their condolences to Mrs. Bennington.

"It's only proper since we're neighbors," he said. "She may need our help at this time."

"I'll go," Alan volunteered, but Bruce wouldn't hear of it.

"It's my place," Bruce said. "Something might happen to you." He didn't need to add it would leave Janet a widow with two small children. "I don't think I'll be in any danger. Unless, of course, there's someone out there who want all of us out of here, and that seems pretty far-fetched."

"The trouble is all in the south," said Black Deer. "A bad place."

"Bad or good, I'm going," Bruce declared.

The weather was threatening when Bruce said goodbye to Melanie in her cabin, and saddled the gelding that was waiting for him outside in the sharp clear daylight, awaiting the journey south along the bay shore.

"It's not a good time to go riding outside," Melanie told him as he kissed her and pulled on his fur-lined jacket. "A storm is brewing."

"The sky's crystal clear," Bruce said. "There's no sign of bad weather anywhere in the northwest."

"All the same," Melanie replied, "something tells me you may not be able to get back in time for Christmas."

"But that's almost two days off."

"I'm worried. We have a celebration planned and I don't want you to miss it. It will be the first time that little Guy has celebrated Christmas. It's an important holiday for him. You should be here too."

"I'll be here," Bruce promised, then paused. "I see. You don't want me to go. You're thinking of Beryl Bennington."

"I am trying not to," Melanie said with a thin smile. "Please don't go, Bruce. Send Bill Dexter. He can be your emissary. Or send Black Deer."

"You know I can't order either one out there. There's still a feud going on between Bill Dexter and Connelly. And Black Deer won't go near the place, as you know, since the massacre. I'm the logical person to make the trip. It's my place to go."

"I still don't like it. I feel uneasy."

"Give me your blessing, dearest," said Bruce, enfolding Melanie gently in his arms.

She had come to mean so much to him that the intensity of his feelings sometimes disturbed and frightened him. He had cared deeply for Louise in Boston long ago, but that emotion seemed bland compared with what he felt for Melanie. He didn't know how to put it into perspective in his daily life, a small world of practical matters like keeping the mill going, working each day with Alan, all of which had no connection with a passion as ardent as his was now. It wasn't so much physical, he thought, it was more like some indefinable spirit that hovered over him, possessing him. He wondered if he would ever be able to settle into the comfortable domesticity that had always been the dominant theme in Alan's marriage to Janet. But then, he wasn't married, he reminded himself; often it was marriage that overpowered romance, dispelling the mystery. In one way it was just as well that Melanie had refused to marry him. Maybe she sensed something that he didn't, or couldn't, know.

"The blessing I give you is my constant awareness of you," Melanie told him. "I shall see you like a vision in the mirror of my mind while you're away. I will know where you are and what you do."

"I won't be far away. This is only a short trip to Yorkville, not a sea voyage to San Francisco."

"Where you are going is a long distance from here," Melanie said enigmatically. "I wish again that you wouldn't go."

"I must, Melanie, I really must. That poor woman down there may need some help. She can't be getting much support from Connelly."

Melanie sighed. "You are right, you must go," she agreed. "So go quickly. Return just as quickly."

She watched him from the cabin door as he moved across the snowcape, watched until he was only a small black speck on the shore's horizon, then went inside to sit by the fire and brood. It was true enough, she could still see him in her mind's eyes and watch every move he made. She could predict what he would do, which made her melancholy. Even when little Guy rushed over from the cabin next door to begin his usual playtime with her, she was almost unaware of the child. She could sense Bruce pause near the log where she and Dolly had tethered their horse that day of her first meeting with Bruce.

She should leave this place, she knew, for there was more trouble coming. But she was powerless to alter her fate one iota. She could do no more than sit and wait for her destiny to spin itself out. Ultimately she would triumph, but this was little comfort to her now . . .

Bruce rode into camp and proceeded directly to the administration building that housed the Yorkville business headquarters.

A guard was posted at the hall door to York's former living quarters. The mill office was next to it. Bruce identified himself and asked for Beryl Bennington. The guard told him to wait where he was and disappeared into the office.

Presently the guard emerged. "You can go inside now," he told Bruce in a surly voice.

Much like an armed camp, Bruce thought as he entered the office and was surprised to see Connelly sitting at York's old desk. He greeted Connelly.

"What the hell you doing here, Randall?" Egan Connelly asked rudely.

No chair was offered Bruce, but he sat down in one across the desk from Connelly. "I came to see if I could do anything for Mrs. Bennington," Bruce explained. "We just got the news earlier today about Bennington's death."

"We're taking care of her."

"How is she?"

"Nerves." Connelly tapped his forehead. "All nerves. Nothing else. The man was kilt in front of her, and she rode in hysterical. All she needs is some rest."

"Have you any clues to what happened in the forest?"

Connelly grinned at Bruce, baring his yellow

teeth. "Looks like an Indian job. Typical. Who else would shoot a man in the back like that, eh?"

"Almost anybody who felt like it," Bruce replied shortly. "Is Bennington already buried?"

"Yep, this morning." Connelly kept on grinning. "With a prayer and everything. Even used the new church buildin' . . . used to be the old saloon."

It was plain that Connelly hadn't liked his new boss's husband, Bruce decided. But the man would gain nothing by getting Bennington out of the way.

"Who'll it be next around here, I wonder?" Bruce mused. "There's no real law and order around here, is there?"

"I'm in charge, Randall. I don't have to explain or justify anything to you."

The conversation was leading nowhere, Bruce saw.

"Let me speak with Mrs. Bennington," he requested.

"I told you, that's not possible. She's sick."

Bruce had reached the impasse he anticipated and knew there was no way around it. The armed guard was standing just outside; others in the camp would be armed, while all he had for self-defense was the rifle stuck in his saddle holster. If he tried to force the issue either here or outside, he might not leave the camp alive. Connelly wasn't only the ruffian Dexter claimed he was; he could become a dangerous animal that moved by impulse rather than reason.

"Very well then, if that's your final word I might as well go back to Green Bay."

Bruce was on his feet and heading toward the hall door when it burst open and Beryl Bennington stumbled inside.

She was a sight. Her bright hair hung down in tangled disarray; her face was chalk-white, lines of strain marked the corners of her mouth. She wore a dressing robe over her nightgown and her eyes were red-rimmed and frantic. Bruce thought at first that she might be drunk. But when she walked shakily toward him he realized that her condition was due to fright.

"Mr. Randall," she cried out, "I saw you through the window. I'm so glad you came."

Connelly sat motionless behind the desk, watching her closely.

"We just heard the news today," said Bruce. "I came to offer my condolences and ask if there is anything we can do."

Beryl glanced furtively at Connelly.

"No," she said, "there's nothing. I'm fine, just fine. Will you be staying over?" she asked. Her eyes were pleading silently with him.

She was far from fine, he could see for himself.

"I should leave for Green Bay at once," he said. "I don't want to travel in darkness."

She turned to Connelly. "See that Mr. Randall has something to eat at the hotel."

"Yes, ma'am," said Connelly in an unconvincing, obedient voice, and stood up.

Beryl said, "When I'm well, and the weather's milder, I'll come up to Green Bay and visit your community."

This seemed to put an end to the interview.

"Yes, of course," Bruce said, getting the distinct impression that Beryl was sending him a signal of distress, but afraid to be more obvious about it. The guard stood in the doorway to the office facing them, his rifle held in competent readiness.

"Goodbye, Mrs. Bennington, and stay well," Bruce said, as Beryl walked from the room, heading down the hall to her quarters. He heard the sharp report of her door slamming.

"Amos will take you across to the hotel for your meal," said Connelly, at the door.

"Thanks for your hospitality," Bruce replied ironically, and left with the guard.

Outside in the square a stiff wind had risen, icy and knife-sharp. Leaden grey clouds were pushing across the peninsula in the northern sky and it looked like a storm was building up. Melanie had been right about the northwester, he observed. One was certainly on the way. He wouldn't be able to get back to Green Bay today.

As he crossed with the guard to the hotel, leading his horse, Connelly stood on the steps of the administration building watching him. Without having to turn and verify it, Bruce was quite certain that Beryl was also monitoring him from behind the curtained window of her quarters.

At the hotel the guard Amos saw him into a room where he could wash up. Presently a tray of food arrived from the messhall. Soggy and unsavory and barely warm, the food repelled him. Bruce ignored it.

The wind was now blowing vigorously outside. Another guard, a new one, came for his tray. Bruce told him that he was planning to stay overnight.

"What about my horse?" he asked the henchman.

The man said he would stable the gelding for

Bruce. From the parlor window Bruce watched the
guard lead his horse away, feeling peculiarly isolated and distinctly apprehensive. He disliked the
idea of remaining overnight at Yorkville, which
would put him back at Green Bay on the afternoon
of Christmas Eve. But on the other hand he
couldn't make it home in this weather. Staying at
the hotel was preferable to getting lost in the forest and freezing to death.

The storm grew in size and fury inside of an
hour, rattling the hotel like an angry giant. Bruce
lay down in his room in the vain hope he might
sleep. He couldn't. Thinking of Melanie and wish-
ing he'd heeded her advice about coming south, he
promised himself fervently he would listen to her
the next time. Still fully dressed, he dozed off.

Toward early evening he fell asleep. Along
about midnight the storm suddenly abated. In the
aftermath of deep, snow-covered silence, he suddenly woke up.

He got up without lighting the bedside lamp
and groped his way in the darkness to the parlor
and looked out the window. The sky was clear; a
half-moon bathed the snow-drifted square in a soft
silvery aura. There was almost enough moonlight,
he thought, to make it possible for him to find his
way through the forest and up the shoreline to
Green Bay. But he knew that he couldn't get his
horse from the stables at this hour without causing
a commotion; in the process he might even get
himself shot as an intruder. Everyone around
Yorkville appeared to be trigger-ready.

While he was wondering whether or not he
should go back to sleep until dawn, he heard
stealthy footsteps outside on the porch. He stepped

into the hall from his room and saw a figure at the door. Since he was the only person in the hotel, he wondered if perhaps a new guard had just arrived. After an interval, the front door opened and Beryl crept in. She was wearing a grey hooded poncho that nearly covered her face.

"Bruce!" she whispered, and he came forward to meet her.

She put a warning finger to her lips and closed the front door.

"Thank God you're here," she sighed in relief. "I didn't think I'd make it with the guard standing outside. We must be quiet," she cautioned. "We can't risk a light. No one knows I'm here."

"Are you all right?" he asked. She was quite calm now, a vast improvement over her frantic mood of only a few hours earlier.

"I'm—well, I'm better. Not all right yet, but . . . better. Bruce," she clutched his hand, "please take me with you. I'm afraid for my life. I can't stay here at Yorkville another night." She leaned against him, trembling. "I'm—things aren't right since Phil was shot. I think Connelly wants to kill me."

"Beryl, what's going on? I want to know."

"Connelly wants Yorkville. He thinks it belongs to him. That Phil and I cheated him of his rightful inheritance."

"How can that be? As York's widow, the estate is legally yours. Unless there are other relatives?"

"None that I know of. Anyway, that wouldn't mean a thing to Connelly. He wants me to sign over three-quarters of the property to him, then he'll let me go. Not until then."

"That's insane! He can't hold you here illegally. It's outrageous."

"Shhhh! Don't speak, just whisper. Softly. Connelly can do whatever he wants. Not all of his men were killed in the forest. There are others who are loyal to him. You saw the guards everywhere. Bruce, take me away now. He'll shut down the mill operation if I don't give in to him . . . And worse."

He sensed she was withholding vital information.

"Beryl, tell me everything," he urged her.

Beryl laid her head on his shoulder in capitulation. He was quite conscious of her warmth, her scent, of the firm, voluptuous body pressed against him.

"I'm so afraid," she murmured. "I—I'm not certain, but I think Connelly killed Phil."

"Connelly?" he said sharply. "My God, why?"

"I'd better tell you. When the next ship arrives Connelly plans to bribe the captain to marry us, unless I've already signed over the mill as he demands. He claims Henry left it to him."

"He's a madman."

"If we were married, he'd take everything, even my San Francisco holdings. He still might kill me then. Who's to stop him? I loathe the creature!"

"I can't believe all this," Bruce said.

"It's true, I assure you."

Whatever the truth was, Bruce could not deny that Beryl was in deep trouble. He had no choice but to help her. He agreed.

Suddenly she threw her arms around his neck; her soft breath burned on his cheek. He knew instinctively that she was offering herself to him as a gift to help her escape. Part of him longed to re-

spond to the stirring in his loins, part urged him
to control it.

She turned her lips up to his; she reached up and
kissed him, pushing her pelvis against his. Her
mouth was warm and fragrant, her tongue sweet
and hot, exploring his.

This was a moment he hadn't bargained for,
but he found himself quickly succumbing to her
desperate passion. He yearned to undress her,
slowly to lead her to bed and make love to her.
Though this was hardly the time or place for it,
even with Melanie fresh in his mind, he could
barely control himself.

She placed her hand on his fly, fumbling with
the buttons, Quickly her hand crept inside, exploring, hotly manipulating him.

"No!" he said, suddenly pulling away from her.
He had a strong impression that someone far away
was watching them, a spirit too dominant to be
denied.

"Why not?" Beryl said. "Don't you find me attractive?"

"The situation's impossible," he said. "We have
to get out of here in a hurry."

"Please," she begged him, but he had lost the
momentary desire she had kindled. He held her
at arm's length.

"Tell you what," he said softly. "Could you find
my horse in the stables?"

She wrenched away from his grip and struggled
for control of herself. "I think so," she said eventually. "I'll get Henry's horse for myself."

"What about the guards?"

"The watchman in the administration building
sleeps most of the night. He won't check on me

until morning. The outside patrol makes its round every half hour. In ten minutes they'll have a checked out this area, then we can go out the back way to the stables."

Clutching his rifle, Bruce walked to the back door.

"Let me go first," he said. "If we frighten the horses we could get caught."

"We won't be," she replied, more confidently now. "The stable boy doesn't sleep there in cold weather, he's in the next building, and hard to wake up. He won't hear us."

They waited until the guard passed, then crept silently from the hotel, through the soft snow to the barn where the horses were stabled. It was a difficult task saddling the horses in the dark. Once a mare in the corner stall whinnied and they froze, but nothing happened, no one investigated the noise. The animals were docile enough and used to being handled. Bruce and Beryl left the barn in a few minutes and were soon on the trail to the bay, moving slowly through the forest. They emerged from the darkness some forty minutes later, into soft moonlight that lit the bay shore plainly and showed them their way along the snow-mantled beach.

When they had put enough distance between themselves and Yorkville to talk safely, Beryl said, "If you'll put me aboard your next vessel bound for San Francisco, I shall be grateful to you."

"Maybe that's best," Bruce allowed. "You certainly can't stay on at Yorkville now. What wil happen to the mill after you've abandoned it?"

"It will run itself until spring until I send some-

one up to replace Connelly. Anyway, it's bad luck
for me. I hate it."

"What will you do in California?"

"Look after my property down there. Settle
whatever has to be settled about Phil's death."

"Your marriage came as a surprise to all of us,"
he said. "I thought your association with Bennington was strictly business."

"It surprised me, too," Beryl replied. "A mistake,
and I paid for it. Once I got here I realized that I
couldn't go it alone. I married Phil because I
thought it would make things easier for me." She
paused a moment. "Maybe I shouldn't say this
since he's dead, but I think he wanted the whole
estate for himself. From the first hour of our marriage I was afraid for my life. I realized he was
my legal heir, and I didn't trust him. At first I
thought he was in league with Connelly and they
both planned to kill me. Another time I thought it
was his idea alone. Perhaps that bullet in the forest
that killed him was meant for *me*! Well, whatever
the explanation, no one wants me in Yorkville. I
was a fool to think it could work. I shall never go
back!" She shivered under her cape. "It's as though
Henry's ghost has cast his spell over the place,
cursing everything. Everyone . . ."

"The situation could change for the better when
Connelly's ousted," Bruce told her.

"Yes. Perhaps. But I'm not optimistic."

So what would happen, Bruce wondered as they
continued north in silence for a spell. Beryl would
leave; she would sell Yorkville. He would still have
neighbors, strangers, as greedy as those either
dead or alive.

"How will you get rid of Connelly?" he asked.

"I can do it legally in San Francisco," she explained. "Phil and I discussed firing him before we got here. If necessary, I'll raise my own army and throw him out. He won't get away with stealing Yorkville from me. After all, the property is legally registered in my name."

"You're within your rights, of course."

"I'm counting on that," Beryl said. "When is a ship arriving?"

"Captain Kelsey's *Prince Rupert* should dock here today or tomorrow."

"Can you put me up in a safe place until then?"

"Certainly. We have weapons. I don't think Connelly and his men will come looking for you in the heart of enemy territory."

"They might. They're—he's capable of anything. He's as ruthless as Henry."

"If they do come they'll meet considerable resistance," said Bruce. "The Indians are on our side."

"You're a decent man, Bruce," she said. "I admire and respect you. I could never have left Yorkville by myself."

She sounded sincere enough, but he really didn't trust her. He was pleased, however, that she acknowledged his indispensability.

"Coming back to the Northwest Territory was unwise," she said, determining to tell no one the story about Henry's will and how Phil switched the substitute document for the original.

"Don't think about Yorkville," he advised her. "It'll soon be Christmas Eve. We're having a party for everyone. I think you might enjoy it . . . You'll join us, of course?"

"I have only the clothes on my back," she said, "but I look forward to being there with you. Thank you."

After this she lapsed into a thoughtful silence as they rode toward the mill town. Bruce decided not to disturb her, let her alone with her thoughts. She'd been through a great deal.

Their progress north was slow and steady but no one rode after them. They arrived at Green Bay as the morning lamps were being lit in the messhall and the cooks were busy preparing breakfast for the loggers.

Never, thought Bruce, had Green Bay looked better to him. It was indeed his home. All through the journey he'd expected an attack from the rear and was immensely relieved that the journey was uneventful. He could scarcely hope, however, that this would be the end of it, and that he had heard the last of Connelly.

19

As soon as Bruce had settled Beryl in one of the new cabins, he rode back to rejoin Melanie. She was up and fully dressed; she had apparently been up most of the night, sitting in a chair with a blanket wrapped around her, brooding by the fire. She looked tired and distraught, although, Bruce noted, her manner was as placid as usual.

"You've brought her with you," she stated in a flat, emotionless voice.

"You mean Beryl Bennington?"

Melanie nodded.

"You saw me bring her into camp."

Melanie shook her head. "No. I just knew."

He gathered Melanie protectively in his arms and kissed her long and passionately.

"She won't be here for long, I promise. She'll be sailing for San Francisco on the *Rupert*'s return voyage. I couldn't leave her to face Egan Connelly alone."

He went on to explain about Connelly's plan to rob Beryl of her rightful inheritance and the possibility that the manager might have also killed Phil Bennington.

"You can't be sure she's telling the truth," said Melanie.

"Part of it is true, anyway. Enough so that I had to help her escape."

"She brings danger to us all."

"True or not, she was Connelly's prisoner. Surely you know what that means."

"I know what it means and I'm sorry that I spoke so harshly before. But the sooner she goes, the better it will be for Green Bay. She has a dark side to her heart."

"You could be right," Bruce said, thinking it best to placate her, she was that agitated. He had been on the verge of infidelity with Beryl, which Melanie had already sensed, he was certain. This no doubt is what had made her uneasy.

"I must talk with Alan now," he said, embracing her again. "Get some rest so you'll enjoy the celebration tonight."

He wouldn't tell her what he thought could happen this evening, it was too grim a prospect. Anyway, he suspected she would have already divined more about it than he knew, and perhaps this was why she clung to him looking almost grief-stricken when he started to leave.

* * *

"They'll come, all right," Alan agreed a few minutes later in Bruce's office. "The bastards will probably arrive late like you say. I'll talk with Black Deer."

"I want it settled without bringing the Indians into it," said Bruce. "This is important. If they get involved in the incident there'll be bloodshed for certain." Bruce shook his head dolefully, tired from the slow, bitter trip back from Yorkville, and depressed by what lay ahead. "I don't understand greed, I really don't."

Alan thought about the hardships he had endured before he became a school teacher. "That's probably because you've always had plenty and never had to cope with real hardship. Greed is worst when men like York and Connelly have to fight their way up from grinding poverty. No education, no advantages except those they could wrest by virtue of their own strength and cunning. Bill Dexter understands these men better than we do. His early life also was one of deprivation. But he didn't turn out the way these villains did. He takes only what he thinks is his fair share, though he'll fight like hell to get it."

Bruce scowled, not used to Alan lecturing, but accepting the soundness of his observations all the same.

"You mean Bill is a decent man in a way York and Connelly could never be?" he asked.

"Something like that," said Alan. "We'd best not tell Janet about the trouble brewing. She'd have hysterics."

"More to the point, don't tell Dexter," said Bruce, just as Dexter, who had been summoned to confer with them, walked into Bruce's office.

"What won't you tell me?" Dexter asked with a wide, knowing grin. "That York's widow's here in Cabin 8 and it means trouble? I could see that one coming blindfolded. And what's the other good news? Connelly's wolves on her trail?"

"Sit down, Bill," said Bruce, and Dexter straddled a chair saying, "So this is a war council, eh?"

"Definitely not," Bruce replied. "We're only talking about self-defense."

"I was just on my way up to Black Deer's village when you called me in, Mr. Randall. I'm bringing them a few guns for their protection—with your permission, of course. This time the Siwash won't be massacred where they live."

"Bill, this isn't a war," Bruce said. "I don't want you arming anybody."

"It may not be a war yet, Mr. Randall, but it sure will be when Connelly arrives. You ought to know that miserable bastard will stop at nothing by now."

"I'll grant you that."

"Well then, let me take Black Deer the rifles. They don't have one good weapon up there, believe me."

Bruce paused only a moment. "All right," he conceded. "But only to defend the village. They're not to come down here if Connelly appears. Impress that upon Black Deer. In an all-out war a lot of innocent people could get killed."

"I'll do my best, Mr. Randall," Dexter replied with a confident grin.

It was plainly evident to Bruce that Dexter was spoiling for a final showdown with Connelly, and that this time one or both of them might end up dead. Were it spring and in happier times, the en-

counter might take the form of a log-rolling contest at the edge of the boom dam, a more ritual
duel that wouldn't cost lives to their camps. The
unlucky loser might fall to his death through the
spill gates but it was unlikely. This Christmas,
however, it would have to be settled with firearms.

Bruce entertained the unsettling thought that
his attitude toward violence had changed radically
since he arrived in the Northwest. Violence and
sudden death were commonplace; he now found
himself taking them for granted as inevitable, and
he didn't like the idea.

"Do more than your best to keep the Siwash
confined to their village, Bill," he ordered Dexter.
"Make it stick that whatever happens, there's to
be no shooting. Only if and when we truly need
it are they to come to our aid. Do you understand?"

"Absolutely, sir," Dexter said. "I'll caution Black
Deer. What time's the party tonight?"

"From eight to midnight in the assembly hall,"
Bruce told him. "Just as we've announced. Why
do you ask?"

"Just wanting confirmation, sir. Connelly will
know the exact time it's going to break up. We
don't want to mess up his timetable, do we?"

"Or yours," Bruce said pointedly.

"Connelly gets real mad when people play tricks
on him. He's got no sense of humor."

Bruce began to see what he had started by
bringing Beryl with him. The feud was getting
out of hand. Bill Dexter and Black Deer would do
what they wanted, no matter what orders he gave.

"Everything's the same, Bill. We'll have food
and gifts and punch bowls inside the hall 'till a

quarter to midnight. And by that time the bonfire in the clearing will be roaring. We'll all go
outside and form a circle around the blaze and
sing Christmas carols. At the stroke of midnight
we'll say a prayer in unison, then everyone can go
home. Is that clear?"

"Absolutely, sir. Just wanted to be sure."

"And you be sure that Black Deer understands
my prohibition."

"I will, sir," Dexter said, and left.

Bruce sighed. "Sometimes I wonder whose side
Bill Dexter is on."

"Ours, definitely," Alan confirmed. "He's lived
with fights and feuds all his life, and the logging
business is no exception. He has to go about things
in his own way."

"You seem to understand him better than I do.
He's a good man . . . I'm not implying he's anything else. But he tends to thrive on excitement."

"Is it any wonder?" Alan asked thoughtfully.
"I have Janet and the kids, you have supreme authority over everybody on staff. But what has Bill
Dexter got? A long-standing grudge against Connelly that hasn't brought him any satisfaction to
speak of and which would probably come to a
nasty conclusion tonight. It's no use pretending
any different, Bruce. Every man will do what he
wants, orders or no orders. Better call off the bonfire. That would really be asking for it, if they
show up."

"No," said Bruce, "I'll not be intimidated on my
own land by a criminal. The bonfire ceremony will
be held as scheduled. But I do think everybody
should be alerted and told that there may be
trouble tonight, so they can prepare themselves

for trouble. Naturally, women and children won't be allowed at the bonfire."

"Little Guy's going to be upset," said Alan.

"You can tell him that some men might be killing each other on the eve of Christ's birthday," Bruce said cynically, "and don't waste your breath talking about peace on earth, goodwill toward men. It doesn't mean a damned thing."

Alan stared at his senior partner. "What's bothering you, Bruce? I've never heard you talk like this before."

"Melanie and Beryl aren't getting along. I should never have let them meet each other."

"But it was your doing," Alan pointed out. "Say, you aren't, uh . . ." Alan couldn't finish the sentence.

"Interested in Beryl?" Bruce said it for him. "No. She's just another pretty, willful woman who'll take what she wants when she wants it and will throw herself on any man who will provide it for her."

"I understand," said Alan gently, for he knew how much in love Bruce was with Melanie. The only mystery to this was, why didn't they get married when they both so obviously adored each other?

"No," Bruce said irritably, "you don't understand at all. You just think you do." Bruce turned the subject back to the topic of interest. "What can Connelly hope to gain by coming here?" he reflected.

"Bill Dexter probably knows the answer to that better than anyone," said Alan. "And we won't know if it's the right one until later tonight. I've already started men working on the bonfire circle.

It's going to make an impressive sight so let's hope it doesn't snow . . ."

In the new assembly hall, it was Bruce's unenviable task to introduce Beryl and Melanie to each other. To his surprise, the two women played their respective roles admirably. They greeted each other with affable smiles and soon were engaged in mild conversation about nothing much. The thought flashed through Bruce's mind that they could, if they wished, easily compare notes on Henry York's intimate habits, but of course they wouldn't dream of doing so.

Tim and Toby, the Moore twins, gave an impromptu concert on guitar and harmonica shortly after the crowd of loggers began to assemble. Scrubbed fresh and pink in the steaming tubs behind the bunkhouses, and dressed in their best clothes, the loggers were in a festive convivial mood. Bill Dexter had promised that boisterous behavior such as drunkenness, loud or coarse language, fights or any other unseemly act would be severely dealt with by him personally. Another reason the men were subdued was Bill's admonition that there might be some trouble from the rival camp round about midnight. Despite the danger, only a few of the loggers remained in the safety of their bunkhouses. The assembly hall rang with hearty applause as the Moore twins performed numbers back to back.

One of Dexter's crew owned an accordion. After the Moore twins had finished their act, he sat down to play music for square dancing. The punch bowls were replenished several times while these activities were taking place, thus loosening normal inhibitions. In lieu of female partners, the men danced expertly with each other over the rough board floor, first in group dancing and then, when waltzes were played, in pairs, dreamy expressions on their rough masculine faces. They weren't thinking of their male partners. They were summoning up other good times in more civilized places, with the female company of their choice.

As the hour approached eleven o'clock, Bruce ordered the punch bowls removed and food brought in. The buffet supper consisted mostly of sandwiches of cold venison, winter apples, assorted cheeses, cookies, cakes, pies, even some Christmas hard candies brought in to the settlement by the last ship. Tomorrow the big Christmas Day feast would be served in relays so none of the lumberjacks would be left out. But tonight's party was devoted simply to relaxing and enjoying the first Christmas Eve that Green Bay had celebrated.

"How do you like the party?" Beryl asked Melanie at one point.

"I am glad to see the men and the children enjoying themselves," Melanie said rather formally.

"You don't like me," Beryl responded with a determined smile. "I can sense that."

Melanie returned her smile. "I have no feelings about you personally, Mrs. Bennington, though I must admit that I shall be relieved when you go."

"That's understandable," Beryl said, glancing secretively at Bruce, who looked more handsome than usual in a suit and cravat as he sat talking with Janet. He appeared to be enjoying himself.

"I am not trying to come between you and Mr. Randall," Beryl said candidly. "If you're harbor-

ing any such thoughts, please banish them from
your mind. I am most grateful to him for rescuing
me from Yorkville and for offering me asylum
here. However I want you to understand that I am
going away for good," she answered the lovely
half-breed.

"You should never have come back," Melanie
said without emotion.

Beryl realized that the woman's response indicated a far deeper concern than mere conversation, and she responded to it. "You're absolutely
right. My life and those of my friends are deeply
rooted in San Francisco. Let us leave my past out
of this shall we? And go on smiling as though we
were the best of friends."

"It is best," Melanie agreed, closing the conversation.

As the night wore on toward eleven-fifteen, the
loggers increased the tempo of the party, but with
control. One by one, at pre-arranged intervals,
an even dozen of the loggers most loyal to Bill
Dexter quietly drifted out of the assembly hall and
back toward their bunkhouses. They gathered in
Bill Dexter's small cabin where they were briefed
by Dexter and given new firearms from the company arsenal. They waited at the house for his
order to move into their assigned positions at
various points around the clearing and hide themselves under cover of the forest.

As quarter to twelve drew near, Bruce began to
grow nervous. He had noticed the loggers leaving
and at first he had considered trying to detain
them, then realized that he would only interfere
with Dexter's plans for a defense of the camp
which he knew was of the foremost importance.

Bruce waited for the time when he could politely ask everyone except the women and children to go outside and gather round the bonfire. As he did sweat flowed from his armpits, dampening his shirt; he had second thoughts about the bonfire circle. He could see the giant pyre burning merrily through the assembly hall windows, lighting up the entire clearing. But what might be lurking in the deep shadows besides Dexter's men could only be guessed.

From time to time, Bruce watched Beryl sitting quietly next to Melanie, politely refusing all offers to dance. So had Melanie. But Beryl's features were flushed with excitement, Melanie's were remote, calm and composed, unreadable.

When Beryl caught him glancing at her, she returned his look with a soft smile. Melanie would not respond to his gaze at all, which made him miserable. Was she punishing him for bringing Beryl to Green Bay, or did she feel that he had purposely slighted the Indians by confining them to their isolated village, and not inviting them to the party? It wasn't their kind of celebration, he told himself. What probably concerned Melanie most was the threat of open warfare erupting outside in a few minutes. She was as worried as he was—yes, that was it—and her silence was the way she expressed this worry. She knew the Siwash intimately through Black Deer. If she were privy to anything the Siwash planned she would never reveal it to him, Bruce realized. She was a woman of great natural depth, a direct, complex creature who would always be somewhat enigmatic. He would never understand her completely and was better off not worrying about it. Accept what you can, he told himself, and ignore the rest.

Bruce gave the signal for the music to stop at fifteen minutes to midnight and announced that the men would now move outside to gather briefly around the bonfire. There they would all sing a Christmas carol and a prayer would be offered to solemnize the first occasion of Christmas at Green Bay. No women and children were to go outside, Bruce emphasized. They would be escorted to their dwellings at once.

It took several minutes for the group of loggers to file out of the assembly hall and form a circle round the bonfire. When they were all settled and quiet, the Moore twins gave the signal by striking up *Silent Night*, a hymn everyone knew, and the assembly began to join in, sending their voices out into the vast wilderness on the crisp night air. It was an impressive moment, thought Bruce, as he scanned the trees that bordered the clearing and added his voice to the choir.

Alan stood on his right, Bill Dexter on his left. All three wore side arms, as they had agreed, hard-hitting .44 caliber Colt revolvers tucked into their belts beneath their coats. Dexter had only joined the party in the assembly hall a few minutes before it broke up, to Bruce's relief. If there were Indians about, he saw no signs of them in the shadows.

The last notes of the hymn died away in the still darkness.

Bruce held out his hands. "Let us all bow our heads in prayer . . ." If Connelly and his men were skulking about, they couldn't pick a better moment, he thought.

Most of the loggers bowed their heads, and some knelt in the circle as Bruce began his prayer of thanksgiving and praise:

"Dear Father, we thank Thee for the gift of Christ and Christmas, and for all that You have done for us during this past few years . . ."

He got no further. At that point a shot rang out across the clearing and a heavy blow struck him in the right shoulder. As he crumpled to the ground wounded, all hell broke loose.

Bill Dexter turned to kneel beside Bruce with Alan. A second bullet hit Dexter between his broad shoulders, knocking him flat on his face.

Then abruptly Connelly and his men stepped into view in the distance. At this point, Dexter's men materialized on either side of them, their rifles gleaming in the firelight. All were aimed at Connelly and his gang. Seeing that they were only waiting for Dexter's order to fire, Alan jumped up and shouted to Connelly, "Stay right where you are and don't try anything!"

Connelly froze. Behind him and his henchmen Alan could see the figures of six armed Siwash and Black Deer. Damn Dexter, he thought. Now there'd certainly be a massacre with those trigger-happy Indians involved. But no one moved, not even Black Deer.

What happened during the next thirty seconds or so while everyone was distracted could not have been anticipated or prevented by anyone.

Beryl Bennington had not gone to her cabin as she had been told just before the loggers moved outside to the bonfire. She had hidden from sight in the shadows of the assembly hall. Now she ran up quickly behind Alan, reached down and grabbed Bruce's sidearm from its startled owner's belt. Nobody else had detected the move.

Holding the gun close against the folds of her skirt, she marched around the campfire toward Connelly, who held his rifle ready.

All eyes were fixed upon Beryl as she walked, the only moving figure in the tense, motionless tableau.

Connelly gripped his rifle tighter. "Stay where you are, woman," he commanded her.

She kept on moving closer until she was about fifteen feet from him, then stopped dead in her tracks with the gun still hidden from view. Raising it suddenly, she pointed the pistol in the direction of the startled foreman and fired. The heavy bullet hit Connelly squarely in the chest. The wounded gunman attempted to regain his balance, then gasped and clutched his chest and fell backward with a thud. He was dead when he hit the ground.

The crowd was stunned. No one seemed to know what to do next except Alan, who realized what might happen if no one quickly took the situation in hand. Beryl's intervention had brought the conflict to a point where it either could end now or immediately explode into carnage.

"Drop your guns!" Alan shouted to Connelly's gang of marauders. To a man, they threw down their weapons.

The Siwash moved in behind them, taking them prisoners. Black Deer brought them forward to the circle while Dexter's loggers covered the move.

Greatly outnumbered, the Yorkville vigilantes dropped their rifles by the fire, docile and submissive, fearful of their fate.

Clutching the pistol to her breast, Beryl leaned over Bruce who asked faintly, "What happened?"

By this time Melanie had appeared. She brushed Beryl aside and supported Bruce as he sat up.

"Help me get him to the cabin," she begged Alan.

"How's Dexter?" Bruce asked about the inert form on the ground next to him. In the quick exchange of gunfire that preceded Beryl's single shot, Dexter had been forgotten momentarily.

Alan crouched down next to the foreman. "He's dead," he said, then rose and walked over to Connelly. He turned the man over on his back and examined him. Then he walked slowly back to Bruce.

"Connelly's dead, too," he murmured, devastated.

"I'm glad I killed him," Beryl said shrilly. "I meant to kill him because he murdered Henry York and Philip Bennington. He was a monster!"

"Be quiet." Alan commanded.

"You can send me to San Francisco in chains as far as I'm concerned," Beryl went on. "It won't bother me a bit. I'm glad I killed him." She handed Bruce's six-gun to Alan, who tucked it into his belt.

Between them, Melanie and Alan half-carried Bruce to his quarters. Melanie sent one of the loggers who lingered outside the cabin to the mess-hall for a kettle of hot water. Bruce lay on the bed as Melanie ripped off his shirt to inspect the wound; fortunately it was a superficial one, though bloody. The kettle of hot water arrived promptly from the cookhouse. Melanie remained silent as she went to work cleaning Bruce's wound. Seeing that all was well, Alan left.

Bruce said to Melanie, "I guess you'll be telling me we asked for it, going outside like that." When she didn't reply Bruce continued. "It was the only way Dexter could handle it, I suppose, even if luring the Yorkers was risky. Except Bill probably never figured on anyone getting killed. Bill disobeyed my orders about containing the Siwash. Connelly must have known they were surrounding him and his men. That in turn must have scared him into firing at me."

"Black Deer set the trap," said Melanie.

"You knew what would happen?"

"Yes. But no one had to tell me."

"It could have been horrible. I'm lucky. We're all lucky. Thank God the Siwash didn't fire. I give Black Deer credit for that. They might have killed innocent people around the fire."

"Bill Dexter's loss will be mourned by the Siwash," said Melanie. "I am glad that the vision about you was incomplete. It told there would be bloodshed tonight. There was no way to avoid it. I was so frightened you might die."

"I feel terrible about Bill Dexter. He'll be missed in Green Bay. He was a good lumberman and a fine person."

"The Siwash who were massacred in the southern village were also decent people," Melanie observed. "It could not have happened if the white settlers hadn't come here."

"You're right," Bruce agreed. "All of it is pointless, it settles nothing. Beryl York was crazy to shoot Connelly, but then, she had a reason."

"She was fated to do so," said Melanie. "Too bad one of the Siwash couldn't have pulled the trigger, like Black Deer."

Bruce felt that Melanie was trying to tell him something. "Did Connelly murder York?" he asked.

"No." She would not look at him as she carefully bound up his shoulder with an improvised dressing made from strips of toweling.

"I gathered as much."

Melanie glanced at him sharply. "How do you know about it?"

"Intuition," he said. "White people have it too, sometimes. Anyway, his death was inevitable. With all the enemies York made, somebody was bound to kill him sooner or later."

"Now you sound like an Indian," said Melanie, smiling at him for the first time since he returned from Yorkville, "even if you weren't fortunate enough to be born one."

"I've learned something about how an Indian thinks since I met you," he said. "Give me credit for keeping my eyes open, at least."

"Then you know who avenged the Siwash massacre by killing York. And York's men?"

"Let's say I have a good idea. But the truth of the matter is that it is no longer important."

Melanie's relief was immediately visible, as if a shadow had passed from her brow.

"Why does that simple statement make you so happy?" he asked.

"Because it means that we can be married. There was always York's death and the death of his four assassins between us," she told him. "You don't blame the Siwash for evening the score?"

"No one ever evened a score by killing," Bruce

said, "but the loss of York is certainly nothing to grieve over. The lawyer's death is a different matter entirely. And Beryl elected to deal personally with Egan Connelly."

"What will you do with her? Your laws aren't as simple as the Siwash code."

"Just what I intended to do anyway: send her away aboard the *Rupert.*"

"Will she have to answer to United States law in California for Connelly's murder?"

"It's highly improbable. She's innocent in the eyes of God, as far as I'm concerned," Bruce said. "I'll sign a statement saying that she fired in self-defense and Guy Kelsey will witness it. Which in a way is the truth. There's not a man in camp who wouldn't support her testimony, or a court of law that would convict a woman as beautiful as Beryl of cold-blooded murder if they knew all the facts."

"With Connelly dead and Mrs. Bennington leaving, what will happen to Yorkville?"

"It may have to close down for good," Bruce said. "I really don't know. It's up to Mrs. Bennington."

That night, between fitful naps, Bruce thought long and hard about his future. With the lumber war settled for the time being, life might be relaxed and pleasant around Green Bay once more. He and Melanie could found a dynasty, small though it may be. He knew she wouldn't be comfortable in a big city, anymore than he would. Or if she preferred, he would sell his interest in Green Bay and move somewhere else. It was too complicated a question to settle in one night, he reflected. It would take care of itself, as Melanie would say, and so thinking, turned over and drifted off to sleep.

Early next morning Bruce called on Beryl. He made the visit with great reluctance, for he had no idea how he should handle her; he was for once completely at a loss for words.

He had been deeply disturbed by her violent and public act. He wasn't quite sure she knew what she had done or what her motive was for doing it. Until the murder of Connelly—it was too deliberate to be called anything else—he had entertained the notion of getting to know Beryl better. In the dim recesses of his libido, Bruce felt a nagging attraction to Beryl; but whether this included making love to her was unclear. His regard for Melanie remained unchanged; it was something quite apart from his present compulsion. And although he found Beryl's violence last night revolting, a vestige of his initial physical interest was still active as he knocked on the door of Beryl's quarters.

She greeted him tensely; rumpled, hollow-eyed, pale and nervous. Obviously she had slept very little. To his surprise Beryl's first remark concerned his well-being.

"Are you all right?" she asked him, glancing at the sling that Melanie had made for him.

"Fine. I mend quickly," he replied. "It wasn't much more than a scratch."

"Thank God. At first I thought you were dead," she said. Beryl perched on the edge of the bunk, wringing her hands, all color gone from her cheeks.

"I did a terrible thing last night," she burst out suddenly. "I don't know what to say or do about it. I have absolutely no excuse for my actions. I'm perfectly sane, and I didn't lose my wits for a single second during the shoot-out. In fact, it was precisely the opportunity I had been waiting for. I knew what I was doing when I took your pistol and headed for Connelly, and it wasn't to avenge your shooting."

"I know," he said to placate her.

"But you don't know!" she cried out. "I didn't love Henry, for God's sake. And as for Phil, he was a smart and sometimes charming man. We got off on the wrong foot after we were married in Yorkville. But I didn't want to see him dead. There's no doubt in my mind that Egan Connelly killed him because he married me." She paused briefly, folding her hands in her lap. Beryl looked at Bruce steadily. "Even now I'm not certain whether I actually intended to kill Egan, or merely stop whatever he planned to do. If I could—"

"The point is, Connelly's dead," he reminded her, "and it was your hand that killed him. And what's even worse, our most valuable man is dead, too. And I almost got it along with Dexter."

"I thought you had," Beryl admitted. She must have decided against expanding on this thought. She let out a brief, forlorn moan, then said, "I'm confused. I feel remorse and satisfaction at the same time. Tell me, am I under house arrest?"

"I see no need for extreme measures," Bruce said. "You couldn't get very far on your own. You're free to wander about anywhere you like at Green Bay."

"Thank you. Then I take it you don't blame me for Connelly's death?"

"That's another matter. Taking a life is a grave

responsibility no matter what the consequences. You might be to blame to a certain degree. I would say this is a question of conscience, first of all. What formal guilt a court of law might attach to your action is something else again. A judge might well consider it justified. But as you know, a formal court has yet to be established in the territory, so we're talking hypothetically."

"Connelly was a fiend," Beryl said with conviction. "I just know he killed Henry and Phil."

"You don't know for certain, Beryl."

"Perhaps not. But I may as well tell you—I wanted Connelly dead. Partly for Phil's sake, as well as for my protection."

"I assumed as much," he said. "We all consider eliminating people like Connelly at one time or another in our lives. Those who say they haven't ever given it a thought are plain liars. Actually, if you want my personal opinion, you've rid the area of vermin. We can all rest easier in our beds at night because of you. I'm sure Connelly was more or less unhinged ever since he discovered he wasn't getting a share of York's estate. Let's hope his death has defused this explosive situation—that is, the raiders are now without a leader. They no longer have any reason to feud with us."

"What will you do with the men who were with Connelly last night?" she asked.

"They'll be shipped out of Green Bay as soon as possible. They're confined for the time being to one of the ships in port; they won't bother you right now. But you will be sailing back together on the *Prince Rupert*."

"That frightens me a little."

"It's necessary that you arrive in San Francisco when they do. That way, if they spread tales you'll have time to get the evidence legally entered in your favor to protect yourself."

"Protect myself—? What do you mean?"

"I'll sign a deposition about the shooting incident. You would be well advised to file it with the San Francisco courts. That would squash any possible charges that Connelly's men might decide to bring against you for their own benefit."

"It sounds depressingly complex, but thank you for your concern. With two husbands of mine murdered in so short a period of time, the authorities might demand some explanation from me. When is the *Rupert* due in? I'm anxious to leave as soon as possible."

"As I said, Captain Kelsey should get here late this afternoon. He'll sail back to San Francisco in two days."

"Then there's plenty of time for someone to gather my belongings."

"Alan will send a couple of men down to Yorkville today. You'll have to give them explicit instructions where to go and what to bring back."

"Thank you, I shall. I only need my clothes."

"No personal papers?"

"I brought all the important documents that pertain to Yorkville with me when we escaped."

She picked up a cloth packet lying on the table by the fireplace. Extracting a document, she held it out to him.

"Would you please look at this?" she requested. "It's Henry York's last will and testament. It leaves everything in his estate to me."

She paused, staring intently at him. Almost as if, Bruce thought, she expected to see doubt in his eyes.

"You may want to read it," she urged. "It's quite legal, I assure you. This is the same document that Connelly wanted to destroy after my husband was mysteriously shot."

"There's no need for me to read it, Beryl."

"Yes there is," she insisted. "It's the basis for a second document, which does concern us, you and me."

Oh God, he speculated, was she grasping at straws, at some desperate hope that their mutual interests might bring them together? He would have to correct that misunderstanding immediately.

"I'll look at the second document first, if you don't mind," he said, and took the sheet of paper from her hand.

"I was up all night writing and rewriting it," she explained as he unfolded the letter. "I wanted it to be as legal as possible in the event anything happened to me."

Quickly he scanned her tense, spidery scrawl.

"I want you to run Yorkville," she said as he inspected the document. "The paper confers upon you proper authority to do so in my absence. You will share the profits and operating expenses with me on a fifty-fifty basis. The paper guarantees that I won't ever interfere with the physical operation of the mill. You have a completely free hand in its management. And if I should die before you do, then the entire Yorkville holdings are all yours, free and clear."

He finished reading what she essentially had just told him.

"There now," she said, "doesn't that make you want to eliminate me for the fabulous riches you'll be getting at my death?"

She chuckled softly, making him even more uncomfortable.

He said, "Are you sure you want to handle it this way?" He knew she could well have second thoughts later on about her generosity.

"Yes, I'm sure. I have no living relatives on either side of my family. My father died in a fire shortly after I met Henry York. There was never a satisfactory explanation how the fire started. I've always suspected that it was arson. My father raised me a genteel young lady, and on his death I was helpless. In those days Henry was a perfect gentleman; it was reasonable that I marry him. My ignorance of business made me glad to wed a man who did well.

"I've never been positive, but I believe Henry saw me as an investment, a way to make his fortune. Oh, he wanted me, well enough, but he wanted my father's property as a grubstake for the north woods venture even more. And he almost got the property. At least, on the strength of it he managed to borrow enough to set himself up at Yorkville—and of course he brought me along with him. You know the rest, or most of it."

On paper, the arrangement seemed sound enough to Bruce. Beryl had given it much thought. But to simply hand over a valuable property like Yorkville to him must mean that she was either a bit mad or else still in a state of shock from recent events. He questioned the soundness of her mind in giving him such a free rein.

"After what you've been through, you're still willing to trust me to such an extent?" he said. "Owners have been killed for far less than the stakes are worth here."

"After my experiences at Yorkville, you look like the soul of honesty to me," she said in a low, seductive voice.

Ah, he reflected, maybe she had some strange idea that he might become husband number three.

"Well," she asked, "do you like the idea?"

"I'd be a fool not to."

"All right then, it's done. This is your agreement copy. I'll keep the original document."

"But remember, I'll understand if you change your mind, and wish to abrogate the agreement at any time. Then we'll part with no hard feelings and no cash settlement. Shouldn't this be specifically stated in the contract?"

"I see no need," said Beryl. "I trust you, and I know that I won't change my mind. You'll honor what's already written. Now, please sign where I've indicated, and I'll sign opposite your signature."

Bruce signed the two papers and watched Beryl sign beside him.

"There," she said. "Are you pleased?"

"Very much so," he replied. "Ever since I arrived in Green Bay my dream has been to unite the two opposing camps in friendship. I never dreamed that they could become business partners, at least not while York was alive. And although I hoped for it I wasn't sure that you'd want to join in a mutual venture with us, after he died. Then when I went to visit you I despaired of seeing Green Bay to the edge of our boundaries where it would eventually become at least physically united with Yorkville. It was an idle dreamer's fantasy, I thought. Until this minute. Now you've made it a reality, and—ironically enough—not only with this document, but by killing Connelly as well."

"I'm glad that something good has come out of misery here," she said quietly. "I too arrived with grandiose plans. But Phil and I failed each other through pure and simple greed, nothing more . . ." She stood in the center of the room, holding copies of the two documents in her hands, staring at them for several seconds. Then she handed one of them to Bruce, looked up at him and smiled sourly.

"Three important men in my life are dead," she declared, "and I can't shed tears over any of them?"

"Three?"

"Yes. Henry, Phil, and Egan Connelly."

"Connelly?" he said. Why would she consider him important? Treacherous, yes; threatening, certainly; but hardly important.

"Egan Connelly . . ." Her face grew flushed, and the words came tumbling out. "I think I can trust you with the real story about Egan—I've never told anyone until now. He was my half-brother, my father's illegitimate son by another woman. My father never recognized Egan as his heir. So Egan thought that forcing a repugnant marriage on me would avenge my father's neglect. I also think it was Egan who was responsible for the fire that killed my father, and that Henry must have known something. If so, he didn't breathe a word of it to me."

Bruce was stunned by her admission. "If you have proof of your charge," he said, "you could testify to it in court. This posthumous evidence of Egan's character would exonerate you for his killing, I would think."

"I have no wish to drag the sordid details of a family scandal into public spotlight. If only out of respect for my dead father's memory."

"You could stay in the north," he told her. "Remain in Yorkville, do some of the things you'd planned there."

"No," she protested sharply, "I would die here all too soon if I stayed on. I want to forget every wretched acre of this entire peninsula. It's been a nightmare for me."

"In that case your future is in your own hands. What do you want to do with your life?" Bruce asked.

"I have no wishes. Wishes are for the hopeful and I am sick of life," she said, sobbing.

He wanted to touch and console her, but he was afraid where that might lead. Instead, he folded his copy of the document once over and slipped it into his pocket. He would show the remarkable agreement to Alan immediately.

"You'll be all right," he said, and at that she ran to his arms and laid her head tenderly against his good shoulder. But only for a moment.

She pulled away from him and said, "Thank you for everything—Now please go . . ."

He left to gather together her personal effects and arrange for their delivery to the *Rupert*.

Where did the truth end and lies begin? Bruce

wondered as he went off in search of Alan. He had arrived in consternation only a half hour ago, ready to accuse Beryl of the deliberate murder of Egan Connelly. He was leaving her after hearing a bizarre tale that might even have justified her act, if it was to be believed. But he also left with a rich prize, an agreement that would eventually help to make his dream city a reality one day. With much judicious planning, with the love and help of Melanie on his side, their children growing, he might even be able to buy Yorkville from Beryl in the not-so-distant future and make it part of his dream.

From the violence of his apprenticeship at Green Bay had come the murders of Henry York, Bill Dexter, Egan Connelly and other ambitious Americans, as well as the terrible massacre that would never be forgotten by the Siwash or himself. But even violence had its compensations. From barbarity, rising like some phoenix from the ashes of the mill fires, had come fresh hope, a renewal of personal faith. He was beginning, Bruce thought, to see at last what destiny meant, to see himself as part of it.

20

CAPTAIN KELSEY and Marian arrived when the
Prince Rupert sailed into Green Bay on Christmas
morning with a shipload of fresh supplies, including wine and gifts. Even with the bother of un-
packing, Guy and Marian Kelsey were in plenty of
time for the late afternoon Christmas banquet that
Bruce was holding in the assembly hall. With a
little crowding, the whole camp could be accom-
modated there.

Tables of rough boards were set up and covered
with sheets, decorated with boughs and berries
and candles. Benches on seesaw legs served as
seats and everyone sat down happily to a feast of
baked ham, mashed potatoes, pickled peaches,

fruitcakes, pies and candies—all part of the fresh
provisions that the *Rupert* had brought on this
voyage. Not to mention, of course, casks of hearty
red Spanish wine from the California vineyards.

Before the banquet was served, Bruce offered a
eulogy for Bill Dexter, followed by a prayer for
the repose of his soul. Dexter's men had buried
him in the cemetery that morning just as Connelly's body was being carried back to Yorkville
to be interred there.

The only person absent from the banquet was
Beryl Bennington. She remained in her cabin by
choice, feeling that it would be unseemly for her
to make an appearance. "The women might not
like it," she told Bruce, and this was just fine with
Melanie, Janet and Marian. They were relieved
that she hadn't shown up; her presence would have
put a damper on this joyful occasion, reminding
them of the recent bloody skirmish.

Everyone ate heartily. The events of last night
were all but forgotten. Toward the end of the
banquet, Bruce rose to make a toast.

"First of all," he said, "let us drink to Captain
Kelsey and his lady. They have graced our table
in the past and will hopefully do so again in the
future. Also I propose a toast to our faithful and
long-suffering cooking staff, who must turn out
three meals a day whether we work or not, and
who have today outdone themselves. And another
to our loggers, who in fair weather and foul, have
gone out into the forest to bring home our liveli-
hood. And finally, to our friends and neighbors,
the Siwash tribe, who will soon be settled in a
permanent village and taught to work alongside

our regular employees. To your good health, and the health of Green Bay, let us all drink . . ."

The company stood up, raised its glasses, and drank to Bruce's toast.

After they sat down again, Bruce continued, "This is also an auspicious day for us in another way. I have just had the good news that a merger between Green Bay and Yorkville is being worked on. The two camps will remain separated by the width of the peninsula, but they will be joined together in management, eventually perhaps by ownership. This will mean an end to our recent trouble and friendly competition should begin to take its place . . . I tell you this after the tragic occurrence last evening so that we will have something pleasant to anticipate in the new year."

Bruce's speech was greeted with polite applause, for the news came as an unexpected surprise, but not as great a surprise as what immediately followed.

It began as a deep underground rumbling, emanating from the ground below, like the sound of a dozen freight trains rushing at them from all directions.

Marian Kelsey was the first to react, screaming shrilly and clutching little Marian, whom she had only seen for the first time that day, in her arms. Simultaneous with Marian's scream, the floor of the hall began to undulate slowly at first, then faster and faster, like a ship deck on a rough sea. It stopped after several seconds with an abrupt heave.

For a moment all was still. Then the building

began to sway, gently creaking and groaning. Next the ground beneath them seemed to drop away sickeningly, several feet, or so it felt. The hall windows burst inward, sending a shower of glass shards over the assembly.

By this time pandemonium had taken over. The terrified loggers fought each other to get to the double exit doors. It was all Bruce could do to protect the women and children from the torrent of frantic bodies scrambling for the doors.

Then, quite as unexpectedly as it had begun, the tremor subsided, leaving the assembly hall still swaying back and forth, while the hysterical crowd pressed on through the exit into the clearing outside.

There was a respite of some thirty seconds before the next shock struck the camp. This one was much more severe. The earth seemed to buck and ripple like a vicious bronco. A corner beam in the roof of the hall broke with a loud crack, sagging downward from the weight of the roof, threatening to collapse at any moment.

The second shock took no more than ten seconds to play itself out, thankfully, or there would have been even greater panic. Even so, several loggers were injured getting through the doors.

With Alan's and Guy's help, Bruce managed to fight through the struggling mass and reach the women and children, seeing them safely outside to the large clearing where the remains of last night's bonfire lay scattered.

Outside, the loggers were running aimlessly in all directions. Some shouted at one another; others muttered to themselves. No one knew quite what to do, or where to seek safety. Some of the men disappeared among the swaying trees, and others, the sensible ones, moved to the center of the clearing with the women and children and remained there.

Alan calmed the children as best he could, disgusted with the selfish behavior of those who abandoned the women and children and fought instead to get out of the hall. Captain Kelsey stood by Marian, Janet, Melanie and the children, so Alan and Bruce could be free to decide what to do next.

The messhall and cookhouse had sustained some damage, Bruce noted. Loosened by the excessive winter dampness, a hemlock's roots had been wrenched from the soil and the tree had fallen across the building's roof, smashing it like an eggshell.

"What are we to do?" Melanie asked, grabbing Bruce's arm and trying to remain calm.

"Stay right here for the time being," Bruce told her, just as another shock took them by surprise—the third one; quick, sharp and extremely brief. Another tree fell away from the clearing and toppled across one of the cabins at such an angle that it brought down the entire roof, driving it so forcefully into the cabin's interior that it took the log walls down with it, almost leveling the structure.

"Oh my God," Bruce muttered to Melanie, "that's Beryl's cabin!" He turned to Alan whose arm was flung around Janet. "Come with me!"

The two men ran toward the fallen trees. As Bruce and Alan ran, they noticed fires starting up in the various buildings, either from stoves or fireplaces.

When they reached the ruined cabin they pulled frantically at the jumble of logs, calling out to passing loggers for aid. Several men stopped to help, attempting to push the logs aside so the men could crawl inside what was left of the building.

Bruce tore at the logs with his bare hands until his fingers were raw and bleeding. He called out as the Moore brothers were passing by, and the twins came to their aid. Ultimately it took the strength of six men to move the splintered logs sufficiently to allow crawl space for rescuers to enter the cabin. The logs were safe only as long as the ground remained still.

"Cross your fingers, I'm going in," Bruce said.

Alan begged him not to. "Another good jolt and you'll be crushed to death," he said.

"That's a chance I'll have to take. She may still be alive in there."

"She can't be," said Alan. "It's too damned dangerous, Bruce. Don't go."

"I have to," Bruce said. "I brought her here. And you can't go inside, not with a family."

Ignoring his safety, Bruce crawled under the broken roof. He could feel the heat of the fireplace through the broken beams and knew that it would soon begin smoldering, and then burst into flame.

Several feet into the ruined cabin he found Beryl's body. He could barely see in the gloom, but with his hands he determined that her head was crushed by the roof's heavy center beam. Obviously she was dead. Either she'd been unwilling to leave the cabin when the quake began, or too frightened, and thus became its hapless victim.

What a poor, ill-fated creature she was, he

thought, having to die like that. But then, she'd said she was sick of life; perhaps she had welcomed death.

It was too difficult to drag her body out now; maybe later. Then he remembered the cloth packet of documents; he'd better get them if it were possible. Groping around in the debris next to Beryl's body he felt the packet lying close to the splintered table on which it had rested. He shoved the packet into his belt and crawled out of the wreckage to safety.

"She's dead," he told Alan and the others. "Let's turn our attention to the injured, and put out the fires."

Fires were springing up in several of the buildings around them. With the Moore twins and Alan, Bruce began to check all buildings that were either damaged or afire. The cookhouse was in flames. Two men were trapped behind the huge stoves, nearly asphyxiated by smoke inhalation before they could be dragged out into the open air.

There were no more shocks, only slight tremors from time to time, enough to remind them that the earth was still in command of the situation and could kill them at any moment in case they forgot.

Bruce ordered all uninjured personnel to make a systematic search through the camp for any casualties they might have missed. Eventually the rescuers returned to the clearing, which was now beginning to assume the appearance of a refugee camp. Victims were huddled in blankets, or were bundled in whatever warm clothing they had been able to find, safe for the moment from fire and falling trees.

Ten minutes after the last shock, Bruce heard

another unfamiliar sound of nature. It reminded him of a sound he loved as a boy, the whisper of wind rushing through high trees. But glancing up, he saw that no wind stirred the tree tops; their crowns were motionless as they had been, before the earthquake lashed them back and forth.

"What's happening?" Bruce asked Alan.

"I don't know. Something sounds strange. More like a torrent or a waterfall."

Bruce then recalled something he'd once heard about giant waves induced by submarine earthquakes near the coast of the South Pacific. A sailor Bruce met claimed that these waves swept in from the sea at prodigious speeds on the heels of a quake, leaving widespread devastation in their wake. Thousands drowned in populated areas close to the sea, and the sides of nearby mountains were scraped clean by the towering deluge of water. The Japanese had a special name for the wave, he recalled. The physical make-up of the coastline and the severity of the quake that impelled the wave would determine the fury of the colossal wave and the devastation it would inflict.

It was too late now to do anything about escaping to higher ground behind the camp, Bruce realized, to climb up a hundred feet or so among the giant boulders that lay a short distance to the rear of the community. The Indian village was on still higher ground, Black Deer had insisted upon it. The Indians would be safe. Where he was now, Bruce and the others could only hope and wait out the fearful, agonizing seconds until the giant wave struck them. Bruce could see the black water of the bay through distant trees and wondered how long it would be. The *Rupert* faced toward the open water. With the help of God, she might ride it out.

The sound grew and began to resemble the roar of a nearby Niagara cascading over the brink.

Guy Kelsey knew what the sound meant.

"It's a *tsunami* running up the shallow bay," he said, standing next to Bruce. "A tidal wave; the Japanese get them all the time. It could beach the *Rupert* high and dry, maybe even destroy it!"

Bruce and Kelsey exchanged anguished, helpless glances. There was nothing they could do but wait for it.

A hissing, tumbling wave with a twelve-foot crest swept down the curve of the bay at fifty miles an hour. The camp was built only a few feet above the regular water level; the wave swept past the settlement and sent a six-foot surge of sea water through the clearing, smashing trees along the way, but not with as much power as Guy Kelsey expected. It stopped halfway into the clearing, leaving a line of dirty foam and jetsam in its wake as it receded.

The sawmill at the water's edge might have suffered considerable damage, Bruce realized, perhaps putting them out of production for a while. That was all right; there was very little production during the next two months anyway. At least, no lives would be lost; no one was working at the sawmill tonight.

The wave lifted the *Rupert* high on its crest for a moment, then dropped the boat like a child's toy onto the muddy bottom of the bay with a ground-jarring thud. The brig was exceptionally well-built, and that alone saved it from destruction.

Kelsey heaved a sigh of relief when he saw the *Rupert* floating upright and intact. The wharf south of the ship had sustained minor damage, apparent in the moonlight, but it wasn't vital.

"There'll be another wave soon," Kelsey told Bruce, "but not as large. I'm going aboard."

"Is that wise?" Bruce asked. "Maybe you should stay here."

"My responsibility is with my ship," said the captain. "I must go aboard to see what's happened and to learn if the men are safe."

He strode off purposefully through the debris of small driftwood and branches that the wave had left behind.

Loggers were bringing the injured into the clearing. Many suffered cuts and bruises, some had broken limbs. While Janet watched the children, Marian and Melanie attended to the victims as best they could.

Bruce called for volunteers among the able-bodied. The Moore twins and several other loggers joined Alan to search the cabins and check for fires. The *tsunami*'s assault had sloshed enough water into the cabins, fortunately, to snuff out all fires.

As cold and wet as they were, none of the survivors cared to sleep under shelter. So far, Beryl was the sole fatality, but everyone was aware that Green Bay might suffer more quake shocks, and bigger and higher waves could follow. Some of the loggers went to the bunkhouses for blankets, but no one lingered indoors a moment longer than was absolutely necessary.

The survivors built a bonfire where the Christmas Eve ceremony had taken place. Dry wood was dragged from atop a huge covered pile of cordwood behind the cookhouse, and soon a hearty bonfire snapped and crackled, and soon many exhausted people gathered around it to keep warm.

Everyone began settling down for the remainder of the night. The moonlight had disappeared; no survey of total damage could be assessed before dawn.

Captain Kelsey had returned from the ship with an optimistic survey report. The second wave, he said, had been almost invisible. "And the brig's as good as new," he added, "outside of a few knocks. Nobody was hurt."

"Will you be able to sail on schedule?" Bruce asked.

"I hope so. Unless the area is struck by a larger quake or a wave of disastrous proportions. I heard about one that scoured a whole mountainside bare across the strait a few years ago. If this is the end of it, then we're going to be all right. If we have more trouble, the *Windfall*'s due to dock at Green Bay in a couple of days; we'll simply wait here for her arrival. Captain Blount can carry most of us back with him, if need be. That includes the York-ville raiders I was to take off your hands and any others who're fed up with it here. I might just insist that Janet and the children go with Marian."

"I would hate to see Janet and the children go," said Bruce, "but if the situation calls for it, all right."

Kelsey eyed Bruce speculatively. "What is it," he asked, "that makes you want to stay on here? I imagined that once you made sure this operation was running the way you wanted it, you'd be ready to leave it in competent hands and move back to civilization."

"I thought so myself, Guy. But a curious thing's happened. This is now my life, all that it will ever be. And I've never felt it more strongly than today, in this moment of near-disaster, despite all the tragedy that's plagued this enterprise. Human frailty, acts of God, none of these are going to put Territorial Mills out of business, or turn the town of Green Bay back into forest," Bruce said.

"Well, I certainly hope Marian can persuade Janet to come with us and bring the children."

"Janet may not want to leave, and I doubt very much that you could persuade Alan to go, either. He feels very much as I do about Green Bay."

"I wonder why?" Kelsey mused. "But I suppose it's related to the feeling that I have for the *Rupert*, and for the other ships I captained."

"With you, it's the adventure of the voyage and the mastery you have over the ship and the sea," Bruce said. "With us, it's the distant dream of a great city rising here and replacing these forests."

"But that's a fantasy, Bruce. It's impossible, or at least it's not possible in your lifetime."

"Maybe not," Bruce conceded, "but that doesn't take any magic away from the dream."

"You mean, after all that's gone on, you're going to stay? Why not clear out, sell your holdings to some other eager settler and come down to San Francisco? You've made a very decent profit so far from this venture. There's no need for you to stay on and endure hardships any longer."

"Guy," Bruce said patiently, "they're not hardships to me. Besides, only yesterday Beryl Bennington worked out an arrangement with me that gives me a whole new reason for going on here."

"An arrangement?" said Kelsey.

"Yes, concerning Yorkville. I should send a party down in the morning to see what's happened to their camp."

"What kind of an arrangement are you talking of?" Kelsey asked, and Bruce told him.

"Good God," Kelsey exclaimed, "what an incredible piece of luck! You now own both communities."

"*If* the document stands up in a court of law. It's written in Beryl's own hand so it might."

"Let's hope so, for your sake. Yorkville wouldn't be damaged in any case. Lying on the other side of the peninsula, it was protected from the wave, at least. Whether it escaped damage from the earthquake, would depend upon where the quake originated, beneath us or somewhere else on the peninsula. Bruce, now that you own the only two logging communities on this neck of land, why don't you simply let your men run it and bring Melanie and come back with us?"

"You still don't understand how I feel, Guy. I want you to marry the two of us here, today. We're staying even if we have to stay alone here with the Siwash."

"*You* are getting married?"

"Any objections?"

"On the contrary, I'm delighted, even if I can't quite see you as a backwoods father. I have to hand it to you, Bruce. You're finally conquering your Boston background."

"Give me time," said Bruce, "and I'll be a real rustic."

"You know, I thought at first you were only in the lumber business for the money."

"That was true, at first. Now it looks as if I might

never leave the Northwest. I love it here. Probably has to do with the Randall pioneering instinct."

"When do you want to be married?"

"At noon, if that's all right with you, and God doesn't sweep us away before then with another earthquake."

"Fine. Now I've something to look forward to," Kelsey wrapped the rainslicker he had brought from the *Rupert* around his shoulders and curled up against a pile of logs. "I'm going to catch forty winks. I'll need the rest to sustain me against the brandy we'll be drinking after the ceremony."

Dawn came in an hour; a light misty rain fell, turning the morning a bright, pearly grey.

Kelsey woke Bruce, who had fallen asleep under a blanket, and asked him to come aboard the *Rupert* while he inspected it further by daylight. The two men found no hull damage; the ship was sound and watertight. Once the *Rupert* was completely unloaded, it could sail out on schedule, much to Kelsey's relief.

When it was full daylight and the rain had stopped, Bruce and Alan made a thorough inspection of the camp. As Bruce had suspected, the sawmill had sustained some minor damage, mostly to the wharf facility and the mill roofing. Once the machinery was cleaned and oiled again, the mill would go back into operation.

Black Deer came down from the northern Indian village that morning to report that all was well with his people.

"We were frightened by the sound of the big water but our hill is high enough to be safe," the

Indian said. "And the shaking ground did not disturb our tents. We will set up tents for you, if you wish."

Bruce was tempted to ask Black Deer what he knew of the murder of Henry York. But such a question would gain him nothing, he knew, except the ill-will of Black Deer, if the Indian thought that Bruce blamed him for the bloody deed. Besides, what did it matter now?

"Something I want to show you, boss," Black Deer spoke quietly, drawing Bruce aside. It must be serious, Bruce decided. The Indian had only called him boss a few times, and at important moments. "It is secret," Black Deer confirmed.

He reached into his pocket and pulled out Henry York's watch. The gold fob with the flashing diamond set in the elk's tooth glistened even in the dim morning light.

"Gold watch," said Black Deer solemnly.

"So I see."

"Is it not beautiful?" asked Black Deer.

"Whose is it?" Bruce countered.

Black Deer shrugged his shoulders. "I have seen it on Mr. York when he lived," said the Indian. "A very fine watch. Too fine for me."

"How did you come by it?"

"Found in Connelly's pocket before men take him to Yorkville for burial," Black Deer explained, looking Bruce straight in the eye.

Well, thought Bruce, if that was the way Black Deer wanted it, he could do no less than accept the story graciously. After all, he had no way of knowing the real truth, not ever. He wondered if Melanie had advised Black Deer to explain the watch in this fashion, but there was no logic to such an idea. Black Deer was making a sincere effort to dissociate himself from the watch.

"It belongs to you now," said Black Deer. "You are new owner of Yorkville now. Take it!"

"I don't think I want it," Bruce said flatly.

"Ah, but there is something good about it," Black Deer pointed out. "It has its own life, it captures time. There is no curse on it, it is more like the taking of a trophy that marks the end of a war for the victor. It speaks at last of peace. As long as you hold this watch, boss, your people and mine will live in harmony. Ask Cloud, she will tell you this is true." Black Deer smiled, dangling the watch before Bruce's eyes. "Go ahead. It is yours . . ."

Finally Bruce held out his hand and took the watch from Black Deer. "May it be as you say," he spoke solemnly. "May it end bloodshed and hatred! I thank you."

Black Deer turned and walked away. The cycle of vengeance was now symbolically completed, Bruce understood, the ritual of the watch's transfer purifying all. Let it be, he thought.

Later Bruce told Alan the story.

"Who do you think killed York?" Alan asked.

"Connelly perhaps, maybe Black Deer. Who knows? We'll do without explanations now, and go about the business of rebuilding Green Bay. It'll take a month or more, and next time we'll build the cabins much sturdier, so they'll stand up better."

"I'm glad you used the plural," Alan said. "My in-laws have a plot afoot to take my family and me south with them."

"I know. I didn't want to influence you one way

or the other. I was prepared for the possibility that you and Janet and the children might sail back to San Francisco aboard the *Rupert*."

Alan looked at his partner in disbelief.

"That's the worst joke I've ever heard you make. Even if we weren't in business together I'd stay on. And Janet feels the same way I do. I want to be around for the real work. One day, all this green gold will be chopped down, and by that time we ought to have the start of a real city going, a fine, bustling Northwest metropolis. What a helluva good time we'll have planning it all," Alan said enthusiastically. "We ought to solemnize the occasion with a drink or a ceremony. Today without fail . . ."

"Odd you should say that. Guy is marrying Melanie and me today."

"By God, that's marvelous news!" Alan said sincerely, clapping his friend and partner on the shoulder. "You can start building that family tonight. And you better be quick about it. I'm already two heirs ahead of you."

"Don't worry, I'll catch up," Bruce promised. "In fact, I'll do you one better. I'll wager that in five years I'll have twice as many offspring as you have."

"That's a bet I'll gladly take," Alan said, and the two men laughed and shook hands on it . . .

Beryl Bennington was buried that morning in a wet, freshly dug grave. Interred along with her body, wrapped in a shroud, was York's gold watch. A fitting place for it, Bruce decided.

At noon, Melanie Cloud and Bruce were married by Captain Kelsey on the *Rupert*'s open deck.

Since the wharf was damaged, the loggers clustered on the shore to watch the simple ceremony aboard the brig.

There were no more large tremors, although myriad small aftershocks continued all that day and for weeks afterward. This didn't deter Bruce and Alan or the majority of loggers who decided to stay on from starting work at once on the new Green Bay complex.

Bruce made a trip to Yorkville and found that the camp was barely damaged. Alan, Janet and the children would be moving down there in the early spring, to take up permanent residence in the lower portion of the dream city the two men intended to build.

Captain Kelsey and Marian sailed away on the *Rupert* after the *Windfall* arrived in port, carrying the precious title papers to Yorkville and its forests back with them bound for delivery to Bruce's attorney-agent in San Francisco. They also carried Henry York's sole will, as it would henceforth be known.

Two weeks later Melanie told Bruce that she was pregnant.

"Your city has begun," she announced. "We will soon have two families, one for each camp. But we need more than that. Why not follow Beryl's suggestion and bring in wives for the loggers who want to settle here? We'll give them each a cabin and a plot of land. What do you think?"

"A splendid idea," Bruce approved. "In a few years we'll have families scattered all through the forests between the two camps, with a good wagon road connecting them."

"Bruce, there's another matter. You don't have

to stay on here because of me, if you don't want to stay. I'll go anywhere with you."

"This is our only home," said Bruce. "It's where we met, where we'll live and where we'll die. We're more than just loggers and boomers, a stew of different races and creeds and backgrounds. We're the new settlers, from now till our city is built, and after."

"What about Black Deer? Nothing has yet been settled about the Siwash. The village can't remain all-male forever," said Melanie.

"I was waiting for you to say something about that," Bruce told her. "In a few days I'll ride south with Black Deer and some of his men and they can choose squaws from other villages and bring them north. We'll give Black Deer land for a model village he'll be proud of. Then he and his men can settle and work at Green Bay, learn skills from our men, be trained to live in the new world we're making. There'll be no more tribal conflict here, white or red."

"You know what I love best about you?" Melanie told Bruce. "You're a romantic, a dreamer, but underneath it all, you have the faith and strength and courage to have a decent chance to make your dream come true."

"What else can I do, when the dream's as real as this one is?" Bruce asked logically, and wrapped his wife in a loving embrace . . .

EPILOGUE

The partnership of Bruce Randall and Alan Travers grew and prospered during the next decade, making millions in revenue from the lumber industry, but pouring the majority of their profits into the rural expansion of the peninsula.

Bruce managed the northern portion of the vast property, Alan the southern division. Both men made all decisions jointly regarding policy and growth for the communities. True to their mutual dream, houses sprang up along the busy roadway that linked the two communities on opposite sides of the peninsula. As the forests were logged out, farms sprang up in their place, and families flourished. The overall peninsular territory became known up and down the Pacific Coast as the Northwest Development Company. The original names of Yorkville Mills and Territorial Mills were put aside once and for all. Later Bruce and Alan decided to call the two communities North Bay and South Bay, the district names that remain today.

Schoolhouses were built in the two townships almost as fast as the families arrived. A friendly rivalry developed between the two districts, which was stimulating to both settlements.

Finding the two communities devoid of racism and respectful of the right of the individual to worship God as his fathers had done, settlers flocked to the area. They discovered a healthy, happy place in which to live and work and settled permanently on lands awarded them by Bruce and Alan. Small businesses began to prosper, encouraged by the partners who offered enterprising merchants the same opportunity in the as-yet undeveloped territory that they would have found in San Francisco, but without the stiff competition.

By 1880, Bruce Randall decided to retire from active participation in the business, turning his responsibilities over to his oldest son, Alan, a married man with a family of his own by this time. Bruce and Melanie decided to take a year's leave, visiting New England and Europe. They got as far as New England, grew homesick for the Northwest, and returned home after a month in New York without ever going abroad, never to leave the Northwest again.

A few years later, in 1884, Alan Travers turned his responsibilities over to his son Guy. Janet and Alan took an extended voyage to the Pacific islands and the Orient. They found Hawaii much to their liking and decided to settle there. But although

they bought land and built a house on the island
of Oahu, they too could not resist the magnet of
the Northwest and returned to the peninsula to
spend their declining years there.

Bruce Randall died of a heart attack in 1886,
Alan Travers in 1892. The two widows, Melanie
and Janet, continued to live close to one another
and enjoyed the shared experiences of their grand-
children and great-grandchildren.

Both Bruce and Alan are remembered for their
distinguished pioneer efforts in helping to tame
the Northwest Territory, but especially for their
ardent conservationism. They pioneered the practice of replanting logged out areas and preserving
as much of Nature as their ownership would allow.

Black Deer and his people were eventually settled in a parklike area around the lake where Bruce
and Melanie had first made love. In a sense, the
younger Siwash became thoroughly domesticated.
Many young males were integrated into the lumber
industry as skilled workers and intermarried later
with the children of white settlers, so that the
Siwash tribe was all but absorbed into the dominant culture.

The partners' dream of a great metropolis like
New York rising on the land that had once been
Yorkville and Green Bay materialized in a way that
neither Bruce nor Alan could have imagined. It
developed further south, beyond their land, but
eventually spread north to encompass all of the
peninsula, from Port Gamble south. Today it is
known as Seattle, largest city in the state of Washington, and in the Northwest Territory of the
United States of America.

THE END

THE WILDCATTERS

JOHN FAUST, huge and powerful, a sometime bare-knuckle prizefighter, ready to mortgage his soul for the black gold locked beneath the hardscrabble Texas soil—ready to destroy his own son for the one woman that could never be his.

BROM TORGESON, deadly as a rattlesnake, he struck it rich early in the game, but nothing would satisfy him until he has brought his sworn enemy, John Faust, to his knees—with the cruelest weapon ever fashioned by mortal man.

BRYNA TORGESON, elusive and beautiful, she ruled these mighty men, giving her body to the son and her promise to the father—but always holding back the one thing more precious than the black treasure that drove men mad with desire.